On The Brink

Cloverleah Pack Series Book 10

By Lisa Oliver

On The Brink is a work of fiction. Names, characters, places and incidents are either the product of the author's imagination or are used fictitiously and any resemblance to any actual persons, living or dead, events or locales is entirely coincidental.

The following businesses/trademarks have been mentioned in these stories:

Eton Dress Shirts - Eton Shirts, US.

Pontiac Trans Am - Pontiac, General Motors

Samuel Adams Utopias - Boston Beer Company

Satya Paul Design Studio Tie - Satya Paul

The Golden Girls - American sitcom - NBC, Hallmark Channel, Lifetime.

Dedication

Firstly, thank you to my lovely readers who have been so amazing during recent events. Your support, enthusiasm and love for my characters keeps me going every day.

And to Phil – this book wouldn't have been written without you. You know that, but you probably don't know how much I appreciate your help – especially with some of the grittier scenes.

And to my marvelous editors; two of you this time. My dearest friends Judy and Sue Ann. You take my words and make them shine. Thank you.

Table of Contents

Author's Note

As mentioned at the end of the last book in this series, Angel in Black Leather Pants, this book starts about midway in the timeline for that book. You may recall Kane, Shawn, and some of the others in Cloverleah went to San Antonio to help when Scott and Madison were kidnapped and no one could find them.

Part One starts in San Antonio with the introduction of Raff (the rare Red Wolf) to Damien's pack and follows onwards to the kidnapping and everything that happened afterward. As you know, Madison meets his mate in this book too, but his story is told more fully in his own book which will spark the spin-off from the Cloverleah pack (The Gods Made Me Do It series) and include mates for some of the other non-Cloverleah men we have come to love. Part Two takes place in Cloverleah where Raff and Nereus meet Teilo.

Some details will be replicated through some of the books—it can't be helped if I am going to keep the story lines straight, but they will be told from a different perspective. I do hope you enjoy this.

PART ONE

San Antonio

Chapter One

"What was it you promised me, about working too hard and leaving me in bed on my own in the morning? One overnighter in the club and you're reverting to your old bad habits," Scott glared at his mate. Damien might be the biggest alpha in the land and he ruled the biggest pack in the States, but his gruff demeanor didn't frighten Scott. Although both men now lived on pack grounds about twenty minutes' drive from the club, an issue with a supplier had them staying in their apartment above the club overnight. Scott didn't mind that, but he was agitated after living next to nature for a while. He'd forgotten how bad the smell of exhaust could be in the city. Waking up alone brought back old insecurities.

"I'll only be another half an hour," Damien said. His desk was a mess of papers, which Scott could've cheerfully thrown in the trash can. "Go down to the restaurant and get breakfast. By the time your plate is clean, I'll be done."

"I'd rather go out for breakfast," Scott stuck his chin in the air. He scanned the office. Malacai, Damien's second and Elijah, the pack doctor were sitting and watching the show. "I'm sure Malacai and Elijah will come with me. Won't you guys?" Scott grinned. It was good to be Alpha Mate sometimes. He wouldn't get turned down.

"Yes, boss," Malacai said drily.

"You're not going without enforcers," Damien warned but Scott could see his mind was on other things. That was all right. Scott would make sure he had his mate's attention once he'd had something to eat. If Damien didn't want to leave his desk, Scott would fuck him over it. Pleased with his little plan, he sauntered around the offending piece of furniture and plopped on Damien's lap. "Kiss me," he demanded.

Damien was always happy to oblige, and it was Scott who had to tear himself from those wicked lips before he forgot his resolve. "Later," he said, standing and giving his cock a nudge.

Damn mating hormones. Scott thought as he got his dick under control. Damien's grin wasn't helping and Scott almost decided to forgo the outing. But when Damien said quite clearly, "take enforcers with you," in that low voice that told Scott he didn't want to be ignored, Scott decided an outing was exactly what he needed. The enforcers were getting too lax, and it had been a while since any of them had to put up with guarding his precious person. Scott sniggered as he sauntered down the hallway. "They'll have to catch up with me first," he muttered. Scott didn't mind making things difficult for the enforcers, but he knew better than to upset his protective mate. That didn't mean he couldn't have fun.

"So, breakfast," he said cheerily. "I know exactly where I'm going. I'm sure you remember the place, Malacai; it's where we had our first cup of coffee together, the first morning I was here."

"That food did smell good, and the coffee was excellent," Malacai agreed, tucking Elijah under his arm. "But if you think we're getting out of here without at least four men following us, you're sadly mistaken."

"Unless you have them on speed dial, they'd better move fast. I'm hungry," Scott said, sprinting down the stairs to the club entrance. Of course, being the good little second he was, Malacai *did* have the enforcers on speed dial, but Scott was determined not to let the extra breakfast guests bother him. He didn't get a lot of time away from Damien by choice, but this unscheduled breather was a lovely change, and Scott whistled a random tune as he wandered the four blocks to the café he had in mind. If he was being rude in ignoring Malacai, Elijah, and the four flustered enforcers as he went; no one commented.

/~/~/~/~/

Scott glared at Elijah, "Egg whites? All the food you can have in a Texas Slam breakfast and you want egg whites?"

"I like egg whites." Elijah looked at Malacai for confirmation.

"He likes egg whites." Scott knew if Malacai could have figured out how to pull his mate on his lap in public, he would have.

"Why? It's not as though we have to worry about cholesterol." Scott couldn't understand why Elijah was ignoring all the wonderful food options the little café had. The smell of bacon and sausage in the air was making his stomach rumble.

"I know. I told you, I just like egg whites."

"I suppose you aren't having sausage either." Scott shook his head.

"Am too. Their chicken sausage patty is to die for."

"Chicken sausage?" Scott made a choking sound. "I suppose you're going to have the gluten-free English muffin too."

"Oh, I haven't tried that. It sounds good." Elijah picked up his menu again. "Scott? Stop banging your head on the table. You'll give yourself a headache."

Scott lifted his head and glared. "I'm trying to remember which reality I'm in. You can get six of whatever breakfast items you want and you're ordering egg whites, chicken sausage, and a gluten-free English muffin?"

"Well, no."

Scott brightened. Maybe there was hope for Elijah yet.

"I'm ordering the egg whites, chicken sausage, gluten-free muffin, oatmeal, plain yogurt and two strips of turkey bacon."

"I think I'm going to cry." Scott put his head back on the table. Malacai laughed.

"Oh," Elijah said innocently. "Do you think the turkey bacon with the chicken sausage is too much?"

"Never mind," Scott sighed. He knew when he was beaten. "Remind me again why I brought you along."

"You may be right," Elijah continued ignoring Scott's

question. "Maybe a nice seasonal fruit would be good."

"It's going to be an apple." Scott practically shouted. He resisted the urge to wipe the smile off his friend's face.

"Oh, yummy. Apples." Elijah actually clapped his hands; Malacai laughed harder.

A waiter approached the table. "Are you ready to order?"

"Oh yes," Elijah said, sitting up and giving the waiter his best smile. The Little shit was so darn cute. "I'll have the egg whites, chicken sausage, gluten-free muffin, oatmeal with plain yogurt and an apple if it is in season. Oh, and do you have green tea?"

"Sure, what kind?"

"Organic tropical?"

"Got it in yesterday."

"I'll have that, thank you."

Scott gritted his teeth. At least the other orders weren't as bad. Glaring at Elijah, he waited until everyone else had finished putting in their requests before giving his order. "Bacon strips, ham steak, hearty breakfast sausages, honey jalapeno bacon, pancakes with extra syrup, Texas-size buttermilk biscuits smothered in white gravy and your bottomless cup of coffee."

"Got it," The waiter snapped his order book shut with a smile. He was probably imagining the tip. "I'll bring your drinks."

As he walked away, Scott whispered to Elijah. "That's how a wolf eats."

"Fat ones," Elijah whispered back. Scott glared; Malacai laughed and a couple of the enforcers suddenly found their phones interesting. Just another day with the San Antonio pack.

/~/~/~/~/

Logan's growl was muffled. Raff stopped, pressing his back up against the wall, cursing his decision to try to find a temporary job. He was hungry and so were the pups, but damn it, he should have known he wouldn't be safe. He wished Logan hadn't followed him, but the blessed pup had a protective streak a mile wide. *I shouldn't have gone into the bookstore. That rainbow flag was a dead giveaway. I should know to stay away from anything that could label me.* Raff shuddered as he remembered the job offer he had received in the store. As if he was desperate enough to get on his knees. Maybe one day, but not today.

Raff could hear voices coming down the street and he flapped his hand at Logan, willing him to be quiet.

"Damn it. He has to be here somewhere."

19

"Come out, come out, wherever you are, faggot. If you're good maybe we won't kill you and your little dog too...." The words were followed by the high insane giggle that warned Raff to run in the first place. Logan growled again in response and Raff bit his lip. Why did teacups have to be so damn loud? Raff couldn't explain to his precious pup there was no way Logan could take on the six men determined to hunt them down. Raff knew he could even the odds; shift into his wolf form, but red wolves were a small species; even the shifters and Raff knew he was smaller than most.

"He's got to be here somewhere," the voice sounded closer. "Split up and check down every alley."

Raff trembled and cursed himself for doing so because Logan took that as his cue to bark.

"Over there!"

Fuck. So much for a break. Raff ran, the men hot on his heels. Who knew six humans could run so fast? The cold air did nothing to cool him down; Raff was covered in sweat and panting hard. He might survive an attack, but he knew Logan wouldn't quit until they killed him, and that thought made him run faster. Logan's former owners had nicknamed the pup, Killer before they dumped him. Killer had no clue to his real size and thought he was a massive alpha instead of a teacup poodle. Killer might have been the reason Raff was running; pissing on that blond ape's leg was probably the final straw, but Raff kept running. He wasn't going to let Logan get hurt or worse.

Raff rounded the corner and then skidded to a stop. His plan was to turn right at the intersecting alley and hide behind the projecting wall, hoping his pursuers would keep going. But it was the wrong alley. Shit. He was in a delivery yard. Raff had nowhere to go.

"Well, well... look what we caught, boys. The little bitch and his mutt."

Couldn't be calling me the mutt, so I must be the little bitch.

"Look, I'm sorry. I'll pay for what he did and..." Raff caught his breath long enough to reply.

"Oh, you'll pay." Raff had no time to register the giant fist that knocked him back against the wall until he fell. "Fucking abomination. We don't want the likes of your kind here."

Logan lunged at the main attacker and Raff winced as he heard a pained yelp when the man threw him against the brick wall behind him. Raff swung out, but he was trapped; one man catching his arms and holding his body open as the others pounded into him.

"You'll learn faggot... one by one, we'll take you out. You're going to send a message to that fucker with the fancy club."

Raff couldn't believe what he was hearing. He was being beaten for an association he'd been doing his level best to avoid. Raff knew about the Alpha in the private club hidden from public gaze with black windows. He knew what Alphas did to red wolves. Sex slaves or death. Not an option Raff wanted to consider. His genetics were enough of a curse as it was. He knew the Alpha was gay, but Raff's size wasn't going to do him any favors. The big alpha would probably tear his throat out.

Fuck, if only I could shift, Raff thought frantically. *I could at least make them hurt before they killed me. Why the fuck am I protecting our species when my own pack threw me out and that alpha in the club will rip my throat out if he knows I'm here. Maybe death by Alpha was a better option.* Raff's legs finally gave way and his assailant let him drop to the ground.

"So what should we do with the bitch before we kill him?" Another man asked. Raff's eyes widened; he was terrified and gulped at the thought of the situation getting a lot worse. The idiot was asking for votes? Somehow Raff's gut was telling him death by assailant was going to be better than what that man was promising with his eyes. The smell of lust made Raff's nose twitch, and he thought he was going to sneeze.

"I gots a hard-on from the fight," the man continued, as though his reaction was perfectly normal. "Maryann wouldn't give me none last night. He's got a hole just as good as anything else. Might as well use him. Hell, he'll probably like it."

Raff trembled and tried to back up but the wall stopped him from going anywhere. *Not rape. Anything but rape.* He wouldn't...he couldn't...

"We got time," the man with the hard dick wouldn't shut up. "Ain't no one going to come back here for hours. Truck's not due in 'till 4 pm. No one takes a break out here because Gerry locked the damn doors when his staff kept sneaking out all the time. We got plenty of time for me to get my rocks off *and* make him hurt."

Raff's eyes went monochrome and the sound of his shirt ripping hit the air. He couldn't stop it; couldn't control it. He was going to shift and that could mean the death of him and Logan. But at least wearing fur would stop him being raped unless that guy was kinkier than normal.

/~/~/~/~/

Scott took another bite of the jalapeno bacon. He picked up a fork full of biscuit and gravy and waved it at Elijah. "You can't tell me you enjoy that as much as I enjoy this."

"I can and I do." Elijah picked up a slice of apple.

"Is he always like this?" Scott asked Malacai.

The only answer he got was a grin. Scott wasn't sure if they were pulling his leg or not. He was getting the distinct impression his friend was putting one over on him. He wouldn't put it past Elijah to get back to the club and order a juicy steak with a bacon side.

"Hey! Come back here!" The man at the front door yelled at a tiny dog as he shot between the man's legs into the restaurant. The waiters converged on him, but the little guy was fast; dodging legs and arms. The waiters ended up in a tangled heap on the floor; Brad, the one Scott was sure was gay, was grinning from the bottom of it. Scott winked at him. He took another bite of his bacon as tiny teeth sunk into his leg above his boot. "Hey!" He shook his leg.

The pup proceeded to have a frantic conniption fit. He ran back to the door, then back to Scott, his high-pitched howl going nonstop. *Okay. Something's up. I get the message.*

Scott shot up from his seat. "Put that on our tab and include a good tip." He ran for the door hot on the heels of the pup; ignoring the muttered curses as the enforcers and Malacai threw down their forks and hurried after him; Elijah safely in the middle of the muscle mass.

Scott dashed around the alley after the pup. He had just enough time to note six men holding a *wolf* captive before he jumped into the fray.

One of the enforcers said to Malacai, "You know, it's only six humans, he can handle it."

"Yeah... you want to explain the bruises to Damien?" Malacai was rolling up his shirt sleeves.

"Hell no."

Scott wouldn't say it, but he was glad of the support. He needed to get back into training again. It was at times like this he missed his twin, Troy. Making a mental note to call him as soon as he got home, Scott looked around as the man he was hitting bit the dust. The delivery area was littered with bodies; none of whom looked like they would be getting up anytime soon. He turned to the small red wolf shivering against the wall. Scott could hear the enforcers muttering.

"A Red Wolf,"

"By the Gods, it's a Red Wolf."

"I thought they were extinct."

"Isn't he pretty?"

"Those eyes... Never saw eyes like that."

The crystalline amber eyes were filled with fear as they focused on Scott.

"It's okay. We aren't going to hurt you," Scott crouched down as close as possible. "Please shift back. You can't run through the city like this and your pup is worried about you."

The trembling got worse.

"Please, I give you my word no one will hurt you."

Elijah came up beside Scott, crouching as well. "I'm a doctor," he said quietly. "Can you let me look at you? I can do it in your current form if you prefer, but it would be better if you shifted. Scott won't hurt you. That big guy over there, Malacai, he's my fated mate and I promise you, he'll keep you safe and so will Scott. Scott is true mated to our Alpha. You won't come to any harm. Please, little wolf. You need help."

The trembling slowed, but the wolf didn't shift.

"You can smell we aren't lying to you," Scott tried again. He'd never seen a wolf shifter so skinny before and he felt guilty for the huge breakfast he ordered. "None of these men will hurt you. Smell them. They will guard you with their lives because I told them too and because they know I have an overprotective mate who will break their heads if I'm upset." Scott heard Malacai mutter something under his breath but it was pitched too low for even his wolf's ears. The Red Wolf seemed to snicker. Could he hear that? Damn his hearing was fantastic even for a wolf.

Scott watched as the pretty little wolf slowly shifted into a man just as pretty as the wolf form had been. The crystalline eyes were still clouded with fear, but Scott smiled. Human was something to work with.

"Malacai?" He called over his shoulder. "You're the biggest. Can I have your shirt and will someone call Damien and have him send pants and a shirt? It's freezing out here and humans won't handle a naked man too well. Some boots and a jacket would be a good idea as well. The pavement's frigid."

The teacup poodle was curled up in Red Wolf's arms.

"Your little friend found us for you," Scott said, hoping the man would talk. "He's a very determined pup."

A soft voice replied, "That's why the former owners named him Killer before they dumped him.

He's pure Alpha. His real name is Sir Logan Barksalot. I call him Logan."

Logan growled when Scott reached a finger out to touch him, but Scott wasn't Alpha Mate for nothing. He persisted and eventually the little dog, and the man he was attached to were getting along fine. By the time clothes arrived for the wolf known as Raff, Scott heard the whole story of the chase and the beating.

"Get their ID's," he said to Malacai, waving at the men who still hadn't gotten up. "Find out who they are and Damien will deal with them later. They need an attitude adjustment." Scott could feel his wolf pushing to shift and deal with the bastards. Looking after Raff had to come first.

Elijah touched his arm. "I think he's going to be fine but I want to check him out in my office."

"I can't!" Raff panicked. "I have to go back to my room."

"We can protect you." Scott offered to take Killer... Logan... Nah... Killer fit him better. His owners were right. The little poodle was hugely protective of Raff. "We won't let anything happen to you and you can join the pack."

Wistful hope came into those lovely eyes. Scott felt his protective instincts ping hard. "I... I have to go back to my rooms. I could come back later if you let me."

"We'll go with you."

"No. I'll be fine."

"Look, I'm not forcing you to come with us but surely you know how dangerous it is. I mean look at what Damien sent with me just to walk a couple blocks; all this for a cup of coffee and breakfast. You're even more valuable and surely you can see we have the means to take care of you. I want to." Scott put on his best puppy eyes; the ones that made Damien melt. Raff was weakening...

"I need to go home. I have three more pups," Raff admitted quietly. "I don't want to be a bother to any of you."

"If Killer has brothers and sisters, they're welcome," Scott said, not sure how Damien was going to take to having natural dogs in the pack. But he was determined not to let the little wolf out of his sight. His gut was telling him Raff was important, and he'd never ignored that feeling before. "We'll get them together."

"It's more his pack," Raff looked down at Killer with a smile; his whole face lit up. "They aren't related. I... look, you don't want to come to where I live. It's not so great." Raff looked up and Scott could see his cheeks were red. He wasn't sure what to say. Raff looked clean; Killer's coat was healthy. How bad could it be?

Elijah spoke up. "We need to go with you and believe me, you now have a pack to care for you," he said, stepping forward. "Scott rescued me from a stinking hole my own mother put me in and kept me in for four months. I was in the dark, alone with almost no food and definitely no way of getting clean. The stench was enough to blind a man. Where you live can't be any worse than the smell of that hole. Now let's get your pups and your stuff and find you somewhere safer to stay."

Scott took the timid nod as a win, and although he'd have a lot of explaining to do with his mate when they finally got back to the club, he knew in his gut he'd made the right decision.

Chapter Two

Raff stood stunned, looking around the room. He barely noticed Scott slipping out the door. The keys for said room were clutched tightly in his sweaty palm. *This is a freaking palace,* Raff thought. In reality, it wasn't. It was a one-bedroom apartment; but for Raff, who'd been living in a tiny room, sharing a bathroom with drug addicts and alcoholics it ranked right up there with a mansion. It even had central heating. Killer barked and tugged at his pants. "We've really landed on our feet, Logan. You have no idea."

Forcing his feet to move, Raff played with the buttons on the television remote; he couldn't remember the last time he watched a show. He wondered if the Golden Girls was still showing; it'd been a while since he'd had a good laugh. Killer was tugging him again and Raff noticed Buddy and

Butch had already found a way onto an armchair and were snuggled up together sleeping; Joey was sprawled out on the couch. Seems it didn't take a lot for his furry friends to feel at home.

"But you'll want feeding, won't you?" Raff glared at the persistent ankle biter. "Let's see if there's anything in the kitchen for you." It's not as though he had any money to buy food; it's why he'd been job hunting in the first place. Scott told him he could order whatever he liked from the club restaurant and Alpha Damien grunted his agreement. But Raff saw the look on the huge man's face and didn't want to do anything to upset his tenuous position in the pack. Damien accepted him into the pack on Scott's say so; Raff's face red with mortification from Scott's description of his living conditions. The back of his neck still burned from where Damien touched him.

"Oh, my lord," Raff stared at the cupboards in amazement. He'd never seen such an array of foodstuff outside of a supermarket. He hurriedly opened the large fridge which was stocked with meats; some cooked, some raw; three different types of cheeses, a tray of eggs, two huge bottles of milk and the bottom drawer held four large dog food rolls; a premium brand Raff had drooled over every time he'd braved a visit to the store.

Suddenly the enormity of the events over the past eight hours hit him and Raff fell to the floor, tears streaming down his face. Killer climbed up on his knee and started licking his face and Raff chuckled in spite of himself. "Oh, Logan. This could be a new start for us," he whispered. "No more scrounging for food; no more being scared in the night." Killer huffed. He wasn't scared of anything.

"I miss Mom and Dad," Raff said, keeping his voice low. "I miss the pack, I miss…." Killer barked and licked his face again.

"You're quite right," Raff said, straightening his spine. "No point in worrying about stuff we can't change. You heard what Scott said. Get settled; get used to our new home and then if I want to, he'll help me get a job. I don't know… I'm not sure how it's going to go working in the club, but Malacai said no one would touch me unless I wanted it. What do you think?"

Killer jumped off his knee and stood in front of the fridge door, his head tilted to one side. Raff sighed and got to his feet. "At least I know where I stand with you. Go and get the others; I'll grab your bowls out of my things. We'll all be eating well tonight." *And hopefully, for some time to come,* he thought as he pulled out a dog roll from the fridge and started hunting for a large knife.

/~/~/~/~/

Damien curled his huge body around Scott's and Scott wished he could purr. "Did you get the red wolf settled in okay?" Damien asked gruffly. Scott stretched his body out along his mates and wiggled.

"Yep. I think he's a bit overwhelmed about everything. He... he's been told a lot of bad shit about alphas and their treatment of wolves like him. Then there was that attack today and that hovel he was living in...how could his pack kick him out like that, especially looking the way he does? He's lucky we found him."

Damien's capable hands turned him, so he was looking into bright gray eyes. His mate wasn't a pretty man by any stretch of the imagination, but those thin lips had brought him so much pleasure over the months they'd been together and from the warmth, in Damien's eyes he'd be feeling them again real soon. "That little wolf will be safe here and if anyone begs to differ, they'll deal with me personally. I wish he'd come to us sooner, but the Fates move in mysterious ways and he's here now. This pack will look after him; we will look after him." Scott felt firm hands on his ass; oh yes, things were going nicely. But Scott still had one major niggle to voice.

"Do you think he'll be safe working in the bar? I'd suggest the kitchen but if Killer escapes the apartment and finds him in there, Chef will have a fit and there isn't a lot else he can do around here," Scott ran his hands down Damien's hips. His mate had muscles upon muscles and Scott knew every one of them.

"Malacai will watch him in the bar and make sure any trouble-makers keep their distance. Raff might not know it yet, but he's got people watching his back. It's all those damned enforcers could talk about; how pretty he is and what a cute little wolf form he has."

"Just the enforcers?" Scott's hand found his target and Damien's eyes glowed. "Raff's got amazing eyes."

"I prefer cheeky blonds with bright blue eyes," Damien snarled and lunged forward, his lips catching Scott's with perfect precision, and for the longest time they were far too busy for conversation.

/~/~/~/~/

Raff lay in his new huge bed, staring at the ceiling, the dogs arranged over his legs fast asleep. Killer was sprawled on the pillow beside him, flat on his back, his mouth open and his little paws twitching as though he was chasing something. Knowing Killer, it wasn't a rabbit. *He's probably imagining himself leading the pack on a run,* Raff thought fondly.

He should be sleeping too. The bed was ginormous and so comfortable with clean sheets and four huge pillows. His stomach was full for the first time in months. Raff spent almost an hour in the lavish tub that took up half his bathroom, and he found plenty of comfortable clothes in the dresser. Raff's own stuff was being laundered, yet another free service offered to people who lived at the club. The chatty young blond, Cody, who'd brought him his dinner pointed out the phone, told him which numbers were on speed dial and for the first time in a long time, Raff felt... safe.

"Could it be?" He whispered in the dim light. "Could this place be home?" Killer snorted, coughed and rolled over, slapping Raff in the face with a paw. Raff chuckled and cuddling Killer in his arms, he finally fell asleep. For once, nightmares didn't bother him.

Chapter Three

Raff jumped as he heard the bushes behind him rustling. He turned to see Buddy dragging what looked to be an old jacket out from the undergrowth. "We're not taking that back to the apartment with us," he warned. Two days since Scott had saved him, and this was his first time outside of the club. The dogs were all litter box trained, but Raff knew they could do with some exercise. Killer was developing a paunch with all the good food he'd been eating. Raff's inability to resist puppy eyes didn't help.

"They find the darndest things, don't they? Give it here," Elijah laughed as he tried to tug the coat from Buddy's teeth. When Raff mentioned he wanted to walk the dogs, Elijah and Malacai had volunteered to come along, and while Raff knew it was more for protective reasons than friendship, he'd been happy to agree. Malacai didn't say much, but there was a smile on his face. Raff knew with Elijah around, Malacai wouldn't let anything happen to either of them. The man was a devoted mate.

"How did you and Malacai meet?" He asked as he helped Elijah rescue the jacket and tossed it in the nearest trashcan.

"He held me after Scott got me out of that hole I was telling you about," Elijah said with a smile. "I was a hell of a state, smelly, skinny and half dead and here I was getting a boner being in this huge man's arms. Confused the hell out of me. I tried so hard to hide it."

"I take it Malacai felt the same way?" Raff risked a quick look at the big man who was throwing a stick for Killer. Killer didn't want to chase it; at least not until Joey, Buddy and Butch did and then he raced after them barking madly.

"Do you know how we know when we've found our fated mates?" Elijah asked quietly. Raff shrugged. Mates were arranged in his pack; pairings designed to increase the size of the pack. He'd never heard of fated mates until Scott said Damien was his.

"It has to do with scent. I wanted to wallow in Malacai's scent, but of course, I didn't smell like myself. After I'd showered, though...," Elijah grinned.

"So you smell someone, and they smell really good...." Raff felt there must be more to it.

"And your dick hardens so fast it makes your head spin and you get all growly and possessive if anyone so much as looks at your mate." Raff's eyes widened. Elijah wasn't any bigger than he was.

"It's a mate thing," Elijah said, "We all do it, even us little guys."

"And none of the bigger guys mind?" Raff couldn't believe what he was hearing. Oh, he knew Elijah was telling the truth; his ears, eyes, and nose were highly acute in either form. He'd just never come across a pack where his size wasn't seen as some huge disadvantage.

"Mates trump everything," Elijah said, watching his wrestling on the ground with the tiny dogs. He was so careful with them. "When you find yours, there's nothing you won't do for him, or them for you."

"Him," Raff said quickly. "That's why... you know... with my pack."

"You have no idea how many men we have in our pack who went through the same thing," Elijah said, slinging his arm over Raff's shoulder. *As if we really are friends.* "You'll see; hell, I was in the same boat. Scott and I originally came from the same pack, along with his twin. Troy, the twin, got banished because he was caught with a guy; Scott disappeared about six months later when Troy found a new pack and somewhere for them to work. If Damien hadn't wanted Scott to try reconnecting with his family...." He broke off and giving into impulse, Raff hugged him.

"Scott's dad lives in this pack now too," Elijah said after hugging Raff back. "He met his mate, a younger human woman and they live in a house on the pack grounds. We'll have to take you out there sometime soon. You'd like Scott's dad; he's been really helpful with some of our younger pack members."

Raff wasn't sure what to say but then it didn't matter because Killer came running straight past him, growling and barking madly. The hair on the back of Raff's neck stood up, and he made to run after his dog, but Malacai held him back.

"Someone was watching us; Killer caught his scent before I did," Malacai said grimly. "Stay here."

"Come on," Elijah said, tugging Raff's arm. "Let's collect the other pups before we lose them too."

The park area was large; edged with trees and bushes of all sizes. Killer was long gone from sight, and it didn't take long for Malacai to disappear. Raff started to tremble; his fragile feelings of safety shattered. He shouldn't have come out. He shouldn't have left his apartment...

"Here, hold this one," Elijah ordered, and Raff found himself with an armful of Joey; his Chihuahua cross. Buddy and Butch were sitting at Elijah's feet, looking up expectantly. "And here come the reinforcements," Elijah added as four men headed their way. Raff was glad Elijah seemed to know them. His fight/flight had kicked in and he was all for running back to the club and never leaving it.

Elijah was just explaining what happened when Malacai appeared out of the trees, Killer struggling in his arms. "I want every inch of those woods covered," Malacai snapped to his enforcers as he got closer. "It's one of ours but I don't recognize the scent. Whoever it was didn't want to be found, and he had no good reason for spying on us the way he did."

"Yes boss," all four men snapped a quick salute and took off running.

"You're hurt," Elijah said, and Raff could see Malacai had a scratch down his face. It wasn't deep but Malacai seemed happy enough for his mate to fuss over him.

"There's no point in calling this one Logan," Malacai said handing Killer back to Raff. "He was damn mad when I caught him and brought him back. He'd got the scent of whoever was watching us, and he was hell bent on finding him."

"Killer did that to you?" Raff was horrified. "I'm so sorry."

Malacai laughed. "I wouldn't worry about it. It'll be healed by the time we get back to the club and besides, I like my mate fussing over me. I would've let the little bugger keep running but there's a busy road on the other side of those trees and I didn't want him run over. Let's just say there's a lot of alpha spirit in that little body. He doesn't like being told what to do; reminds me of Damien, actually."

Raff managed a tight smile and kept an even tighter hold on Killer as they headed back to the club. But his mind was in turmoil. He didn't know what was worse. The thought his precious pup could've been hit by a car; the idea that someone was watching them in the park or that Killer might decide to take a chunk out of Damien. None of those thoughts helped calm his jittery stomach.

/~/~/~/~/

Raff was half-dozing on the couch, sort of watching a reality show on television when someone knocked at his door. Frowning, Raff muted the television and pushed Killer off his lap, much to the small dog's disgust and hurried to answer the door.

"Alpha Mate, Scott," Raff added when Scott frowned at the title. "Is something wrong? Has something happened? Oh, my god, this is about Malacai isn't it? Killer didn't mean to hurt him. Malacai said it was okay. Is the Alpha angry at me? Do I have to go? I'm sorry; of course, I have to go. I'll just get my things; we'll get out of your territory…." Raff turned from the door, but Scott's hand caught his arm.

"Whoa dude; has anyone told you, you panic too much," Scott said. "Calm down, take deep breaths," Raff didn't realize he'd stopped breathing. "Now, sit down and tell me what horrible sin you think you've committed. I saw Malacai not ten minutes ago and there was nothing wrong with him that I could see."

"I... er...." Raff knew he had no choice so he sat on the couch; Scott right next to him and explained what happened earlier that day.

"So let me get this straight. You thought, because your adorable little poodle..." Scott scratched Killer's tummy and the dog batted him with his paws to keep going. "Because he scratched our pack second who probably shouldn't have grabbed him in the first place; you thought we were going to kick you out of the pack?"

"Malacai's important in this pack. He's second only to you and the Alpha. I'm just... I'm nobody," Raff's voice dropped to a whisper.

"Oh Raff, sometimes I just want to hug you so hard," Scott said before he did exactly that. Raff found himself pressed against a well-muscled chest; strong fingers ruffling his hair. Just as he thought his lungs would burst, Scott pushed him back a bit and Raff gasped.

"Now you listen to me young man," Raff didn't think Scott was much older than he was, but he listened anyway. "You are important and not just because you're a rare type of wolf. Yes, Red Wolves are damn near extinct and the council will have kittens when they find out you're in our pack, especially since you're gay, and they can't breed from you. But Damien will handle them. We have friends stronger than the council. But your genetics

55

has nothing to do with why I brought you here."

Raff's eyes widened. He thought the only reason he'd been taken in was because he was in pack territory. He hadn't given his genetics a thought, and maybe he should have. But Scott hadn't finished talking.

"You need us," Scott said gently and Raff could see the sincerity in the Alpha Mate's bright blue eyes. "And in a way, I think we need you too. This is a good pack, but most of the men here are either dominants strutting around thinking their shit doesn't stink, or subs looking for a master." Raff blushed. He'd been on the streets a while. He'd often been mistaken for a sub and some guys found his no hard to take.

"You're different," Scott stroked Raff's hair from his face. Raff couldn't remember the last time he was touched with any kindness.

"You remind me of Dean, an omega I know from my old pack in Cloverleah. He's like my younger brother, and I feel the same about you."

"You've only just met me," Raff said quietly, although he could understand what Scott was saying. From the first day, Raff knew the Alpha Mate could be trusted.

"Which is why I'm telling you this now," Scott laughed. "You might not like me once you get to know me. I can be a brat at times." Somehow, Raff didn't think that was possible. Scott's face was as open and honest as the day was long.

"I had an older brother once," he said hesitantly. "He didn't... they didn't... my family wasn't pleased I was gay." That was an understatement, but he didn't think Scott needed to hear the rest of it.

"In this pack, it's almost a prerequisite," Scott said easily. "We do have straight guys here and there are women and children in the pack as well. But a good seventy-five percent of us are gay. You'll see more when you come out to the pack grounds next time we have a run."

Running with other wolves; Raff's wolf was keen, but Raff was still leery. Maybe it wouldn't happen for a while.

"Anyhow, now we've got that sorted, the reason I came to talk to you was to let you know I haven't forgotten about your job. John, the bar manager has said I can train you to work the bar. But, Damien told me we've got visitors arriving tonight, and he wants me to meet them," Scott glanced at the clock on the wall. "In fact, they are probably already here. So, if it's all right with you, we'll meet up tomorrow about lunchtime and I can start showing you all you need to know then. Is that okay?"

Okay? Raff could barely keep from babbling his thanks as he let Scott out of the apartment. As he shut the door, he leaned against it and then leaped in the air, and let out a "whoop." The dogs stirred and Killer raised his head from the cushion Scott had put him on but Raff hurried through to the bedroom and started pulling out the drawers in his dresser. He had to find something suitable to wear. He had a job to train for.

Chapter Four

Scott hummed as he hurried down the stairs into the club. He was glad he'd had a chat with Raff. The little guy reminded him so much of Dean it made him homesick for Cloverleah, but he shoved those thoughts away. Damien was sitting between his two friends. Scott watched them from the bar and tried to guess who was who. The one sitting taller than Damien with hair that flowed around him like water was his bet for Nereus. As he got closer, he saw the sea blue eyes. Yep. Had to be Nereus.

His attention turned to the one that had to be Sebastian. Wow; Scott mentally fanned himself. His dark military attitude complemented his friend Nereus's laid-back manner. Just as muscular but different. Scott couldn't put his finger on it. It was as if Sebastian kept slipping from view. Gray eyes, so dark they almost looked black, focused on him and for the first time in ages, Scott blushed under the intensely interested gaze. What was wrong with him? He was mated. He loved Damien. Why the hell was he blushing?

"Hey," Damien drew his attention with a smile. "I want you to meet Nereus, son of Poseidon and Sebastian, son of goodness knows who, but we don't ask."

Scott came from behind the bar to stand next to his mate. Giving them a charming smile, he said, "Hi. I'm pleased to meet you both."

"You are so much like him." Sebastian murmured then leaned toward Scott and said. "Well, aren't you a luscious...."

Scott didn't even have a chance to blink before Damien roared and tackled his friend. They crashed into the table, smashing it completely.

Sebastian scrambled to his feet first. "See, I told you he's unreasonab..."

Damien yanked him back down.

Nereus gave a loud sigh. Scott felt his arm nudged and he let Nereus lead him further down the bar. "Let the boys get reacquainted."

Damien went head first into the stage wall. The wood broke. Other wolves were standing around; including an angry looking Malacai, but no one interfered.

"You have insurance, right?" Nereus strolled behind the bar and started looking at bottles.

"Ah..." Scott flinched when it was Damien's turn to throw Sebastian across the room. More plaster shattered.

"Don't worry; they are practically unbreakable when he's fighting Sebastian. Makes me think Sebastian actually likes him."

"They do this often?" Scott was beginning to think there were a lot of things his mate hadn't bothered to tell him about their visitors.

"Yeah."

Tables flew as the two men rolled across the floor; they seemed evenly matched.

"Really?" Scott turned to face Nereus. He had to see his expression. Only to be handed a bottle of Samuel Adams Utopias. Expensive stuff. Scott blinked.

"I'm good for it. Damien usually runs a tab for me." Nereus grinned. "So, how do you like being mated to Damien?"

"I… it's, oh God…not sound system!" Scott's eyes were drawn to the wreckage after another loud crash rang through the room.

"Yep. Have a swig. Sebastian will pay for the breakage. He actually has more cash than I do."

"And they do this every time they meet?" Scott was getting over stunned and heading for furious. He thought Damien cared about his club.

"Yep, ever since Damien was a pup. There was this redhead who was with the German settlers who... Maybe I shouldn't tell you this." Nereus had the grace to look embarrassed.

"Oh no, feel free." Scott could feel his anger burning his gut, and the beer wasn't helping. "I've put up with the harem. A redhead from 100 years ago won't faze me."

"Actually, that was more like 170 years ago."

"How old is my mate?" Scott yelled. He chugged back the Samuel Adams and slammed the empty bottle on the bar.

Damien and Sebastian didn't notice.

"Ah... he didn't tell you? Oh dear. To be fair, he was a very young pup." Nereus gave him another bottle of beer.

"Forget that. Get the whiskey. No, not a glass. Give me the damn bottle."

Nereus wisely kept his mouth shut. They both watched the destruction of the club until the fighters rolled too close to the bar.

"You said they're indestructible?" Scott asked Nereus.

"Yeah. They are."

"Good." He whacked Sebastian over the head with the whiskey bottle.

Damien staggered to his feet. "Thank you, babe."

Scott whacked him with the same bottle, leaving both men slumped on the ground. He picked up the phone. Malacai was on the other side of the room, but he didn't want to yell. "Malacai? Damien and his friend are through celebrating their reunion. Could a few of the enforcers carry them to their beds? And call contractors; find out fast they can put the club to rights and how much it will cost."

He paused then said, "Yeah, it won't be an easy job."

Hanging up, Scott asked Nereus, "Are you two staying here or at the pack house?"

"The pack house is fine. If you don't mind, I would like to grab a shower before we go there?"

Scott decided he knew a thing or two about dealing with angry boyfriends and Damien needed to take lessons. "We'll be here until my mate wakes up. Use the third door on the right of the hallway."

Nereus nodded and fled.

Malachi strode over and growled, "What the fuck caused this?"

"They got reacquainted." Scott was pissed off enough for both of them.

"This is going to cost a fortune." Malacai shook his head as he grabbed Damien under the arms.

"Put Damien in our room. Put Sebastian in the unoccupied apartment, but knock because Nereus is grabbing a shower. I'll be here."

"Ah, do you need my mate?"

"I have it on good authority they are indestructible but it probably can't hurt." Scott scooted around a broken table. "I'm going to find him. Tell Madison to meet me in the office."

"Right." Malacai got Damien to his feet, and an enforcer struggled with Sebastian. Scott wandered off to find Elijah. Personally, he didn't care if both Sebastian and his mate proved bedridden, but even with a pissed off attitude, he still had an inbuilt need to care for his mate.

But he was looking forward to letting his mate know exactly what he thought of the fight after Elijah gave them the all clear.

/~/~/~/~/

Scott was talking to a contractor about immediate repairs when Madison entered the office. He held up a finger. "Yes, if you could. An estimate would be nice. I can't stress how important it is this is fixed immediately. If you can do it in two days, there will be a nice bonus for you and the workers. I'll have the manager wait for you. He has my authorization to approve it. Thank you. I'll tell him to expect you first thing in the morning."

Madison practically bounced. "What happened down there? It looks as if the entire pack went at it. Why do these things always happen when I'm away?"

"Love the new clothes," Scott ran a practiced eye over his PA. He was looking smarter than usual. "Damien and an old friend got reacquainted."

"Reacquainted?" Madison's voice was faint.

"Yep. Reacquainted. Now I need you to..." There was a knock at the office door. "Come in."

Nereus grinned around the door. "They're still resting peacefully."

"Good," Scott was still angry. "Have a seat. I'm just getting quotes. Sebastian will be paying half."

"Only fair." Nereus smiled at Madison. "Hello."

Madison squeaked. Scott hadn't realized he was capable of a noise that high.

The smile became devastating as Nereus cocked his head and his right eyebrow went up. All Scott could think was he was glad he was mated. No one stood a chance when that guy smiled.

"Nereus, this is our PA, Madison; Madison who will be taking my notes. Won't you, Madison? Madison!"

Another squeak was the only answer.

"Madison?" Scott said, "Write!"

Madison nodded.

"Maybe it's better if I leave?" Nereus said smoothly. "You can fill me in on the costs and stuff on the way to the pack house."

Madison found his voice. "You aren't staying here?"

"Scott invited us to the pack house. But of course, we'll be here a lot." Oh, that Nereus was good. Madison was damn near creaming his jeans. Scott smirked.

"Oh good; I mean how nice."

"If you want Nereus, why don't you go down to the kitchen and order dinner for us. Whatever you like." Scott decided getting Nereus out of the room was the only way to get any work out of Madison.

"Sure." Nereus took Madison's hand. "It was so nice to meet you pretty wolf."

Madison squeaked then cleared his throat and said, "Yes, I'll look forward to meeting you again. I mean I look forward to meeting with you again. I mean..."

"I understand." Damn it the laugh was deep and sexy. Scott was worried he'd have to scrape Madison off the floor. "I'll order, Scott. For our rooms?"

"Ours. We have a large table in the apartment. I don't mind replacing it if necessary. The apartment could do with remodeling."

Nereus laughed and left. When the door shut behind him, Madison dropped in a chair. "Oh, my Gods..."

Scot grinned. "Close. Very close."

"What? I mean oh, my. He was... he is... I..."

The man had rendered Madison speechless. Scott wondered if he could be persuaded to stay.

"He's Nereus, son of Poseidon and a friend of Damien's. Do not drool on the carpet."

"But he's... he's... I..."

"Look. Let's get this finished and then you can go plan how to impress him. We are going to the pack house but as soon as the contractors are done, we'll be back to inspect."

"Yes! Oh my Gods, yes. I mean of course." Madison pulled himself together. "We will make sure that everything is finished as fast as possible."

Oh, I bet you will. Scott grinned. "Now. About what needs to be done and what I want you to do...."

Chapter Five

Raff hummed as he shined the glasses. It'd been five days since Scott offered to train him in the bar, but of course, things didn't quite work out as planned. First, there was the little matter of the bar getting trashed. Raff heard the rumors; something to do with Damien and a friend. Raff didn't get the details because he didn't encourage gossip, but he saw for himself how substantial the damage was.

Then Scott was needed at the pack house. Damien had a history with one of his friends... apparently, they fought over the silliest of things. Raff didn't understand how anyone could be friends with someone if they were arguing all the time, but word among the pack was the contractors were needed at the pack house once they were done with the club. But despite all the uproar, Scott didn't forget his promise and the bar manager, John, visited him personally, introduced himself and started training Raff the moment the debris was cleared.

So, Raff had a job, and he found he was good at it. It wasn't difficult being friendly to nice people, and he's quickly mastered the art of pouring beer on tap, and how to make the more common drinks. Most of the shifters who frequented the club had stopped by to say hello. Once they realized Raff wasn't a sub, they pretty much left him alone, but Raff wasn't encouraging attentions either. His life was a thousand times better than it had been just ten days before and if he wanted someone to cuddle up to at night, Killer was always happy to oblige.

"Three beers and get something for yourself." Raff hurried to comply, keeping his eyes down. He didn't drink, but John told him it was okay to take the money for a drink as a tip. The man waiting to be served wasn't one of the "most shifters" he'd been thinking about. There was something about the tall, dark shifter that upset Raff's wolf, and as he grabbed the beers from the fridge he quickly scanned the bar to see if Malacai or one of the other enforcers were nearby. Noah was sitting at one of the tables close to the bar and caught Raff's eye. He winked and kept an eye on things while the man paid and stepped away. Raff nodded his thanks to Noah and went back to polishing glasses. The evening shift was going to be busy because the Alpha and his friends were coming in to inspect the renovations. Raff was glad Elijah offered to feed Killer and the other dogs. He was going to be rushed off his feet.

/~/~/~/~/

Scott would always remember exactly where he was when Nereus realized he had a mate. They were on the staircase in the club; sixteenth stair from the top. He and Nereus, Damien and Sebastian were heading down the stairs, after enjoying a somewhat peaceful meal in their apartment. Nereus stopped talking in the middle of a sentence; his body completely motionless. "Are you okay?" Scott asked quietly.

Nereus simply nodded.

Behind him, Scott could hear Damien and Sebastian squabbling about something. Gods, they should have been brothers the way they fought about everything from the state of the economy to the proper way to brew coffee. Scott glanced up and saw Raff with his hands full of glasses pinned against the end of the bar by a human. Raff was shaking his head and Scott could read his lips enough to realize he was saying "No, please go away, I'm not a sub."

Damn it. Scott felt a rush of protectiveness. He scanned the room and saw Malacai and the other enforcers rushing toward them to pull the man off Raff.

The only problem was the idiot human stuck his hands in Raff's pants at the same time Nereus realized that *his mate* being accosted and struggling to get free. Scott grabbed Nereus's shoulder as the bigger man lunged. "Malacai and the enforcers are on their way," he said urgently.

His words had absolutely no effect. Nereus shrugged off Scott's hand as he roared at the top of his lungs, "Mate!" and it didn't drop off. The sound was like a sudden surge of the ocean breaking through a wall.

At last Damien had enough sense to pay attention to Nereus, but he was too late. Reaching past Scott, it was Damien's turn to yell, "Nereus, no!"

Whatever it was Nereus was doing, he didn't stop. Damien must have realized he was too late because Scott felt big arms surround him, yanking him off his feet and Damien flew back up the steps behind Sebastian yelling at the top of his lungs, "Go. Damn it! Sebastian, move."

Well, how about that; for the first time since Sebastian got there, he and Damien were in complete accord. Scott opened his mouth to ask what the fuck Damien thought he was doing when every club door slammed open with a resounding bang; water rushing through them. Scott's eyes opened wide, and he latched onto Damien. "Shit!"

"Yeah." Damien stood at the top of the stairs.

Malacai changed direction and grabbed his mate, making for the highest point he could find. The enforcers grabbed twinks and something solid to hang on to. A whole lot of enforcers were going to get lucky tonight with the way the smaller men were clinging to them.

The man groping Raff washed out of the room; Raff struggled to hold on to the bar. He failed. Scott gasped as Raff lost his grip. It was like watching a slow train wreck. Without hesitation, Nereus dove into the water. The last thing Scott saw was a shimmering fishtail as the man moved through the water to grab a very wet Raff. Raff had enough sense to grab Nereus's neck and held on tight as they vanished in the flood.

Madison, a very wet Madison, in his new teal leather bar shorts and mesh tee shirt washed past, his arms flailing. Scott struggled to get free, but Damien held him tight. Shit, Madison was going to be...

Sebastian let out a roar and did a perfect dive off the balcony.

"What the fuck?" Scott looked at Damien. "I didn't think Sebastian liked anybody."

"No clue." Puzzled, Damien looked over the balcony rail.

Scott joined him in time to see Sebastian grabbing what looked like a drowned Papillion. Poor Madison. His immaculately coiffured hair was plastered to his face, and black lines ran down his cheeks where his eyeliner ran. "Oh dear."

Damien started to laugh. "This is priceless."

"Madison's going to be furious," Scott said struggling not to laugh at the dejected picture Madison made. "He so wanted to impress your guests. He was drooling over Nereus the night they arrived."

"Nereus is drool worthy and apparently mated to our red wolf." Damien's laughter picked back up. "And so is Sebastian."

"To Raff? I didn't think Nereus and Sebastian were mates."

"They aren't. Sebastian's mated to Madison!" Damien dissolved in laughter again. Scott couldn't understand why Damien thought the situation was funny.

"I don't get it."

"Long story. I wouldn't wish it on Madison." Damien wiped tears from his eyes. "But Sebastian has met his match. Madison is going to rule that house."

"But if they're mates, doesn't that mean Sebastian will be here from now on? I can't see Madison leaving." In fact, Scott was sure nothing would pry Madison from his position as the Alpha's PA, not to mention his position in the pack.

Damien stopped laughing, and it was Scott's turn to start. The look of horror on his mate's face was priceless.

/~/~/~/~/

Raff felt strong arms lift him from the flood water and a deep voice said, "You're safe, my little wolf."

Crisp clean smells flooded his nose. Salt air with just a hint of salt water taffy and coconut. Mate? Mate! He had a mate. His mate. *Keeping me safe. Calling me his little wolf. My mate.* Before Raff could get his thoughts straight, his wolf lunged and his teeth dropped. He sank them into his mate's shoulder and groaned as he felt something snap inside of him. Nereus gave a yell; surprise and then pleasure as the smell of spunk hit the air. Raff howled; his happiness too big to contain. He wasn't alone anymore. He'd found the man meant to be his... or rather, his mate found him.

The water subsided around them and Raff realized he was still cuddled in his mate's arms. That realization hit him at the same time as the ramifications of what he'd done and he covered his face with his hands. "Oh, I'm sorry. I... I shouldn't have bitten you without your permission. I'm so very sorry. I should have asked. I just reacted. I thought I was going to drown. That horrible man grabbing me... all the water coming from nowhere. I thought... I never expected to have a mate. The flood... Your smell... My wolf just...."

Raff realized he was babbling and tried to shut up but his feelings were overwhelming. The rude human at the bar; the flood out of nowhere, realizing he needed to shift to swim and his wolf too scared... and now this; claiming his mate without permission.

Raff felt his hands being tugged from his face and his mate shook his hair so it flowed like the water around them. "I couldn't be happier. I've found my mate. All mine. Forever." A beautiful smile broke.

Gods, he's so big. Raff trembled and the next thing he knew, the strong arms around him grew tighter and a large hand was rubbing up and down his back.

"You're cold. Where's your room?"

"Next to Scott and Damien's apartment." Raff felt a surge like the incoming tide and suddenly they were in front of his door. Killer must have smelled him because the pup started to howl from the other side; his little pack joining in.

"Pups?" The big man quirked an eyebrow and Raff finally realized what swooning meant.

"Dogs. I rescued them and they rescued me."

"I'm glad." The door opened and Killer rushed out trying to jump up to Raff. When that failed, he bit the man holding Raff. "Ouch. And he's got teeth."

"Killer!" Raff struggled to get down.

"Killer?" His savior laughed as he carefully let Raff find his feet. "Let's get you dry." Raff noticed his mate was dry already and wondered about the huge fish tail he thought he'd seen.

Large hands explored him as his wet clothes were pulled off. Raff's body tingled all over. "My little wolf." The bigger man's voice was almost reverent.

"Raff. My name is Raff. Are you Nereus?" Raff might not have encouraged gossip but there'd been enough subs drooling over Damien's friends. Madison was the worst of them and Raff spared a thought for his new friend. Madison had high hopes of attracting one of Damien's friend's interest and Raff hoped it wasn't his mate's. *Too late to worry about that now.* Raff looked at the bite mark on Nereus's neck. Already healed; the scarring permanent and he felt a flush of pride.

"I'm Nereus, yes. It means water. My father didn't have a lot of imagination. Your name means Red Wolf," Nereus smiled. "It's so fitting."

Nereus bent his head, and Raff's body tingled as he knew what was coming. He was a virgin; something he should probably mention, but he'd lived around wolves for most of his life and shifters weren't shy when it came to matters of intimacy. He closed his eyes, holding his breath.

One light touch of lips on lips and then another. Raff sighed and wrapped his arms around Nereus's neck and that seemed to be the signal his mate was waiting for. Those lips came back and Raff found himself devoured under a passionate onslaught. Nothing could've prepared him for how wonderful it felt, or how his body would respond. Raff's skin was on fire. He could do nothing but hold on; he'd never been kissed before, but if he never got kissed again, he would always have this. And just as suddenly, Nereus stopped and Raff opened his eyes. Then Nereus winced and Raff looked down. Killer's teeth were sunk into Nereus's ankle.

"I'm sorry, but I think that's enough biting for one night, don't you?" Nereus carefully picked Killer up by his scruff and put him outside the door. "He'll be fine?" He asked before he let go.

Raff nodded. "Yeah, he knows how to get into Scott and Damien's room. He'll sleep there."

"Good," Nereus purred as he sauntered back into Raff's personal space. "Now, where were we?"

/~/~/~/~/

Scott woke at the soft whine. He leaned over the side of the bed. Killer whimpered. Scott reached down lifted the poodle onto the bed. Killer cuddled against him then curled up as he settled into the bed. Scott's eyes slowly closed.

/~/~/~/~/

Damien stirred and pushed closer to his mate. His hand slowly stroked down Scott's side as he snuggled against him. Scott gave a soft murmur. He kissed his mate's neck as his cock hardened. He let his hands keep moving, searching for Scott's dick. His mate's fur... Fur? Damien's eyes flew open. Scott wasn't furry.

Killer was enjoying a nice dream when the hand groped his ass. His eyes flew open in shock. He knew who it was. That Alpha wannabe. It wasn't enough the pervert had a wonderful little beta for a mate, now he was groping Killer's ass. The pup proceeded to do what any self-respecting Alpha would do when he was being groped by anyone. He sank his very sharp tiny teeth into the offending hand.

"Shit!" Damien jerked back, rolling off the edge of the bed and hitting the floor hard.

Scott rolled over. "What? What happened? Haven't we had enough crap to deal with tonight?"

"That little bastard bit me."

Killer peered over Scott and growled.

"What did you do to him?"

"Why does it have to be my fault?"

"You did something to him."

"I thought he was you."

"And?"

"Fine! And I groped him."

"And you didn't expect to get bitten?"

"I didn't expect him to be there in the first place."

"You groped him."

"It was his fault for being there." Damien glared at Killer who he swore was smirking at him from Scott's side. "I am going to kill that little..."

"He's a freakin' teacup poodle. He isn't even a foot tall. Are you honestly going to fight a teacup poodle who bit you because you groped his ass?"

"I thought it was your ass."

"On my front?"

"No. I mean I thought it was your dick."

"My dick isn't furry. My dick isn't furry even when I'm furry."

"Damn it, Scott..."

"Get back in bed. And leave Killer alone. He's not your type."

Damien crawled back into bed. "Scott…"

"No, I am not throwing him out. Raff and Nereus need some alone time. They've just met and they're mates. I need some freaking sleep because I've got to call the contractors back in the morning and boy, will that be an interesting conversation. You can put up with Killer being here for one measly night and if you don't shut up, I'll grab the other puppies too and you can sleep on the couch."

Damien grumbled while Scott settled back asleep. He would swear that damn dog was watching him, and smirking. The little shit. He was going to have to sleep with one eye open.

94

Chapter Six

Nereus couldn't believe it; having lived a life longer than any mortal could understand his mate was finally in his arms, under his lips... and driving him to ecstasy faster than he could blink. As one of the five acknowledged sons of Poseidon (there were many others), he'd never been sure if he qualified for a mate. But one of the Fates must like him, because here he was, in a pack house in Texas of all places, sucking the tongue of a gorgeous little wolf like his life depended on it. Something he could do tomorrow, and the next day, and the next because the guy would never leave him.

As he captured a moan, his mate was so deliciously responsive, he recalled that split second when he knew his life was about to change for the better. Half bored with Damien's and Sebastian's antics, he was thinking how happy he was

Damien finally mated. Scott was a wonderful man and a fun person to be around. Something Damien definitely needed in his life. They'd been chatting... he couldn't recall about what; but he'd felt it – a tug like a silent siren song. Totally in tune with his environment, his eyes scanned the club patrons; it was as though Raff was standing in a spotlight. He was the only person worth looking at in the room.

To see his mate struggling against the unwanted attentions of a brute; Nereus never felt his anger rise so fast. He called for the waters without thinking; fuck. Raff could've drowned. *What had he been thinking?* But then he always assumed wolves could swim.

"Have you changed your mind about me already?" Raff's soft voice broke through his thoughts and Nereus realized he'd let his anger and worry get the better of him. That wasn't fair to his new mate.

"Of course not," Nereus smiled at the quiet young man in his arms. And he was young; by the Gods Raff was young, but he was all man. Tiny, but perfectly formed. "I'm sorry. You deserve every ounce of my attention. It just crossed my mind that I'm going to owe Scott and Damien a lot of money for the mess in the club."

"That was your fault?" Raff's eyes, a gorgeous shade of amber, glowed. "Wow, um. Look, I don't have any money yet, but I've just started working in the bar...."

"Oh no, no, no, sweet thing," Nereus shook his head, still smiling. "I'm... I've got plenty of money; more than enough to rebuild this place a hundred times over if necessary. It's just I've spent the last five days teasing Sebastian about his repair bill. He's going to give me shit about it, that's all."

"I could pay half," Raff offered. "I could get Scott to garner my wages. It's my fault you...." He waved his hand. "Did whatever it was you did."

"I called the waters," Nereus could tell his mate was curious about him and despite his cock's constant nagging that Raff was naked and they should get to the good stuff, he led Raff over to the couch and arranged his mate on his lap. Nereus felt his heart settle and a sense of peace come over him as Raff curled up on him. "I'm a demigod of the seas," he explained. "All water is mine to command. There are pipes underground, the river's not that far away; any available water will come when I call."

"Just as well it's night then," Raff giggled and Nereus's heart leaped. It was such a sweet sound.

"Imagine being in a canoe or something on the river when the water suddenly disappears."

"I'm usually a lot more careful," Nereus said ruefully. "My dad would have my hide if I caused too many incidences." He brushed Raff's dark hair, thrilled at how soft it was under his fingers. "I knew the instant I came down those stairs that my mate was in the club. I looked around and it was like a beam from the heavens opened up and pointed me in your direction."

"That is such a romantic thing to say," Raff looked up at him, studying his face. Nereus knew he didn't have anything to worry about. Thousands of men and women alike had thrown themselves at his dick in the past. But Raff was different; permanent, and Nereus felt an uncharacteristic twinge of worry.

"You are also amazing to look at," Raff added, his gaze warm. "But then you know that already. I know I've already bitten you, and our mating is a foregone conclusion, but are you honestly happy the Fates chose me for you? I'm not worldly or clever; I don't have any money. I've only been in this pack just over a week, and the only friends I've had for a long time are my dogs."

"What about your parents? Surely you were born into a pack?" Nereus wished he hadn't asked when sadness marred his mate's face.

"They didn't want me," Raff whispered. "I wasn't good enough for them."

"And that's why you're worried you're not good enough for me, is that it?"

"I'm a virgin," Raff's voice couldn't be any quieter, but Nereus let out a whoop loud enough to wake the dogs sleeping on the other end of the couch. One of them, a Maltese growled and Raff said quickly, "it's all right Butch." The dogs settled down although the one called Butch gave Nereus what could only be called a dirty look.

"I'm sorry; that was uncalled for," Nereus felt his cheeks heat up even though his cock was jumping in excitement despite being trapped in leather. "But really, honestly... you are legal, aren't you?" It would suck if he wasn't.

"I'm twenty-two," Raff said hotly. "I know it's pathetic; I should have had a hundred guys by now, but I wanted to wait. I wanted my first time to be with someone special. There's nothing wrong with that."

"There definitely isn't; in fact, I think it's amazing," Nereus assured his anxious mate quickly. "I... I'm almost as old as the sea itself; I have had sex in every possible way with more people than you could count," Raff growled, low and deep and Nereus carried on quickly. He'd forgotten Raff's wolf side for a moment. "But the one thing I've never done is shared my body with someone who cared about me beyond what they could see. I can have that with you."

Raff tilted his head and studied him and Nereus relaxed under his gaze. His mate didn't know him; didn't know how Nereus refused to lie under any circumstances, much to his father's chagrin. But Nereus believed he'd been born with enough advantages in life without having to take advantage of anyone else.

"It's not been easy being you, has it," Raff said at last and Nereus was stunned. Was it possible no one had ever taken the time to really look at him before? How could this one little man see something he'd hidden for centuries? "You are so amazingly stunning; your hair, your eyes; even your scruff is adorable. You were perfectly crafted and yet how many people have touched you here?" Raff laid his small hand over Nereus's heart and he wanted to melt right into the couch.

"My father, my brothers," Nereus rested his head back on the seat, unable to meet Raff's eyes. He felt as though Raff could see his soul and it was unnerving. "Less than a handful of others over the centuries. Sebastian's probably my closest friend but people who've bothered to stick around after the sweat has dried?" Nereus shook his head. "My father once said love was mortal foolishness."

"That's so sad. Did you believe him?" Nereus felt a brush of warmth over his heart and realized it was coming from Raff's mouth. The heat from that tiny touch could be felt right down to his toes.

103

"No." Nereus swallowed as Raff's fingers started tracing lightly over his bare chest. He'd been dressed for clubbing; a shirt hadn't been necessary when a flex of his pecs could have subs falling over themselves. "I prayed to every deity that would listen, to bring me a true mate."

"And now you have one," Raff said, his breath ghosting across Nereus's chest. "A broke, rather insignificant wolf shifter; I almost feel sorry for you. But I do have one thing precious I can give you," Nereus looked down to Raff looking up at him. Raff's cheeks were a pretty shade of pink. "I wasn't talking about my virginity," he said, stumbling over the last word. "I give that to you gladly because we're mates. I was talking about my heart. I don't care if you can command the waters, or have a man creaming his pants with one raised eyebrow. Yes, I heard the gossip about you in the club." It was Nereus's turn to blush. "I'm not interested in how much money you have in the bank, or what position you have anywhere. My wolf sees you; your spirit and from the moment I bit you, you became mine and I will cherish you till the end of days."

Raff's face was flushed and Nereus watched he worried his bottom lip with his teeth. Nereus was amazed at the courage held in one tiny body. He'd never met anyone who could give his heart so freely, expecting nothing in return. "You have given me the greatest gift," he said, pouring all the sincerity he could into his words. "I will never ever give you cause to regret it."

"I know," Raff said brightly. His hands moved and Nereus felt a tentative brush across the bulge in his pants. He bit back a groan. "Can we go to bed now, because the smell of your lust is driving me crazy."

"I am yours to command," Nereus said fervently; Raff's joyous laughter tickling his ears as he found his way to Raff's bedroom; his mate still wrapped around his body.

/~/~/~/~/

Raff was nervous; who wouldn't be? In all his years, when he dreamed of giving his virginity, he never imagined it would be with the son of a god, or that the man in question would be the one fated for him. It was a dream come true if Raff ever dreamed something so fantastic. The best he'd ever hoped for was for someone who wouldn't laugh at his size; would take the time to chat to him for five minutes first and who would maybe cuddle afterward.

I have a mate; mine forever. I wish....

Whatever he wished for went right out of Raff's head as a hot body covered his. *When did he get naked?* There were definitely no clothes in the way. Raff could feel his skin lightly stimulated by the hairs on Nereus's arms and legs, and the curls around Nereus's dick tickled his balls. His arms were still wound around Nereus's neck and as he looked up, Nereus's smile was warm but his eyes were heated.

"There are so many things I want to do to you," Nereus's voice was the warmest of caress. "I want to take hours simply getting to know every spot that makes you gasp. But I find myself at a bit of a disadvantage."

Raff frowned. Nereus had already spoken about being experienced; there was lube in the drawer by the bed and given the heat branding his belly, Nereus was hard enough to do the deed. "What's wrong?" He whispered, wondering if his inexperience was showing.

"If I move an inch, I fear I'm going to come all over your belly before we even get started," Nereus confided in a low whisper.

Biting his lip, Raff tried not to laugh; worried it would upset his mate in some way. But he couldn't help himself. Nereus's face was so serious but his eyes were twinkling and as Raff gave in and laughed out loud, Nereus chuckled. "You are just that sexy," Nereus explained.

Raff wasn't sure about that; as a wolf shifter, he thought he was rather plain. But with Nereus looming over him, his thin hips cradled between Raff's thighs, Raff felt powerful, desirable and that gave him courage. "Kiss me," he said.

Nereus's top lip was almost obscured by the hair on his face, but his bottom lip was deliciously soft, plump and ripe for sucking on. His mate tried to hold himself aloft, but Raff wasn't having it. His arms tightened around Nereus's neck, and when he wrapped his ankles around his mate's hips, Nereus groaned. "Sweet one, please; I'll come."

That was Raff's intention, and he hung on tighter, wriggling his body, the friction on his cock so good he hoped Nereus felt the same. They quickly found a rhythm, grinding against each other and Raff's wolf howled in his head. Yes... almost... with a loud cry Raff climaxed and a mere second later, Nereus's body tightened and the sticky warmth on his stomach increased.

"You... you... you little minx," Nereus gasped as Raff sank back into the mattress. "You... I... I was gonna...."

"You still can, can't you?" Raff said as he got his body under control. "You telling me you can command the waters but you can't orgasm twice in an hour?"

"Why... you...." Nereus shook his head, his chuckles running through Raff's body, firming his cock again. "You are perfect for me."

Chapter Seven

Nereus hadn't been boasting when he told Raff he'd been intimate with more people than he could count. It was a fact of his life. But he couldn't remember coming from simply rubbing off on another person's body. He probably had as a teenager, but once he hit adulthood, his cock was usually encased in a hole before it performed. Men, women, both; he'd never been overly fussy, but as he grabbed a washcloth and a couple of bottles of water, he felt a trickle of unease at taking a virgin. He was a big man in every department and if he'd been with a virgin before, it'd been unintentional and he'd never known about it.

Gods, I was a callous bastard in my day, he told himself off sternly as he came back into Raff's room, entranced by the beauty on the bed. Raff's shoulder length dark hair was a mess on the pillows; his bright red lips were puffy and the surrounding skin covered in beard rash. *Might have to think about trimming it,* he thought ruefully, running a hand over the hair in question. Raff clearly had sensitive skin.

"You're not tired, are you?" Raff asked, "Only my wolf thinks it would be pretty awesome to bite you while you're actually fucking me."

Nereus shook his head as he climbed back onto the bed. It was big enough to hold an orgy. "Why would I fuck you when I can finally try this making love concept so many humans talk about?"

"I'm easy either way," Raff said, but Nereus could tell from those amber eyes, there was a huge part of Raff who wanted nothing more than to be loved. His father be damned; Nereus believed and as he bent his head and took Raff's lips, he kept his actions gentle, sensuous, knowing he had all the time in the world to get things right.

Raff took his cues and ran with them. Work-worn hands traced lightly over the dips and grooves in his body. Raff's lips were pliant under his; none of the pushiness of before and now Nereus's urgent need had passed he could take the time to enjoy his mate.

His mate. Hot damn. There was so much to enjoy. Raff wasn't a muscleman but there wasn't an ounce of fat on him. Nereus could trace his ribs and there was a decided dip in Raff's stomach region. His mate's life hadn't been easy as evidenced by the calluses on his hands and the roughness of his heels. But all the skin in between was warm, inviting and so freaking suckable. Determined not to cause Raff's face any further discomfort, Nereus trailed his lips and tongue down Raff's neck and onto the body below; the hint of salt from his sweat coating his tongue.

Nereus groaned; as a creature of the sea, salt was an aphrodisiac. Resting his hands lightly on Raff's arms to keep him in place, Nereus's nose, lips, and tongue sought out more. Raff's body was hairless and nothing got in the way of Nereus's search. Under the arms, the backs of his knees, and there, in the groves of Raff's pelvis Nereus found the strongest concentration of all. His hands were now needed to hold Raff's legs apart, but his sweet mate wasn't going anywhere.

Indeed, Raff's fingers clutched the covers, his head thrown back, his thigh muscles tight under Nereus's fingers. Nereus used his nose to nudge Raff's balls aside, his tongue working long stripes in the gully of Raff's groin.

"Nereus, please."

Sweet words; cock inflaming words under any other circumstances and in that respect, they were no exception, but Nereus had only just started. Carefully flipping Raff onto his stomach, Nereus let his tongue map out the ridges and groves of Raff's spine, his moans rippling along Raff's skin as he found pockets of Raff's unique taste along the nape of his neck and in the cute little dimples framing the base of his spine.

Raff was moaning in earnest at this point, writhing on the covers, trying to find release. Nereus cupped his thin hip bones securely in his hands, raising Raff's ass for further exploration. A quick slide with his thumbs and his goal was in sight – perfectly pink and tight. Nereus whimpered and quickly muffled the sound by burying his nose between Raff's tight cheeks. Raff's scent was stronger here as well and Nereus lapped it up, loosening the tight muscles he was desperate to penetrate.

"Lube. Drawer. Hurry, please, you bastard."

Bastard? Maybe it was time to move things along. Lord knows Nereus's cock was ready to stage a protest. Not a strike, but the ache in his balls intensified and yet he knew the next stage was crucial. Without proper prep, he could scar Raff's psyche for life and cause serious problems in their mating. Propping up Raff's butt with a handy pillow, Nereus lay over Raff's body, his fingers working down low, while his mouth kept Raff busy up top.

"Please, Ner… Please." *Ah, youth; all about speed and satisfaction*. But as Nereus ran his tongue around the shell of Raff's ear he could see the wolf in his mate's eyes and the tension rippling through Raff's body.

"Soon, sweet one," he rasped in Raff's ear. "Just let me…." Heaps of lube, a spot of magic; *thank you Dad,* and Raff was ready. "Breathe out. Push out and relax," he whispered as his cock found its goal. "Oh, fuck." Too much magic? Too much lube? Nereus wasn't sure but his cock slid right in; Raff barely flinched.

It was Nereus's turn to pant. He'd forgotten the heat inherent to shifters; not to mention the strength of the muscles holding him firm. "I'm never coming out," he mumbled as he blanketed Raff's back.

"Just move."

Shaking his head at how feisty his mate seemed to be when he was horny, Nereus was happy to oblige. Worrying about his mate's virginity was one thing; that was gone. That didn't mean he had to plunder Raff's body like a bull in a gate. Settling into a sweet rhythm

Nereus focused on the next bit–for him at least. A mating was special, sacred and had to be done just right; at least that's what he'd heard among the lesser Gods. Raff's constant moans, the way his body rose to meet his with every thrust was not making thinking easy.

Wrong way! His brain screamed helpfully and Nereus pulled out. Face to face, cock engaged, orgasm imminent, now what? Raff's wolf was taking over; Raff's cute fangs were showing over his lips and his eyes glittered like crystals. He was close and Nereus knew exactly how he felt.

"*Ego te pro meo; et nos unum sumus,*" he yelled, knowing words were necessary but not having a clue what to say. Greek would have been better, but Nereus was not a multitasker. "I take thee for my own. We are one; forever and a day and may the wrath of Poseidon fall on those who try to come between us."

Nereus felt a burn on the base of his spine, like a hand pushing him deeper into Raff's body. Raff's back arched and suddenly Nereus yelled as Raff's teeth hit their mark. The sensation of cool water covered Nereus's body, soothing him as his balls pumped his seed into the man who'd be his forever. His heart was still pounding so fast, Nereus wasn't sure he'd survive. But fuck, it didn't matter. After a full body orgasm, he didn't have the energy to care.

Raff disengaged his teeth; his eyes half closed as he wrapped his arms around Nereus's neck and gently licked the wound. Nereus slumped over him, then rolled to one side, keeping them together. It seemed to take forever for his heart and lungs to slow enough to speak.

"Are you okay? That was a little unexpected."

"What was?" Raff panted. "If that's what sex is like, no wonder everyone does it so much."

"It's never been like that for me before," Nereus admitted.

"The intense orgasm, the heat, the water or the tattoos?"

"All of it," Nereus panted a bit more. "Hang on, did you say tattoos?"

Raff pointed at a mark on Nereus's chest. A trident with a dolphin jumping through the prongs was etched above his heart. "You've got one too," he said, although Raff's was smaller. But it was a matching mark and Nereus smiled. No one would doubt who Raff belonged to.

"I'm not complaining or anything," Raff said, "but could you look at my back? I feel like something's burning my butt cheeks and I'm sure that's not normal."

Unwilling to leave the warmth of his mate's body any sooner than he had to, Nereus leaned around Raff's body, trying to keep his cock in place. Sure enough, Raff had another tattoo on his ass–two huge waves cresting over into his tight little crack.

"Bloody Dad," Nereus shook his head. "Looks pretty, though." Raff laughed and slipped his hands around Nereus's butt.

"Have you got one?" Raff was almost asleep, but his eyes still held a twinkle.

"I'll get a washcloth and you can look," Nereus said, carefully pulling out and stumbling off the bed. He'd barely made it two feet from the bed when Raff was laughing again.

"What? What is it?" Raff was laughing too hard to tell him. Nereus summoned a mirror and tried looking at his back, but it wasn't easy. Then he saw it.

"Property of Raff," in gothic script across the top of his butt cheeks.

"Your dad gave you a tramp stamp," Raff giggled.

"I'll kill him," Nereus snarled as he stomped into the bathroom. "I'll fucking kill him." But as he caught a glimpse of it in the larger bathroom mirror, he admitted to himself it did look pretty cool. Not that he'd ever tell his father that. The man had interfered with his mating enough and he just hoped Raff never realized his dad had been in the room. He had a feeling Raff would be mortified.

/~/~/~/~/

Raff woke with a start; the sound of snoring loud in his ear. *Killer's loud,* was his first thought, but it wasn't Killer curled up on the pillow behind him. The body stretched around him was a lot, lot bigger. *My mate!* Slowly the events from the night before flittered through his brain and Raff carefully turned, unwilling to wake his bed partner.

Nereus looked beautiful in the half-light; the scar from his mating bite visible to Raff's keen eyes and the tattoo on his heart... perfectly placed. He wasn't sure how much of a part Nereus's dad played in their marks, but he whispered "thank you" and thought he caught a whiff of the sea in reply. Maybe Gods really were everywhere. Raff never thought much about the spiritual side of life. Wolves knew they were one with nature and his human side was always so busy worrying about food and a roof over his head.

Which was something he was worried about now. Would Nereus want to stay with the pack or would he expect them to move somewhere else? Maybe his house was under the sea? Raff remembered the flash of fish tail he saw, right before Nereus appeared in front of him in the bar. He gulped and instinctively snuggled closer to Nereus's body. He couldn't swim in his human form and his wolf couldn't breathe underwater. Raff couldn't see his wolf being happy swimming with fish... and sharks... oh my goodness, how could he have forgotten about sharks? They ate dogs, so it wasn't a stretch to think... Raff's wolf cowered in his mind.

"I don't live in a house under the sea," Nereus rasped, his blue eyes slowly coming into focus. "I have houses all over the place, all on dry land. But seeing as my new mate lives in a pack, I don't think we'll be going far. Now stop worrying and pucker up those lips of yours."

"You don't mind staying around here?" Raff knew he was a bit of a worrier; he'd worried all his life. First about keeping his family members happy and his orientation a secret; then trying to cope with keeping himself and his precious dogs fed and housed. His dogs. Shit. He always fed them the moment he woke up. Killer would be furious; Buddy would be doing that hang-dog look he'd perfected so well and Joey....

"Kisses," Nereus said firmly. "Everything else can wait five minutes."

Raff dutifully lifted his head. From the moment Nereus's lips touched his; he knew his mate was right. If he could have this; his mate holding him and caring for him, then maybe life wouldn't be so hard.

Life won't be hard anymore; I won't let that happen. Raff's eyes flew open to see Nereus was still watching him although their lips were still entangled.

We have a mind link?

Yep.

Nereus seemed smug. Raff was stunned. No one in his home pack shared a mind link although none of them were true mates either. *Oh wow; oh my god, I'm really not dreaming.* Even though he knew he was mated and had the twinge in his ass to prove it, it was as though it hadn't sank in until now.

The tattoos not enough for you?

Nereus seemed to be laughing through their link, but Raff didn't care. He flung himself into their kisses, determined that would be his first order of business every day. His beloved puppies would just have to wait in line. They didn't make him feel like he did in Nereus's arms, which was just as well because that would be *eww*. Nereus's laughter flittered through his mind again and Raff wondered if he should talk to someone about filtering his thoughts. After the kisses. And maybe more, because despite not having a frame of reference, Raff was quickly coming to realize Nereus's kisses were a whole body affair and parts of his body were reacting faster and with more urgency than others.

Chapter Eight

It was after ten by the time Nereus and Raff made their way down to breakfast. There were kisses to finish; then Nereus thought it'd be a great idea to introduce Raff to blowjobs, because when his mate said he was a virgin, he meant in every way. Nereus had barely finished swallowing Raff's come when the sweet man wanted to reciprocate. Nereus wasn't an idiot and clumsy though he might have been, Raff learned fast. Then they needed to shower, and the dogs needed seeing to. By the time they hit the stairs to the club, Nereus was ready to eat.

"There doesn't look like there's a lot of damage," Raff said quietly.

"What?" Nereus had forgotten all about his little incident. But Raff was right. Apart from a rather high tide mark running around the walls, everything else looked fine. People were sitting around tables drinking coffee and eating pastries. "Either that or someone's been busy overnight."

Nereus led Raff into the restaurant. Scott and Damien were already at a table. Damien scowled as they walked in. Time to face the music. "Would you order for us, sweet one? I'll have a large breakfast platter, heavy on the bacon and a triple-shot espresso." Nereus didn't see why Raff should have to handle the wrath of an Alpha. Raff looked worried, darting glances at Damien, but he stood on tiptoe and pecked Nereus on the cheek.

"Be right back."

Nereus watched until he saw Raff talking to a smiling man at the counter before making his way over to the Alpha pair. "Good morning," he said with a smile, as he sank into one of the empty chairs. "Everything's looking good this morning."

"No thanks to you," Damien immediately started the offensive. "You had no reason to let loose like that, last night. We take care of our pack members, and the enforcers were already on their way to deal with the asshole who assaulted Raff before you let loose with your freaky powers. My club was a dripping mess."

"When one finds their mate, they don't expect to find said mate being physically and sexually assaulted by someone else," Nereus said calmly although his blood still boiled at the manhandling he'd seen. "Was that guy pack or what? Because I'm thinking a trip to Davy Jones' Locker would be a perfect punishment unless you've already handled it."

"The guy was human," Scott said quickly as Damien started to growl. "No one claims to have seen him before and no one can find him since he got swept out of the club door with the tide. All John, the bar manager could tell us, was that the guy had been in earlier asking about Raff specifically, wanting to know what he looked like and when he was working. John didn't tell him anything, but someone clearly did."

It was Nereus's turn to frown. Glancing over his shoulder to make sure Raff was still busy, he turned back and hissed, "You think my mate was targeted specifically? That he's responsible for this? He was two seconds away from being seriously violated."

"I don't think it was Raff's fault. No one asks to be attacked," Damien growled. "But we know nothing about him except he was close to being homeless and under attack when Scott found him. I couldn't scent any deceit on him when I admitted him to the pack, but you have to admit this looks suspicious."

"What I think is you're letting brutal, violent humans into this club, and then blaming Raff for the way he looks," Nereus kept his voice down. "He's a rare breed, yeah? Special to your kind? How do you know one of the assholes in your pack isn't behind this? Have you even asked Raff about it?"

"No, they haven't." Nereus turned. Raff's face was white and his eyes were full of tears. "I heard what you said Alpha. I don't want trouble for your pack. I'll go if you can just give me time to collect my things. I'm sorry. I never wanted to bring trouble to anyone which is why I stayed by myself."

"You've got nothing to be sorry for," Nereus reached over and tugged Raff into his lap. "You need your pack and you shouldn't have to leave."

"I've lived without a pack for almost two years," Raff's voice was so quiet it was hard to hear, but Nereus knew Damien and Scott could hear every word. "My home pack didn't want me because I wouldn't mate with the lady they picked out for me. It's not surprising this pack doesn't want me either. I don't want to cause any trouble."

"You're not causing trouble," Scott said firmly, glaring at Damien before getting off his chair and crouching in front of Raff. "You were a victim last night, just as you were the day we met. We just haven't had a chance to talk to you about it and Damien hasn't had his coffee yet. What can you remember about the human who assaulted you?"

"He smelled funny," Raff clearly didn't want to talk about it and Nereus was amazed he was trying. He rubbed his hand up and down

Raff's back, hoping it would help. "Like, not cologne or anything... more like drugs... as if he was on something."

"The enforcers don't let guys like that in here," Damien said.

"Which simply means he took it while he was here," Scott snapped back. "What else?" His voice was a lot softer speaking to Raff.

"He ordered a drink and then told me he'd give me an extra fifty bucks if I blew him in the alley." Raff looked up at Nereus, who could feel his anger burning and was trying not to show it. "I didn't go. I wouldn't do that sort of thing."

"I know sweet one. I'm not upset with you. Assholes piss me off," Nereus said.

"He wasn't happy when I said no," Raff continued. "He told me all the subs did it; that I'd lose my job if I didn't make him happy. I could smell he was lying. I was trying to catch the eye of an enforcer, but the guys at the door were busy, and there was some sort of ruckus in the restaurant... so everyone was occupied."

"He was adamant he wanted you to go outside of the club; not in the bathroom or one of the rooms in the back here?" Scott asked.

"He said outside in the alley. He kept insisting and then he grabbed me."

"See," Scott said to Damien, standing up and then taking his seat. "Someone was trying to get Raff *out* of the club; someone who knew Raff was in the pack. Nereus could be right. You might want to get the enforcers to check the alley. None of our subs go out there for a hook-up. There's no need with the rooms we have here."

A wave of his finger, a couple of terse words and two large men disappeared from the restaurant. A waiter came over with heaped trays of food, but Nereus didn't let Raff take his own seat. He wasn't letting go of his mate until he knew he wasn't in any danger.

"Eat, sweet one, you need to keep up your strength."

With a wary look at Scott and Damien, Raff picked at his food. Nereus was hungry, but every mouthful was like cardboard. He managed half of it, before laying down his cutlery and as soon as he did, Raff stopped the pretense of eating too. Damien sighed and pushed his plate away.

"I'm not accusing you of anything," the big alpha said slowly. "But you told Scott when you were being attacked by those men the day you came here, that one of the men said he wanted to send a message to me as the owner of a gay club. Is that right?"

"That's what it sounded like," Raff said, while Nereus tried to digest the information that his mate had been hurt before. Gods, he was lucky he found Raff when he did. "He was talking about gays, and the club, and being deviants and how they didn't want that sort of thing in town."

"He probably assumed all gay men come here, which is totally stupid because we aren't the only gay club in town," Scott said. "We are the most exclusive, but we have our reasons for that." He smiled.

"I've never had any trouble with people in town before. The businesses around here appreciate how much we do keeping drugs and gangs out of the area," Damien said. "I think that first attack was an opportunistic hate crime. But last night was different. Trying to get one of our members out of the club; I've never known anyone to do that with any of our other subs."

"Raff's not a sub," Nereus said sharply, "And he was targeted specifically by someone who thought he was. Seems to me, one of your Doms could have the wrong idea."

"You think it was a set-up?" Scott asked.

"I think it has something to do with a pack member," Nereus said. "Look, you've got a lot of guys here. You can't keep tabs on everyone. You told me just the other night at dinner about the shit that was going on at the pack grounds before you both moved out there. What if you've got a rogue here?"

"It might not be someone in the pack," Damien said. "Oh, I'm not saying a shifter isn't behind this," he added when Nereus scowled, "but we've always allowed any visiting shifters to use the club and facilities provided they don't cause any trouble."

"How long have you been working the bar?" Nereus asked Raff. He hated seeing the worried frown lines and dull eyes on his mate and wanted the matter fixed and sorted.

"Only a few days. I was due to start the day after Sebastian and the alpha had their fight. John trained me as soon as the mess was cleaned up, but last night was only my third shift."

"Has anyone made you feel uncomfortable, or done something you didn't like?" It was Scott that asked.

"Not done anything, no…" Raff trailed off.

"Speak sweet one, there is something, isn't there?" Nereus stroked Raff's pale cheek.

"There was a guy; a wolf shifter. He tried to hit on me my first shift. Was real excited because he could scent I was a red wolf."

"You're a pretty wolf; you attracted a lot of attention among the enforcers and probably half the unclaimed Doms as well, I imagine," Damien said drily.

Raff shook his head and his body trembled. Nereus glared at Damien who simply glared back. Scott shot them both an exasperated look and asked, "This guy worried you?"

"Everyone's been real friendly," Raff's head came up and Nereus could see a lone tear run down his face. "Some guys did hit on me, the first time they saw me, but when I said no, they accepted it and were friendly about it."

"This guy was different though?" Nereus brushed a finger through Raff's tear and sucked on it. *Damn... wrong move.* He could taste Raff's sorrow, but it didn't stop his cock from responding.

"He watched me all the time. He wanted me to go with him to a hotel to play and I told him I didn't...."

"Hang on a minute," Damien interrupted leaning forward on the table. "A shifter from here tried to get you to leave the club with him and he specifically used the word play?"

Raff nodded.

"Shit!" Damien leaned back hard enough in the chair it creaked. "It's a rule in this club; no one plays outside of it unless they're with a mate. No one. It's not safe for the subs; we've got no control over what happens and every single Dom and sub in this club respects that. Who is this asshole?"

"He didn't give me a name; said I had to call him Sir."

Nereus wrapped his arms tight around his mate, rocking him gently. The tears were pouring down Raff's face. Raff feared Damien's anger and the unnamed man who'd spooked him so badly. Nereus wanted nothing more than to take his mate far away and never see another fucking alpha again.

"He needs a pack," Scott said softly. Nereus nodded, but that didn't mean he had to be happy about it.

"I'm sorry, Raff," Damien said suddenly. Nereus didn't think he'd ever heard his friend apologize before. "I am angry, but not at you. You should be safe here, the same as any of my other smaller members. I'm annoyed that you weren't."

"Noah might know the man," Raff's head came up, and he faced his alpha bravely. "Last night, the man was in; he frightens me, although

143

that time he only ordered drinks. But Noah was at a table by the bar and he kept an eye on him until the man left again."

"I'll call him," Scott said, but just then the enforcer concerned came running through the restaurant.

"Alpha," Noah inclined his head. "Sorry to disturb your meal but Malacai sent me to find you. One of the subs, Joel is missing. Cody said he hasn't been back to their room in two nights and he's not in the club."

"Close the club," Damien ordered as he stood up. "No one in or out unless I say so. Tell the guys at the door to put a sign up, closed 'till further notice and then get all of my enforcers into the office and tell Cody I want to see him there too."

"I'll take Raff upstairs and find Sebastian," Nereus said, refusing to let go of his mate as he got to his feet.

"I don't know that Sebastian is here," Scott said. "He's been weird since he saved his mate, but Madison might know where he's gone."

"Is Madison Sebastian's mate?" Raff asked.

"Supposed to be," Scott growled as he hurried after his mate.

"We need to go and see Madison," Raff said and Nereus didn't have the heart to refuse him. Although what he could say to his friend's mate, when he knew Sebastian was still in love with a dead man, was anyone's guess.

Chapter Nine

Scott was ready to pull his hair out. There were no leads on the missing sub; the enforcers were running all over town looking for him. With what they'd learned from Raff, there was a real sense of urgency about the search, but of course, Scott couldn't help because he was frigging Alpha Mate. He and Damien had just gone up to their apartment for five minutes peace and quiet and didn't even get to the door when Sebastian stormed out of the one he'd commandeered, looking like shit. "Where's Nereus?" The big man demanded. "I've got to get out of here."

"He's with his mate, just like you should be," Scott snapped, too frustrated to think about being polite. "Do you have any idea what being rejected by a mate can do to a wolf shifter?"

"I didn't ask for a mate," Sebastian yelled back. "It's not my fault the Fates made a fuck up. My true love is dead and has been for centuries. I'm not dishonoring his memory by taking a piddly-assed twink as a mate. My mate will be a warrior; just like my lover was; someone big, capable of looking after himself; instead of worrying about the state of his frigging clothes and water in his hair. The Fates are playing a fucking JOKE on me, and I won't have it. I won't take that twink for a mate if he's the last man on earth."

Scott heard a gasp before a white-faced Madison sprinted past them, dashing down the stairs. "You've gone too far this time, you bastard," he said to Sebastian. He swung around to Damien. "Fucking sort him out; teach him some facts of life or so help me, I will. I'm going after Madison." He raced down the stairs, calling Madison's name.

He wasn't in the club; a quick look told Scott that. He eyed the doors, but the bouncers locked them and Madison was unlikely to have gone there. Hearing a whimper to his right, he dashed around the stairs, remembering the back entrance he'd used his first day in the pack. It led out onto the alley beside the club. Sure enough, Madison was there, his face a mess of tears, trying to get the door opened.

"Madison, don't go. It's not safe." Scott hurried to Madison's side, determined to pull him away from the door, but suddenly he felt a rush of fresh air as a sharp prick lanced his arm. "What the...." Scott tried to turn, but fell against Madison and the two of them landed on the floor. Just before darkness overwhelmed him, Scott saw a dark figure in the shadows.

"You two will do nicely," the man said, as Scott slipped into unconsciousness.

/~/~/~/~/

"You can't force me to mate your wolf," Sebastian struggled out of the wreckage of what was Damien's large dining table.

"No one's forcing anyone," Damien was having similar problems. His leg and arm had gone through the plaster wall. He yanked his foot out, pulling a large chunk of plaster with it. "But you didn't have to be so fucking hurtful. Madison's a sweet man and your words devastated him. He'll never get another mate while you're still breathing and now his wolf's scented you, he can't be with another partner even if it's just for sex. You're a fucking asshole. You should have left him alone."

"I couldn't let him drown. I'm not a complete bastard." Sebastian brushed off his clothes and looked around for a chair. They were scattered in pieces around the floor. He sat on the kitchen counter

150

instead, resting his head in his hands.

"You could have fooled me," Damien staggered to the kitchen and pulled out a couple of beers. He handed one to Sebastian. "How long has this lover of yours been dead?"

"Two thousand three hundred and thirty-nine years. It will be two thousand and forty years next June."

Damien stared at the guy he'd known most of his life, unsure what shocked him more. "And you haven't been with another man in all that time?"

"Of course, I have," Sebastian took a long swig from the bottle. "Alexander and I weren't mates. But he took my heart with him when he died."

"I also vowed never to love again," Damien said. "You've heard me say that often enough over the years, and then Scott came along and, bam, I couldn't be happier."

"Your mate is strong and of the warrior class. I understand why you mated him. I'd consider it if that twink looked like Scott."

"The twink's name is Madison," Damien snarled. "He's older than he looks; has been through a hell of a lot in his life, and then he had the misfortune to end up with a mate like you. Now he can't be with anyone else because you're too stuck up to see value in a person beyond his size."

"I'll get the mating broken; I have connections," Sebastian had the grace to look uncomfortable. "Maybe the Fates will give him another mate."

"And maybe they won't and last I heard no mating could be broken no matter who you were." Damien looked around at the messy apartment. "Scott is going to have my guts for garters because of this." He searched their mind link, wondering where Scott was. He started to growl as he was met with nothing but darkness.

"D, you okay?"

"Scott... SCOTT!" Flinging his bottle to the floor, Damien ran from the apartment, tugging his shirt off as he went. Following his mate's scent, he was in wolf form as he reached the back door to the club. Madison's and Scott's scents were there, but they were fading. His eyes monochrome, Damien's wolf found two darts on the floor, and a piece of paper taped to one of Madison's shoes. Shifting back to his human form, he snarled, "Get me a phone."

/~/~/~/~/

"Don't be scared, sweet one," Nereus said softly as they walked to Damien's office. "You haven't done anything wrong."

"I don't know why he wants to see me at all," Raff whispered, all too aware of how acute a shifter's hearing could be. "I don't know the sub that's missing and last I heard every enforcer in the pack was out looking for him."

"Seems like a lot of them are back," Nereus stopped in front of the office door. "Maybe Madison's had some luck with Sebastian?"

Raff hoped so. Spending a good hour listening to Madison cry because his mate abandoned him after saving him in the flood was hard enough. Listening to him dithering in his wardrobe after Raff convinced him to find the man when he was looking his best was torturous. Raff didn't think it was possible for anyone to own so many clothes.

Taking a deep breath, he knocked on the door and turned the handle when he heard the call to enter. The room was full of people; big people and Raff shrank against his mate as he sidled into the room.

"You wanted to see me Alpha?"

"Take a seat you two. We've had an *incident*."

Raff frowned. He could see the tension in the Alpha's shoulders and there was no sign of Scott. A smaller man, no bigger than himself, touched Damien's arm, and the alpha relaxed slightly. But his next words sent an arrow straight through Raff's heart. "Scott and Madison have been kidnapped. We think it's the same shifter who tried to take you."

Frozen, Raff couldn't get his mouth to work. It was Nereus who answered. "Why do you say that, D?"

"Because in the note he left at the scene, he says he will return Scott and Madison if the red wolf leaves the club on foot and walks out of town."

"That means he must be around here somewhere, right? Otherwise, how would he know if Raff left the club?" Nereus said. "Surely, your enforcers can find them."

"He's blocking his scent," a tall, slender man with long black hair said. "I can't get a bead on any of them and the enforcers have found nothing in a ten-block radius."

"Shifter Guardian, it's an honor," Nereus nodded.

"As it is to meet you, son of Poseidon," the shifter guardian said smoothly, bowing slightly.

"Sorry. These men are from the Cloverleah pack," Damien explained gruffly. "Scott comes from there; Troy his twin, still lives there," he added pointing to a slightly muted version of Scott. "Beside him is Anton his mate; Kane, the Alpha," Raff tilted his head, "Shawn, shifter guardian;

156

Dean, their Omega and his mate Matthew."

Raff's mouth dropped open, and he quickly snapped it shut. He'd never known so many alpha personalities in the one room. His wolf cringed in his head. Even Dean flashing him a shy smile didn't help.

"So when am I meant to leave the club?" He asked. "I'll have to get someone; Nereus can you feed…."

"You're not going anywhere," Nereus said firmly. "Not without me."

"But who'll look after Killer, Buster, Buddy and Joey?" Raff said. "Please, you have to. We don't know how long I'll be gone."

"I'm not sacrificing you, not even for my mate," Damien spat the words.

"Scott would never forgive you if you did," Troy said. His eyes were red-rimmed, but he held his head high and had no troubles staring Damien down. "He's my twin, and I'd do anything to get him back, but I know in the depths of my heart, he'd never allow anyone to be put in danger because of him."

"What about Madison?" Sebastian demanded. Raff hadn't even noticed he was in the room, but now he could see him he saw his shirt was torn, there was a huge bruise on one cheek and he looked furious. "All you're freaking talking about is Scott. Madison's just as important and maybe he wouldn't care if the red wolf is swapped out for him."

"He's my mate," Nereus yelled, at the same time Damien growled.

"You've already rejected your mate, to his face, claiming your heart is buried with some geezer who's been dead since before Jesus, for fuck's sake. You told Madison you wouldn't mate him if he was the last man on earth. So you can shut the fuck up."

"Damien," Dean said softly, and Raff felt a wash of calm flow over the room. Even Sebastian calmed down although if looks could kill Damien would be dead.

"Thank you, Dean," Kane said quietly. "Arguing won't get us anywhere. Raff, it's nice to meet a rare wolf such as yourself. I'm only sorry it has to be under these circumstances. Can you think of any reason why this shifter wants you so badly?"

"Because he's gorgeous," Nereus said and Raff felt pulled onto his bigger mate's lap. With all the attention on him, Raff was grateful for the support.

"No disrespect to your mate," Kane continued, "but all the men in this room are gorgeous and Damien's club is full of willing subs that are just as pretty."

Raff knew that was true, but Nereus whispered, *you're by far the prettiest,* through their mind link and he bit his lips together to stop from smiling. He thought about the visiting Alpha's question.

"Maybe it's because I'm a red wolf," he said hesitantly. "Scott mentioned," he stopped when he saw Damien flinch but Kane waved at him to continue. "Scott said that when the council hears I'm in this pack, they'll probably pitch a fit. We're on the verge of extinction. As far as I know, I came from the only pack of Red Wolves left and there were barely thirty of us. Scott said Damien would stop the council from trying to force me to breed."

"The council might suggest it," Shawn said, "but there would be no force involved and I have very strong opinions about smaller shifters being taken from where they've chosen to live." He and

Dean shared a quick smile and Raff wondered about their history.

"That said," Shawn continued, "It doesn't explain why the kidnapper thinks you could be any value to him. I'm not saying you don't have worth; your genetics are rare. But how could another shifter capitalize on it?"

Raff didn't know either, but he knew he had to get the men in the room to listen to him. Scott was the first person/shifter in a long time that was kind to him. It broke Raff's heart to think his friend might be hurt, tortured or even killed while he stayed safe cuddling his mate. Damien alternated between anger and heart-wrenching sorrow and Troy was trying to stay strong, but it couldn't be easy for him either.

"I still think we should do what the kidnapper said," he said firmly, and he felt Nereus flinch. "It's not like you guys can't follow me, keep track of me, or fit me with a GPS or something. There must be something you can do to keep me safe and bring Scott and Madison home."

Loud voices tried to drown each other out as everyone in the room seemed to have an opinion. Raff couldn't make himself heard no matter how hard he tried and Nereus wasn't helping. In fact, he'd gone deadly quiet and although his arms were as comforting around him as ever, Raff had a horrible feeling he'd upset his mate.

Chapter Ten

As a demigod, there wasn't a lot Nereus *couldn't* do; being what he considered a good person, there wasn't much he *wouldn't* do. But being supportive of his mate's suicidal plan to walk into a dangerous situation none of them understood was something he would not do. And in that part of his mind even Raff couldn't read, Nereus was hurt. Hurt that Raff would even suggest putting himself into danger within hours of being mated.

So he didn't say anything; relying on Damien and the men from Cloverleah to come up with objections to his idiotic plan. It was clear Raff knew nothing of strategy, and while Nereus knew Damien was holding himself together by a thread, and Troy wasn't much better, none of the men would let Raff sacrifice himself. Sebastian was a different story, but Nereus had been his friend for a long time, and it seemed when Madison was finally rescued the angry man was getting ready to eat some humble pie.

Eventually, after a lot of talk, a bit of eating and arguing on all sides, everyone in the office accepted that there was nothing they could do; at least for now. Troy reminded everyone time and time again Scott would do his best to escape. Running around looking for him wasn't any good if no one knew where to look. And that was something that bothered Nereus although he kept quiet about that too. It would take powerful mojo to interfere with Scott's and Damien's mind link. He didn't mention it because of the alternative, Scott wasn't able to respond, didn't need verbalizing. If it wasn't for Dean, there'd have been bloodshed in the club already.

"I think you and Raff should move out to the pack house while this is going on," Damien said. "In fact, I think it would be best if we all go." He looked around the office, his face grim. "The club is on lockdown until further notice. No one in or out. I can't have any of the subs in danger and small seems to be this guy's type. Malacai, I want you to keep half of the enforcers here; the other half will go with me back to pack land. If…." Damien stopped himself and took a deep breath, "When," he added more strongly, "Scott escapes he's going to head for home and once he's away from this… whatever it is that's stopping our link, we can get to him faster with the pack split in two."

"As soon as I have him, I'll zap him to you," Shawn said quietly. "You know I will, and none of us are going home until both men are safe."

Damien nodded but didn't say anything. From the look on his face, he couldn't... not without breaking down and Nereus knew how he felt. After arguing for almost an hour, Raff had gone silent and while he stayed in Nereus's arms he didn't feel happy there. *It's only our first day mated.* Suddenly, he needed to get Raff alone; needed for them to have a firm and frank conversation before misunderstandings got too big to sort.

"I'm taking Raff to his room; we have to see to the pups, pack his stuff and then I'll trans-locate them all to the pack house. Seb, if you want to go with me, be at Raff's rooms in an hour. Not before." He stalked out of the office before anyone could stop him; Raff still in his arms.

"You're angry with me," Raff said as soon as they were clear of the office.

"Not here," Nereus said keeping his voice low. He didn't need other members of the pack knowing their business. Keeping his mouth shut and his eyes off his mate, Nereus had them at the apartment in no time. Killer and the other dogs made a fuss as soon as they arrived and Nereus set Raff on his feet and stood back while his mate rushed around filling feeding bowls and giving his puppies the affection he craved with that part of his soul still aching from what he saw as a betrayal.

It wasn't until Raff was curled up on the couch, Killer in his arms, that Nereus let go. "Yes, I'm angry. How could you? I know Scott is your friend," Nereus started to pace as Raff shrank into the couch. "He's my friend too, but you and me, we just got MATED. And you wanted to walk away from that? Put yourself in danger with some wacko who's got the hots for you?

How the hell did you think that would be okay with me?"

"But you didn't think about me at all, did you?" Nereus continued, well aware his voice had risen to roar status. "No, you just decided, all on your own, that you weren't worth anything and the lives of the Alpha Mate and Damien's PA were more important. You didn't care about what might happen to me if something went wrong and you DIED. All you wanted me to do was feed your wretched puppies."

"I just wanted...."

"NO! There is no excuse." Nereus flexed his hands. He had no wish to flood Raff's apartment no matter how angry he was. "You didn't think you were worth anything. You, honestly, would have waltzed out of the club and into certain danger, and you didn't think about me once. How is this mating even going to work? You told me you'd care about me and then the first chance you have to show it, you throw me and my feelings away. How did you think that would make me feel? Do you have any idea how freaking HURT I am?"

"You're a demigod. I knew you'd save me."

Two tiny sentences, delivered in such a quiet voice but they had the power to drain Nereus's righteous indignation completely. He turned and stared at his mate. Raff's face was white, his eyes red rimmed, and he was holding onto the poodle as though his life depended on it. But his chin was stuck in the air and he met Nereus's eyes without blinking.

"Explain that again," Nereus wasn't going to make any assumptions.

"I owe Scott a lot," Raff said carefully. "But there is no way I would put that friendship before our mating. When the shifter guardian said he couldn't get a trace on Scott or Madison, and the enforcers hadn't found anything, I thought if I did what the kidnapper said then it would give us a lead. Your dad slapped a tattoo on my butt last night. I hardly think it's too difficult for you or him to keep me safe. And I thought... I thought...." Tears slowly rolled down Raff's face and now Nereus felt like an ass. He'd promised himself he'd be on his best behavior with his mate and he'd trashed that promise in just one day.

"They don't have someone wonderful like you to protect them," Raff choked out. "Sure, there's a shifter guardian here but he can only do so much. You're almost a god; your dad *is* one. I thought this way we could catch the man and no one else would get hurt."

"You believed in me that much?" *It's official. I'm an ass.* Nereus covered the distance between them in a blink. He carefully scooped Killer and put the growling puppy on a cushion before cupping Raff's face as he crouched down. "Forgive me?"

"I should have talked to you first?" Raff's eyes were still damp, but they held a glimmer of hope.

"That would have helped; or maybe," Nereus had no problems admitting when he was wrong, "I should have trusted you and realized you had reasons for what you wanted to do."

"It doesn't matter, anyway. The Alpha and the others won't let me go."

"No, they won't and I'm sorry, but I'm glad of that. If you'd died, and I had to go and see Uncle Hades to get you back," Nereus mocked shivered. "Let's just say I don't want to owe that guy a favor and my dad would never let me live it down if I lost you in the first week."

"I'm worried about Scott and Madison," Raff said. "Sebastian looked really angry. Madison was going to see him. Do you think he said something that made Madison run off? Is that why he got kidnapped?"

"I don't know sweet one," Nereus shifted his leg. Staying crouched wasn't doing his knees any favors. "Unfortunately...Sebastian's been waiting centuries for his mate. He expected someone who looked more like Scott or Damien than Madison."

"But that's not fair to Madison. He is who he is. Not everyone finds their mate. Sebastian should be thankful he found his at all."

"Sebastian has very rigid ideas about twinks." Ouch. Raff shrank back into the couch. Nereus's knee was giving him hell, so he straightened to his full height and then pulled Raff up and cuddled him against his chest, aware Raff's feet were dangling a foot from the ground. "Cuddle me," he said softly. Raff's arms wrapped around his neck and his legs locked together on Nereus's ass. "Sebastian's been a soldier for most of his long, long life. It's hard for him to see strength as anything more than size."

"I don't care if he doesn't like me," Raff said hotly. "But Madison's wolf won't allow him near anyone again now he's scented your friend. That's not fair."

"I agree, but I think it's up to Sebastian to sort things out with Madison when they get him back." Nereus felt he needed to reconnect with his own mate, rather than discuss Sebastian's oafish efforts with his. "Any chance I can get a kiss? It's been a long, stressful day, and right now I just want to focus on us."

"I should be packing," Raff's lips twitched. "I have to get the dog's stuff and…." He leaned forward. Nereus met him halfway. *Oh, this is much better.* Nereus could still taste the trace of salt from Raff's tears but Raff's lips were warm, full and totally pliant. *Don't you dare come early, Seb,* he thought as he slipped his fingers under Raff's shirt. He had a lot of groveling to do for his anger outburst.

Chapter Eleven

Scott stirred. Shit. What the hell hit him? *This must be what a hangover feels like. What the hell was I drinking? The last thing I remember was... Madison!* The fog lifted and Scott's stomach lurched as he realized he hadn't drunk a drop. Shit. Trying to move brought the sounds of chains clanking and a decided lack of movement. *I'm chained?*

Scott slowly opened his eyes and sure enough, a large chain between the wall and a collar on his neck. His arms and legs were shackled. Scott called his wolf, but his animal half was muted; subdued and unresponsive. Shifting was out of the question. He screamed for Damien in his head, but there was a void where his mind link had been. *Gods. Not Damien. Don't let anything have happened to Damien.* Scott's heart broke at the thought of his mate in danger.

A laugh was the first clue he wasn't alone. Scott turned his head, wincing as the chains clanged again. That would get annoying real fast. "Having problems, Alpha Mate?"

He recognized the fucking laugh from when he'd been with Madison. "Damien is going to kill you."

"Sure he is. If he could find me," the body attached to the voice stepped into view. "I'm so tempted to keep you. You do make a good Alpha Mate. All I'd have to do is train you and you seem reasonably intelligent. You'd learn quickly with my methods."

Fuck. It was one of the pack members. Why, in heaven's name, did Damien get all the crazies? Scott desperately tried to think of the name but came up blank. "You need to let me go," he said strongly. "Damien won't stand for this; if anything happens to me, he'll tear you apart."

"Nope. As I said, he'd have to find me first and that won't be easy," The man shook his head. Shit, Scott wished he could remember the guy's name. "And he won't be seeing you again unless he hands over the Red Wolf. If he does that, I'll consider letting you and that little fuck toy of yours go."

Fuck toy? Madison! "Where's Madison?" Scott quickly scanned the room, but he and the kidnapper were the only occupants.

"He's keeping another twink of mine company; not that he'll be much company, though. That young man was very disappointing; didn't last long at all. Shame. His screams made my cock hard."

Joel? Oh, Gods. Scott swallowed a whimper. Damien would be devastated.

"I am Alpha Mate of San Antonio. I demand you let me see Madison!" The thought of his feisty PA screaming for his life sent terror through Scott's heart.

"Nope." The man smirked, and it was not a good look. "Your toy is stored safe and sound. Nicely chained, caged and waiting for my special brand of entertainment if your precious Damien doesn't hand over the Red Wolf. He may be an alpha but he doesn't get to keep you, the toy and your breeder. That's just greedy."

Breeder? What the fuck was he talking about? Scott's mouth fell open before his brain engaged. "What breeder?"

"Don't play stupid." The scowl was as bad as the smirk. "I *know*. You alpha types all think you can keep a secret, but my daddy told me. I remember." The kidnapper tapped his head. "I know Red Wolves can have pups. Male or female; they can have pups. That's the only reason Damien took him in; don't think I'm stupid because I know. If that pretty Red Wolf carries anyone's pups, they're going to be mine. Not yours; not Damien's. My pups for my pack."

His expression changed. A sly look crossed his face. "Although if you want to stay here as my Alpha Mate, I could arrange for some of those pups to be yours. After the little darling has had mine, of course."

"Raff can't get pregnant." Scott was starting to think he was dealing with a madman and that did not bode well for his future.

"You keep saying that because you're part of keeping the secret. I *know,* don't you understand? You don't have to pretend with me.

Damien can't have everything. I want the Red Wolf and I will have him."

"Raff's mated. To Nereus. He can't have sex with you. He'll die if they're separated; just like I'll die if I'm not sent back to Damien. We're true mates and true mates die unless they stay together."

The slap had him sprawling; the kidnapper looming over him. "Don't you fucking lie to me. I know better. There are no true mates! My daddy said it was all a lie. My momma claimed she had a true mate waiting for her and she didn't die. Daddy made her pay for that."

"She would die if she had scars like I have from Damien's bite." Scott tried to use his most reasonable voice; not easy to do when he had no way of defending himself.

"She didn't have scars," the man spat on the ground by Scott's face. "She didn't last long either. He took her as a breeder and she was dead by the time I was five. He got smart with the next one. Told me never to get one younger than 16 or they won't last. That Red Wolf is about the right age. Women just don't do it for me and I need pups if my pack's going to grow, so I need him."

Scott fought the urge to throw up. Raff had to be protected. Oh, Gods. He had to get free, and he forced himself to stay calm. "Damien won't hand over Raff, no matter what," he said firmly.

"Then he's going to be missing his Alpha Mate and his favorite fuck toy, ain't he? I'm done talking. I'll bring you a sandwich later. I might feed the fuck toy if I feel like it. Maybe." He grinned and Scott shuddered. "Now you behave. They ain't going to find you. You don't have any scent. Those nice drugs work just fine hiding scents and they won't allow you to shift either."

He laughed as he left the room. As soon as the door closed, Scott started to struggle. He had to find Madison, get to Damien and warn Raff.

Chapter Twelve

Raff heard raised voices. He wasn't sure who they were, but he quickly started walking in the opposite direction. He'd taken the pups out for a breath of fresh air; trying to stay out of everyone's way. The air was crisp and cool and there was a threat of snow in the breeze, but Raff hunkered down in his coat and kept walking.

Scott and Madison had been missing for two long days and Damien wasn't the only one with his temper fraying. The pack lands were beautiful, better than any Raff had seen before but there was nowhere to escape the tension and Raff couldn't help feeling it was all his fault. He followed a well-worn path through the trees and found a patch of grass by a stream. Hopefully, no one else would come out this way.

They should've let me follow that letter's instructions. Damien's not eating, he doesn't sleep. He'll die if Scott doesn't get back soon, and it will be my fault. Raff closed his eyes. Crying wasn't going to help. Nereus was spending a lot of time with Sebastian. Goodness knows why. Yes, Raff was annoyed about it, but not because Nereus was being a good friend. It was the fact Sebastian didn't notice anyone less than six feet tall that upset him. *If he'd not said those hurtful things, not made Madison run away….*

Killer barked and Raff's eyes flew open as the other's joined in. He scanned the clearing and his eyes widened. Peering around the tree was a bear cub, his nose twitching; the intelligence in eyes proclaiming his shifter status. Raff didn't think cubs or pups of any kind shifted so young, and the cub was young; still tiny. But really cute with his gold and black fur. He forced a smile on his face.

"Hey little guy, you get lost or something?"

The shifter shook his head and then looked back at the dogs. Raff understood the longing in his eyes.

"You want to play with my dogs? You can. It's okay. That noisy apricot one is Killer, the black one is Buddy, the white one's name is Butch and the little scruffy one is Joey. I'm sure they'd love to play with you."

The cub took a couple of steps out from behind the tree, his nose still twitching wildly. "I'm Raff," Raff said keeping his voice calm. "These are my dogs; my sort of pack, I suppose you'd call them. I rescued them from a shelter, and they're my family now. Do you have a family?"

The little cub sat down on his furry butt and shook his head. "Oh, you poor thing." For Raff, family was everything. When his family kicked him out of the pack, it'd almost broken him completely. If he hadn't had his dogs to focus on, he would've died of grief. "You can come and play with my dogs anytime you want to."

The cub tilted his head but didn't move. The dogs were bouncing around, trying to get the cub's attention. Maybe he was shy? Raff rummaged around in his bag of dog toys and pulled out a medium sized ball. He liked it because none of the smaller dogs could pick it up and run with it; something Killer often did with the smaller toys.

"Why don't we play some ball?" He said. Killer heard the word ball and came running and then went running back to the cub. Raff grinned and threw it close to the cub. "Can you get it?" The cub lumbered towards it, nudging it with his nose. Killer dived after the ball, knocking it back, and within a minute all five animals were diving and chasing, knocking the ball around and having a great time.

"Oh, thank goodness, there he is," Dean came running into the clearing. Raff hadn't had a chance to talk much with the smallest pack visitor. If Dean wasn't helping Damien stay calm, he was off doing other stuff with his mate and pack. But he came and flopped down on the grass next to Raff as though they'd been friends for years. Raff's heart warmed at the gesture.

"I was supposed to be watching him," Dean said, trying to catch his breath. "But the little guy is fast. He snuck out when I thought he was eating lunch."

"He's not eating?" Raff looked at the cub worriedly; his instincts kicking in. The cub looked healthy enough; his fur was shiny and in good condition and he seemed to have plenty of energy, playing with the pups.

188

"Oh, he eats," Dean said. "He eats too fast that's the problem. I thought I'd have at least five minutes. I only went to the bathroom and when I got back he'd scarpered."

"What... why... where...?" Raff had so many questions. What was a bear cub doing in a wolf pack? Thankfully Dean seemed to know what he was asking.

"His name's Oliver, but he prefers to be called Ollie," Dean said quietly, although Ollie lifted his head when he heard his name. Then Joey knocked the ball against his belly and the game was on again. "He was found in a lab; he's been experimented on. His mother's dead. Some of the guys in our pack found him with a bunch of other shifters and sent them here because there's a doctor here. The other shifters were adults, and they've been accepted into this pack. Ollie... he doesn't have any family left."

"Oh my god, how awful," Raff covered his mouth with his hand, shaking his head. "What's going to happen to him?"

"We've got a couple of bear shifters in our pack," Dean smiled at Raff's look of shock. "Yeah, I know. Cloverleah's a mixed pack; more mixed than most. But anyhow, they're heading here. There's three of them; the two bears and Tobias, a wolf shifter that used to be an enforcer here, funnily enough. A true mate ménage."

Raff had never heard of such a thing, but Dean hadn't finished talking. "Ollie... he has nightmares. He doesn't seem to want to mix with any of the kids in this pack. He stays in his shifted form most of the time. Luke, one of the bears, is a grizzly, just like Ollie. We're hoping that being around other bears might help him. I'm doing all I can, but with Damien the way he is...."

"I can help," Raff said quickly. "With Ollie I mean. I... er... I try to stay away from Damien. I don't think he likes me very much, but I can help with Ollie during the day if you like. I like kids and Ollie seems to be having fun with my dogs."

"What happened to Scott and Madison is not your fault," Dean was looking right into his eyes and Raff couldn't look away. "No one blames you."

"If they'd let me go when the kidnapper wanted me too, then maybe Scott and Madison would be home by now." Raff dropped his head, unwilling for Dean to see his tears.

"They probably wouldn't be," Dean said softly. "The guy who took them; he's a criminal. That sort of person can't be trusted. Damien knows that. Everyone does. Sacrificing you wasn't going to do any good."

"They might have had a chance to catch him," Raff persisted.

"Or we might have lost you too, and then I'd have one more mate I'd have to keep calm. Damien and Sebastian are bad enough without adding Nereus to the mix." Dean smiled to show he was teasing.

"I feel so helpless," Raff stared at his hands. "If I'd just gone with the guy in the first place...."

"You'd probably be dead," Dean said bluntly. "Then we'd have a rampaging demigod running amuck with the water and the whole of Texas would probably be flooded."

Raff giggled in spite of himself. "Nereus does seem to cause a bit of a mess when he's upset," he said.

"Exactly, and I don't think the State of Texas could cope with flood damage, especially if Nereus pulled the waters from the gulf. Besides, who would I have to help with Ollie if you weren't here?"

"You'd let me help?" Raff's eyes widened. "I'll watch him so carefully and make sure he doesn't come to any harm. I'll make sure he eats and...."

"You're a red wolf," Dean said kindly. "No one knows more about family and the importance of kids than you do, I'm sure."

"I used to help with the kids in my pack all the time," Raff said quietly, watching Ollie with the pups. The ball was forgotten and Ollie was following Killer on some insect hunt under the bushes. At least Raff hoped it was insects Killer was looking for. "When they found out I was gay, they didn't want me around the kids anymore. My dad said I was a bad influence."

Dean's arm came around his shoulders and he was pulled into a hug. For a little guy, Dean was strong. "You'll have kids of your own one day and you'll make sure they grow up a lot more open-minded."

"I sure hope so." It was Raff's dearest wish. He just hoped Nereus felt the same way.

/~/~/~/~/

"I've just about had enough of you," Nereus snarled as Sebastian lounged in a chair, swigging a half empty fifth of whiskey. In two days, Sebastian hadn't showered, shaved or changed his clothes. He reeked so bad even Nereus could smell it. "Everyone knows you didn't want Madison as a mate; yet now he's missing you're acting like a love-sick goat whose harem's run off."

"I didn't want to mate him; doesn't mean I wanted anything to happen to him."

"Well something has happened to him and what are you doing about it? Sitting there getting drunk and acting like an ass."

"Goat. Ass. You are full of colorful terminology today," Sebastian sneered, taking another swig from the bottle. "What's the matter? Why are you even here? Your twink's ass boring you already?"

"You've got no right to talk about my mate," Nereus clenched his fists. "Don't think I haven't noticed the way you ignore him every time he's in the room. You're fucking upsetting him and you've got no right. He's kind and sweet and he was willing to sacrifice himself just so Madison and Scott had a chance of coming home. What have you done?"

"You stopped him from going," Sebastian lurched to his feet, his bottle fisted in his hand. "This whole mess could've been over by now, but no, your little twink was far too precious to be used as bait."

"You didn't even want your mate," Nereus said, feeling his anger growing hotter. "Damien told me; told all of us. You wouldn't mate with Madison if 'he was the last man on earth', so you said. Your poor mate heard you say those very words. I can't imagine how much that must have devastated him. At least I had the guts to accept the decision the Fates made for me."

"Guts. It doesn't take guts to fuck a twink," Sebastian said harshly and Nereus wondered how they'd stayed friends as long as they had. "You've been saddled with a mate; saddled with a worthless twink who'll hang like a leech around your neck for the rest of your existence. Now a warrior on the other hand," Sebastian swung the arm with the bottle attached. "It takes guts to mate a warrior. A real man."

"How would you know?" Nereus seethed. He knew his friend was hurting but the impulse to smash the man's face in was riding him hard. "So you fucked a few thousand of warriors. Whoop-di-do. So have I. And you know what I got out of it? Fucking nothing. Same as you. An itch scratched. That's it."

"Like your twink's any better. I'm surprised you can even get you cock up his ass without him crying."

Nereus closed his eyes and blew out a long breath. "I get love from Raff," he said slowly. "He might not have said the words but I sense it every time he touches me; I feel it every time he welcomes me into his body. That feeling stays with me well after my cock's gone down. He cares about me; cherishes me. Something you know nothing about. He completes me, damn it and I will worship him for the rest of my days."

Opening his eyes, he saw Sebastian had moved closer. "I'd rather spend a lifetime of boredom as you call it, being loved by a strong, sweet and wonderful man like my mate than spend five minutes with a toxic mess like you. If you want us to stay friends, then you will treat my mate with the respect he deserves; the same respect I'd give yours if you'd manned up and claimed him."

Suddenly Nereus was beyond disgusted with his friend. Sebastian's behavior was causing a rift between him and Raff and while Raff hadn't said anything, he didn't have to. A two-handed shove sent Sebastian to the floor, the whiskey spilling all over his clothes. "Get your shit together, Sebastian. Wallowing in your own filth isn't doing anybody any favors. Your mate wouldn't want you like this if you begged him on your hands and knees."

Nereus shook his head as he left the room. Sebastian made him feel dirty. Hurting or not, the man had no right to treat anyone smaller with such blatant disrespect. Tuning into his mating bond, he ran down the stairs and headed for the gardens. Nereus needed a hug. A very big loving hug and he knew just the man he could get it from.

Chapter Thirteen

Scott groaned, shook his head and then wished he hadn't. His head still rang from the beating he'd received. It seemed his nutty kidnapper didn't appreciate food being thrown in his face. Scott checked himself over. He was still chained... but something was different. His wolf; he could feel his wolf a lot stronger this time. *He must have drugged the food. It's wearing off.* Trying not to get his hopes too high, Scott carefully rolled his body, so he was on all fours, calling on his animal spirit with every ounce of energy he had left.

The shift was slow; his wolf still groggy, but clothes ripped and Scott felt his animal half emerge. The chains on his ankles and wrists dropped off and he wrenched his neck from the collar with a growl and a quick flick of his head. *Thank fuck for that,* he thought as he shook out his fur. Now to find Madison.

Trying not to breathe too hard, Scott peered through the gloom. He was in a cell of sorts; a different one than before. Two doors; one looked to be solid steel, the other one was wood. A small window; glass, no bars, Scott noticed. The kidnapper had relied on restraints to stop him going anywhere. There was a stench coming from the slime on the concrete walls and what looked like shit in a corner. The only furnishings apart from the chains were a pallet, with a jug of water beside it. Scott edged over and sniffed the water. It seemed fresh but Scott didn't dare take a drink. If there were drugs in the food, it made sense they were in the water too.

He had to find Madison. Scott wasn't sure how long he'd been in the dratted place or how often they'd been moved around. Being unconscious skewed time. There was nothing much to see; that was obvious and Scott's nose couldn't smell anything but fecal matter. Straining his ears, Scott tried to pick up the slightest sound. There, on the other side of the steel door. Scott swore he heard whimpering.

Carefully making his way over to the wooden door, Scott double checked for any sound of human movement. He couldn't hear anything except the thudding of the blood going through his ears. *Steel door it is then*. Wishing his sense of smell wasn't so acute in his furry form, he carefully picked his way across the room.

The first thing that struck Scott about the steel door was there was no handle, no visible hinges; nothing. The door was a thick plate of steel set in the chunky block walls. Shifting into his human form again, Scott tried to get his fingertips in the tiny gap between the door and where it met the blocks, but there was no way of getting a grip. Giving up, he rested his cheek on the metal, pressing his ear against it hard.

Crying. Someone was definitely crying. Scott debated for all of two seconds. He didn't want to attract attention to his awake state, but if Madison was there. "Hello," he called out softly. "Can you hear me?"

A hiccup and then Scott heard Madison's voice. "Scott, is that you? Are you all right?"

"Locked up, but I managed to shift," Scott called back softly. "Got a few options for getting out. How about you?"

"None," Madison sounded scared. "There're chains around my ankles and wrists; my wolf's not responding. The cage bars are thick and too close together for me to get through in either form."

"Are there any other doors? Can I get to you?" Scott rested his hand on the steel, wishing he was on the other side of it. His soul screamed at him to find Damien but he was reluctant to leave Madison behind.

"I don't think so. There're two doors but they both look the same. I've seen the asshole use one of those remote key locks which must be how he gets in and out."

Shit. Scott was hoping for a wooden option. He was fairly sure he could break a wooden door, but he'd just dent the steel ones.

"Is there anything else in there," he said urgently. "Something you can use to get free."

"There's a lot of shit in here, none of it within reach," Madison was starting to sound panicked. "Believe me, I don't want to be in here anymore than Joel obviously did."

"Joel's there with you?" *Please let the kidnapper be joking.*

"Dead." *Shit, shit, shit.*

"Okay." Scott let out a long breath. "Is there any way you can see me getting in there? A window perhaps."

"No. Concrete blocks, two steel doors, a big assed cage and *manacles*." Madison's voice rose.

"Is the floor concrete too?"

"Yes! And there're manacles and whips, chains and knives, and some stuff. Fuck, I don't want to see this stuff."

"Madison. You have to calm down, Madison."

"You have to go and get help. I've got to get out of here. The kidnapper is batshit crazy. He's getting worse. The things he says. He's going to do to me what he did to Joel and you don't want to see the state that poor man is in."

Scott felt tears well up in his eyes. He remembered Joel from the club. A sweet, eager to please little sub who was just finding his feet after Damien removed him from his fuck roster. Poor kid deserved a better end than he got.

"This is fucking Sebastian's fault," Madison was hitting the rambling stage. Scott had seen it before when things didn't go the PA's way. "I'm going to go back to the club; I'm going to tell that fucking Sebastian I wouldn't touch him with someone else's dick on a ten-foot pole and I'm going to beat him till he bleeds."

"Okay," Scott said soothingly. He was getting worried about Madison's state of mind. He wasn't usually violent. "I'll get Damien to hold him down for you when it happens. But look, don't do anything stupid, all right? I'll get back as quick as I can."

"I'm stuck in a cage; what kind of stupid can I get up too?"

Good point. "There's a window in here; my wolf can get through it. I can see daylight. I'll get help."

"You get help ASAP. No fucking Damien when you get back. You get me out first, do you hear me? You promise me you won't do anything but get as many enforcers as you can find and you get your ass back here and get me out. I'm not going to end up like Joel. I'm going to find that arrogant son of a bitch who's supposed to be my mate and I'm going to make him wish he'd never been born... He fucking refused me...."

"I promise. You just keep thinking those positive thoughts," Scott said not sure if he was doing more harm than good. "I'll be back before you know it."

Madison didn't reply; he was still cursing Sebastian, his parentage, and some long dead lover. *Whatever keeps you sane, little guy,* Scott thought. His shift was quicker this time and painless although the smell was gagworthy. Taking a few steps back, Scott put his head down and leaped for the window, his skull breaking the glass. For a long moment, there was nothing under his paws, and then he landed with a jolt.

Thank the Fates, ground floor window. Probably should've checked that first. Taking a quick look around to get his bearings and work out where he was Scott started running for the pack house. He couldn't afford to let people see his wolf form and his clothes were wrecked from his shift. Even going back to get his prized boots didn't appeal. He'd buy another pair.

Scott ran as though the hounds of hell were after him, screaming Damien's name in his head, praying to the Fates his mate would answer.

/~/~/~/~/

"He can't be gone; he was right here," Scott looked around at the cell in despair. The two steel doors Madison mentioned were wide open, the cage and shackles standing empty. "Half an hour; it took me half an hour to get you and get back. How could he be gone?"

"Found Joel, boss," Malacai said, coming over to where Scott and Damien were standing, his face grim. "Could only tell by the scent. There's not a lot left recognizable." He shook his head. "If that's the fate Madison and Raff were facing... shit, I haven't seen anything like it."

"He thinks Raff can give him puppies," Scott sniffed and wiped the tears from his cheeks. He still couldn't believe the bastard had moved Madison in the time it took for him to get help. "The guy's fucking mad."

"Puppies," Damien's face scrunched up in confusion. "He wants those little dogs Raff has? Why doesn't he just get some of his own?"

"Puppies, babies, you know," Scott made a rounded motion over his stomach. "He thinks Raff is capable of getting pregnant. His daddy told him. He swears red wolves, male or female can get pregnant and that it's some big secret that only alpha's know about. He thought I was in on the secret."

"What secret?" Shawn and Kane came over; both holding hands to their noses.

"Let's get out of here," Damien said roughly. He'd been holding onto Scott since he flew into his arms. The frantic kiss Scott got when he shifted made it hard to remember his promise. Damien was all for locking him up again in their room this time, and the thought was tempting. Mind you, Scott was clinging just as tight. He hadn't realized how much he'd missed his mate until he caught a whiff of the Christmas scent he loved so much. "The enforcers are scouring the area for any possible scent. We'll talk at the house once Scott's cleaned up and fed."

"We need to warn Raff and find Madison before it's too late," Scott said urgently. "Neither one of them are safe from this madman."

Damien let out something that sounded like a sob. "Just this once," he said quietly. "Please, just this once, can you do as I ask? Let me see to you and then I promise we'll do all we can for Raff and Madison."

Scott wanted to argue. Damien hadn't been in the cell with him; didn't know how crazy this guy was. But there were dark bruises under Damien's eyes, a three-day scruff surrounding his face, and Damien's cheeks were gaunt. It didn't take a mastermind to know his mate was barely holding himself together. "Just this once," he said. But as they made their way back to pack lands, Scott silently vowed to keep his promise to Madison. He only prayed Damien understood there'd be no sex between them until Madison was found. Racked with guilt at not moving faster, Scott would hang onto his promise to the little guy, if nothing else.

/~/~/~/~/

Madison shivered. He tried to pull the chain loose. No such luck. Of course, no such luck. He had no

213

fucking luck. His mate hated him. Sebastian-the-bastard would rather fuck Scott. Damien would rather fuck Scott. Everyone.... He stifled a sob. No, that wasn't fair. Scott was Damien's mate. He was the one stuck with a stupid, ungrateful, beautiful, strong, sexy... asshole. Sebastian was an asshole. No questions about it.

Why in fuck's name couldn't he get a single break in his life? Chained like a damn dog to the wall. How many places like this did the guy have? Whatever his captor forced down his throat made him feel weak and sick. He couldn't smell anymore; his wolf was comatose. If the pack couldn't find his scent, they couldn't trace him. The sob broke through. He tried not to close his eyes. Every time he closed his eyes he saw Joel.

The door screeched open and then slammed shut. Madison shivered. *Gods. He's here. Sir. Like I'd call someone like that sir.* And from the slamming of equipment against the concrete walls, Madison guessed his kidnapper was not in a good mood.

"They aren't going to do it. Now the fucking Alpha Mate has escaped, Damien won't budge. I'm not getting that little Red Wolf this way. Which means you're useless to me. Fucking useless."

Madison curled in on himself. He'd spent years putting up with Damien's temper, but this guy was a whole new kind of crazy. A fist in his hair had his head pulled up so Madison was forced to stare crazy in the face.

"You're pretty enough," the kidnapper said slowly, licking his lips. Madison felt like a piece of meat. "Yeah, I think you and I can have some fun. I bet you can scream real loud."

Madison spat at the kidnapper's face; hitting his mark. The next second he found himself slammed against the wall. *Fuck that hurt,* but he still managed to keep the glare on his face.

"Oh, breaking you is going to be fun," the kidnapper's grin was evil. "I like fighters. You'll be a lot more fun than the last one. He just begged and cried and screamed. I had to wear ear plugs just to fuck him."

Every instinct told Madison not to take his eyes off the man; even his wolf agreed, and he was half asleep. When the kidnapper left the room, Madison started to relax only to have the door pushed open again; the kidnapping bastard dragging something into the room. It looked like a small cage and Madison's wolf whimpered in his head. The kidnapper sat it upright and attached a rope to it; pulling it into the air. "You'll look real pretty in the coffin."

Gods. Madison kept his mouth shut; refusing to let the whimper in his chest escape. He simply stared at the man, terrified as to what he'd do next.

"I have a lot of other goodies." The kidnapper left and then returned, this time dragging a chest. Madison had seen similar chests in the club dungeons.

The kidnapper sauntered over to Madison and he flinched as the man ran his hand over his body. "We are going to have some fun tomorrow." Madison glared at the bastard, refusing to let the man know he'd gotten to him.

"Oh yeah. You are a fighter. It's gonna be real fun. Bet you're a good fuck too. You would have to be for Damien to keep you as his fuck toy. You are going to make me real happy." The kidnapper laughed as he headed towards the door. "Now don't you go anywhere. Anticipation is half the fun. I'll be back when I'm ready and then we can play."

Madison waited until the kidnapper was out of the room before he started to tremble. *Someone get me out of here. Please, gods, Fates, I don't care who. Wherever you are, get me out of here.*

Chapter Fourteen

Hours later Madison was still uselessly tugging at his chains. The cell was dark, only one tiny light offering any relief from the gloom. Although watching the coffin hanging like a warning gave him the shivers. The kidnapper hadn't been back except to drop off some food, muttering about the red wolf all the while and Madison was thankful for the reprieve he'd been given. Maybe the bastard could keep his anticipation game going long enough to get hit by a passing truck. But who'd save him then? Was anyone even looking for him anymore? Scott escaped what felt like days ago.

Pushing the plate of sandwiches away, the clanging plate was the only relief from the silence. Gods, Madison was sick of fucking potted meat. A tear trickled down his cheek. There was no way he was going to be rescued as long as that asshole kept giving him the scent blockers. He would smell just like a human. Not that it would matter because his mate didn't want him, anyway. No, he couldn't have a nice normal wolf who would appreciate a pretty little twink. He had to get a fucking pain in the ass that was still hung up on some guy from two thousand years ago. Asshole. He sniffled as he rolled onto his side facing the wall.

"Madison."

Great, now he was hearing things. That wasn't the kidnapper's voice and he would have heard that bastard banging open the door. Asshole liked to make an entrance.

"Madison."

He refused to answer.

"*Madison*!" The voice vibrated throughout the room.

Shit. He rolled over and sat up; his wolf immediately recognizing the visitor even if he'd never seen him before. Oh, gods... it was Death. Death had come for him. Death. Thanatos. No more chances to do anything. No chance to find someone who would love him; not like he had anything to hope for that after all he had a mate who didn't want him and... oh gods... Death.

The chains fell off him. Shit, this was real. It wasn't a dream. All because that stupid son of a bitch...

"Fine. Just fucking fine. I don't care." Madison yelled as he threw up his hands. "It's not like it matters anyway, no one wants me. No one's looking for me. The damn idiot who kidnapped me drags me all over the damn place because of Scott and can't take the time to even feel me up, even though he said his full intention is to make me his slave and rape me when he feels like it. But no, he's too fucking busy chasing another man. Throws me in the trunk of his car, drags me off to another location, not because he's keeping me safe; oh no. It's because this other guy is so important to him that he can't get over him after two thousand year... s.... Wait, that's my idiot mate. And let me tell you he is an idiot..."

"I know."

"I put on my best suit; I fixed my hair for him. I take special care of my face, I check for wrinkles every day, well not in here, but what does that asshole tell me? He doesn't do twinks. Like I asked for him? It's what Fate wants you to have because you are the perfect mate for him and come to think of it... it's his fucking fault I am in here right now because the asshole tells me that a twink took his love away from him. It was two thousand fucking years ago, cut me a fucking break. But nooooo he just has to ruminate over that loss, like it was my fault they weren't mates. Instead, he makes it plain he doesn't want me so I had to go running off crying and get Scott and me kidnapped by that weirdo who can't even find time to molest me. Not that I would want him to molest me but can't someone find some damn time to care about me for a fucking change, instead of running all over the fucking place fussing about men they are never going to get? Noooo. Instead, I end up here, chained to a fucking wall with the same exact fucking problem I had with my damn mate." Madison knew he was rambling but if these were his last moments left breathing, he had things to say.

"I'm your father-in-law."

"So now you show up and that means I'm never going to have a mate because I'm dead, not that they will care. The pervert will just throw my carcass in the river and I'll just float along until someone fishes out my body, if they ever do. Damien will just replace me with a new PA just like he replaced me with a younger prettier sub. My own damn mate will be relieved he can go on pining for some stupid son of a bitch that has been dead longer than any wolf in our pack has been alive. All because the stupid son of a bitch wouldn't let go of some bastard...."

"I'm your father-in-law"

"Who has been dead for centuries. I'm done, I tell you, DONE! I am sick and tired of no one paying any attention to me. I'm a wolf; I have feelings just like they have. I have been rejected so damn many times. And you know what? Frankly, it is their fucking fault. I would have been a good mate for Damien. I know he's found Scott, and that's okay but before he found him. I would have been a very good mate and kept him on track but no... Do you have any idea how hard I worked to make myself useful to the dumb son of a bitch? How hard I worked to make him notice I was more than a sub and then he rewards me by making me a PA and replacing me with another sub, not that it was all bad, but it fucking HURT. He never considered for one moment that I had the possibility of being a mate to him when he didn't even know Scott existed. And God knows the man is so damn disorganized..."

"I AM YOUR FATHER-IN-LAW."

Madison's mouth snapped shut and his eyes widened as Death seemed to grow in stature right before his eyes. Then he fainted.

/~/~/~/~/

The warmth of the bed comforted Madison as he stirred from his sleep. "What a stupid dream."

He sighed and slowly opened his eyes. The room was still dark. It must be very early. Hmm... that would mean he would have time enough to go out to breakfast at that little cafe Scott loved before work. Eggs, bacon, sausage, pancakes and maybe some French toast.

"That can be done."

What the fuck? Madison sat up in bed. He blinked as a light came on. Death... well... a very sexy Death, stood in front of him with a tray in his hand. "It wasn't a dream? Am I dead?"

"No, Madison. I wasn't a dream and you're not dead." Thanatos sat the tray on the bed. "Now what would you like to drink?"

"Coffee."

"Perhaps a Mimosa?"

"Oh yes. If this is being dead, I think I can get used to it."

"You aren't dead, sweetheart. You aren't ever going to die." Thanatos laughed. A tray appeared with coffee, water and a pitcher of Mimosas on it. As he poured Madison a drink, he added, "My son is like me, immortal. Since you're his mate, you are also immortal."

"But he hasn't mated me yet." A confused Madison took the drink from him.

"He will."

"Yeah, right." Madison downed the drink and held out the empty glass. "Death... I can't keep calling you Death. What do I call you?"

"Dad? Or Thanatos, but I'd prefer Dad."

"Dad? Dad would work. I haven't called anyone Dad since my father tried to kill me; yelling I was defective as a wolf because I was gay at the same time."

"Dad. No matter what my idiot son does, you will always be my son. Even if he tries to break the mating bond, I will still consider you my son."

"I..." Madison wiped his eyes. "Thank you."

"Eat. Then we'll get you back to your home and we will deal with my idiot son who doesn't realize what a treasure he's been given. You will need every ounce of your grit to deal with him. I'm afraid he's the one who'll benefit from this deal if he can get over himself long enough to mate you." Death faded out of sight.

"Damn. I guess I need to get used to that." Madison focused on his food and took a bite. "Oh God. This is so good." Madison wasn't sure how long his good fortune would last, but at least he wasn't eating potted meat. After the time he'd had, he'd take his wins where he could get them.

/~/~/~/~/

Madison took another look in the mirror... mirrors.... *Oh, this was so fantastic*. Every wall in the dressing room reflected his new look. He stroked the jade green silk suit. *Gods, this had to be so expensive*. His fingers traced the buttons on the Eton dress shirt. Never in his lifetime could he have imagined wearing a $45,000 shirt. His reflection smiled. It suited him. It appeared Dea...Dad had wonderful taste. The room he had been given was full of expensive clothes. Madison touched the tie again. He didn't normally wear ties for the office, but this was the *ultimate* in ties. Diamonds and Gold, a Satya Paul Design Studio tie worth $220,000. Something Madison had only drooled over in magazines. He didn't even want to contemplate how much money he was wearing. He looked like he was oozing the stuff. And Dad had told him to pick out his favorites to wear. There wasn't much left of the rags that had been his favorite outfit. He took a last look at his reflection for confidence and opened the door.

"Very nice." Death was sitting in a large armchair, a magazine on his lap.

"I'll get these back to you as soon as I can get changed into my own stuff." Not that Madison was in a hurry to change. The clothes made him feel ten feet tall and yet the boots only had a two-inch heel.

"Why? After all, they're yours."

"You mean it?" Madison froze. No one gave away stuff worth that much money. Not in his experience anyway.

"They're yours. Everything in here is yours. It's your room."

"My room?" Damn, he needed to shut his mouth because he was coming across as stupid. Turning slowly Madison took in the deep rich colors; he already knew the feather bed was warm and comfortable. Through a partially opened door, he caught sight of the bathroom containing its own sauna, hot tub, and a rainfall shower head; all of which he'd used and absolutely loved. Madison squeaked "This is all mine?"

"Of course. You are my son after all."

"Why are you doing this? You don't even know if Sebastian will claim me. I'm fairly sure, after what he said, he won't ever claim me." Confused Madison plopped on a chair, looking up at his mate's father.

"You deserve it," Death said softly, a small smile gracing his handsome face. "You are my son's mate even if he is an asshole and doesn't accept you, it doesn't change anything. Madison, I know your life; you are a brave wolf who has fought for everything you have.

Damien would have been lucky to have you for a mate until Scott and my son came along. If I want you for my son, even if my other idiot won't claim you, it's because I know who you are and I'm proud of you. And frankly, I just plain like you."

"I... er... Thank you." Madison didn't know what else to say, so he shut up. Truth be told, he was overwhelmed. No one had ever accepted him so readily before. The fact that it was Death... Madison shook his head.

"You ready to face the pack?"

"Yeah." Madison took the travel bag handed him. "What's this for?"

"In case you want to bring something back. I'll create a shortcut from here to Damien's so you can get to work by opening a door."

"You mean I can stay here, permanently?"

"It's your home now. I wouldn't say you were my son and kick you out the door. Let's go see if the idiot's temperament has been improved by your absence."

Madison closed his eyes for a moment and opened them to Damien's club room.

"Madison!" Scott got to him first and pulled him into a hug. "How did you get away? I was so damn worried. We have been searching everywhere. Thank the Fates you're all right, and will you look at you? You look amazing. Who's this with you? Damn, you just appeared out of nowhere. What the fuck?"

There was a chorus of wolves calling his name but Madison's eyes fixed on his mate who glowered at his father standing beside him, a casual hand resting on his shoulder. He didn't notice Cody's face paling and Cody fleeing the room. Typically, Sebastian's was the only glare in the room.

Damien came running over, shaking Thanatos's hands. "I don't know who you are, but thank you from the bottom of my heart. Great to see you're back Madison. You look great. We'll catch up later, I promise, but for now, come on Scott."

"Wait. What?" Scott was wrenched from Madison's hug and thrown over Damien's shoulder. "I kept my promise," he yelled as Damien strode from the room.

Madison felt a shaft of shock as he realized what Scott was talking about. No wonder Damien was in such a hurry.

Chapter Fifteen

Raff chuckled as Ollie tried to stick his furry nose in the plastic container almost knocking him over in the process. "In a minute," he laughed. "I've got to get things set out for the picnic. You can have yours as soon as Nereus gets here. Go play with the others for a while."

Ollie crooned low in his throat and dazzled Raff with a beautiful set of puppy dog eyes. Killer and the other dogs were curled up, half buried in a blanket against the chill in the air; all fast asleep. They were worn out from playing since breakfast. Raff planned to have lunch outside so he could spend more time with the little bear. Ollie's fur protected him from the cooler weather, and if he was being honest, Raff was keen to stay out of the dramas. Scott and Madison might be home and safe, but there were still some frayed tempers in the pack. Sebastian's being one of them and as Nereus was Sebastian's best friend... yeah, Raff had had enough of the whining, drinking, and the man's rude comments.

Besides, his time with Ollie was limited. The three mated shifters from Cloverleah would be arriving later in the day. Raff wondered what he could do with himself once the cub was gone. Nereus hadn't been happy when he mentioned going back to work at the bar. But he wasn't used to sitting around doing nothing all day either.

Realizing he wasn't going to solve any of the major problems sitting on the blanket, and Ollie was looking so sad with no one to play with, Raff tugged the ball out from his bag of tricks. "Come on; I'll play with you then until my mate gets here. I wonder where Nereus is?" Raff knew he could use their mind link to find out, but he was reluctant to "pry" as he called it. There was a part of Raff that still couldn't believe he'd scored a demigod for a mate and while Nereus was kind, sweet for the most part and treated his body like it was something to worship; Raff kept waiting for the other shoe to drop. No one could be that good and that nice all the time.

A sharp nudge to his side had Raff laughing again. Ollie was totally adorable in either form and as Raff rolled the ball and chased after it, followed by a slower Ollie, he decided a clear mind and exercise would keep his doubts at bay for a little while yet. At least, he thought that until he saw Ollie change direction. *Oh no, Ollie's heading up a tree.* Raff raced to stop him.

/~/~/~/~/

Nereus shook his head, grinning as he strode over the clearing and caught his mate around the waist. The man was trying to climb a tree for some reason. "Need a boost?" He asked.

Raff threw a quick smile over his shoulder. "Yes, please. Darn legs are too short."

"What are you... ah, I see," Nereus peered through the pine needles, watching a pair of cute little cub eyes watching him. "How the hell did he get up there?"

"Watch your language," Raff said, but he was still smiling. "He can climb, of course. But the problem is, he gets up there, and then he can't get down."

"So you have too..." Nereus snapped his mouth shut. He'd already learned his overprotectiveness upset his mate. But his jaw tightened and there were rocks in his stomach as he watched Raff climb further from the ground. From memory, wolves didn't climb trees, but Raff was doing a good impression of a monkey.

"Now come on Ollie. You know you want to get down. I've made you some of those honey biscuits you love. You can't eat them up here."

Nereus chewed on the inside of his mouth as he watched his slender mate scoop up a cub that was easily half his size. Ollie didn't want to let go of the branch; his claws were dug into the wood.

"You have to let go, little man. Come on," Raff tugged as he said the last word, just as Ollie let go. *Shit.* Nereus sprang around the tree, barely catching the two of them before they hit the ground.

"Hi there," Nereus said, waggling his eyebrows. "Come here often?" He lowered Raff and Ollie to the ground. Ollie stalked off without a backward glance, heading for the picnic spread. Raff stayed in his arms.

"Did you have a good morning?" Raff asked. He seemed almost nervous, but Nereus had noticed that about his mate quite often.

"Had a chat with the Alphas; Kane and the others are leaving today." Nereus said quietly. "The bears will be here for you know who this afternoon, although Damien thinks they will stay awhile until he gets used to them."

"Yeah," Raff said, looking over to where Ollie was trying to hook a plastic container open with his claws. "I'm going to miss the little guy."

"We could go back with them. Kane's offered us a place in his pack if we want it." Nereus wasn't sure how Raff would take the news. But like it or not, Raff and he were moving packs.

"Why would we leave? You've been friends with Damien for most of his life, and Sebastian will probably end up here too once he gets his head out of his ass about Madison. I don't understand." Yep, Nereus didn't think Raff would accept it was something as simple as an invitation to transfer.

"After the things that Scott and Madison said when they got back, Damien felt you would be safer in another pack and Kane agreed."

Raff slipped out of Nereus's arms as fast as he slipped into them; his face a mask. "Damien never wanted me in this pack in the first place and after what's happened with Scott and Madison, I don't blame him. But fobbing me off on another pack, just because he can't be bothered with me is a bit rude. I thought he liked Kane?"

Nereus frowned. "He does. From what I can see Damien's friends with the whole Cloverleah pack. They seem like a great bunch of guys. Smaller pack than here, of course, but that could be fun."

"Really?" Raff stalked over to where Ollie had given up on the container and was now foraging through the picnic basket. Raff rescued the chicken and pulled out some chopped plums and other bits and pieces; putting together a plate for the cub. Nereus walked over more slowly and it wasn't until he'd sat on the blanket that Raff spoke again.

"I can understand Damien wanting me out of here, but if he and Kane are such good friends, then why would he foist his problems onto a smaller pack? Why doesn't he just banish me and be done with it?"

Nereus shook his head. "Hang on a minute. You think this is some form of punishment? That you've done something wrong?"

"Well, why else would they be trying to get rid of me? I've stayed out of everyone's way; I don't speak unless spoken too. I've tried to help with Ollie because I needed

243

something to do while you've been busy with that friend of yours, but clearly that's not enough. Damien wants me gone because of what happened to Scott and Madison."

"I understand it," Raff continued when Nereus tried to interject. "I wouldn't want me around either after the scare, the pack went through with those two missing, but what I don't understand is why he would deliberately push me on another pack who already knows how much trouble I am?"

"Oh no, sweetie, baby; you have totally got the wrong idea." Nereus pushed the plate of food towards Ollie and pulled Raff into his lap. "No one is punishing you or blaming you. Scott's terrified this madman isn't going to give up on you. Sending us to Cloverleah is for your protection."

"But this pack is so much bigger." Poor Raff. Nereus gave himself a mental thump around the ears for not handling the matter with more finesse.

"If Damien and Kane weren't friends, Damien would be worried if the Cloverleah pack decided to move to San Antonio." Nereus could see Raff didn't understand. "Dean told you the pack was a mixed bag, yeah?"

Raff nodded.

"You already know they have a shifter guardian as Alpha Mate. That's a big deal. His power is freakishly amazing."

Raff nodded again.

"They also have an omega; the only omega in existence. That makes the pack pretty special as well because he's mated and has come into his powers."

Raff's eyes widened and his mouth dropped partly open.

"They also have three wolf shifters who served as Black Ops soldiers;

245

one of which is also half fae and the ruler of the Western States of the Fae realm. He's mated to two other fae who are Sidhe Princes in their realm. The king of the cat shifters, can you believe, is mated to the pack second, and they recently hired six enforcers whose sole job is to protect the pack, one of whom is apparently in the process of claiming a royal djinn as his true mate. All the enforcers are either ex-FBI or ex-mercenaries and that's without the bears."

"Wow."

"Oh, and there's an ancient vampire who happens to be the Regent of the Atlanta coven, but because he's mated to one of the betas in the pack, he's living there now too."

"Holy crap, that is a mixed bag. How can they want someone like me around?" Raff chewed his lip and Nereus couldn't resist pulling the luscious bit of flesh from the teeth and soothing it with his finger.

"They think you and I can make a home there," Nereus said.

"Well, I can see why they'd want you," Raff looked at him, his bottom lip trembling. "But what can I bring to the pack? I'm just a wolf and a small one at that. Most other wolf species see our kind as weak which is why there're so few of us left."

"Oh babe, I wish you'd been with me at the meeting today," Nereus said softly. "I wish you could see you like others see you. Scott was damn near in tears, knowing you'd be safer at Cloverleah but not wanting you to go. Shawn gave a lovely speech about the importance of red wolves and their love of family. Damien pulled on his alphaness and made Kane swear to protect you and to make sure you were happy and settled. Apparently, the fae in the pack are already planning a house for us. Babe, moving to Cloverleah is anything but a punishment. You have two packs who want to make sure you're safe and happy. I'm just 'the mate' who tags along."

"Oh, Ner," Raff's voice dropped and his eyes were shining. "You were always going to be too good for me. You are never and will never be just 'the mate' to me. You're my everything. We don't have to stay in a pack if you don't want to. You said you had houses; we can stay in any of them if you don't mind the pups shedding fur on the carpets."

"I haven't got a problem with packs. But you, do you realize you've never said that before?" Nereus's heart thumped hard.

"You're my everything?" Raff's shoulders lifted, and he ducked behind his hair. "Mates don't lie."

"Oh babe, you have no idea how happy you make me." Nereus wanted to pick Raff up, swing him around and yell out to the world that the precious man with him was his. But Raff was shy, and the dogs were starting to stir, so he settled for a taste of those lovely full lips. Things got heated fast as Raff threw his arms around Nereus's neck and kissed him back with the sort of abandon Nereus was coming to crave. When they were intimate, Raff seemed more confident somehow; such a change from his usual demeanor. Nereus moaned and stretched out his legs, ready to strip his sweet mate bare, but his boot caught fur instead.

"OUCH, damn it," Nereus cursed as small teeth made an imprint on his calf muscle. Raff's cheeks went bright red and his hand covered his mouth.

"Maybe we should have some lunch and take this up later once the visitors have arrived?" Raff's hands slipped from Nereus's neck and he started pulling more things out of the picnic hamper.

"You bought enough food to feed an army," Nereus teased.

"I'm still learning what you like," Raff ducked his head again. Nereus's heart warmed again, and he thought he caught a hint of the smell of the sea. *Yes Dad, I have a pretty amazing mate. Unless you have any ideas on how to boost his confidence, though, butt out.*

"I'll eat anything you put in front of me," Nereus assured him. "So, is it a yes to Cloverleah?"

Raff looked unsure for a moment, but then he nodded. "We can give it a try. It's not as though we haven't got other options."

Nereus gave his mate a quick kiss and kept the conversation to casual matters as the two men, and the cub enjoyed their lunch. All thoughts about his relief at Raff's acceptance, and the worry he felt for his little mate's safety, he kept solidly locked behind a wall in his mind.

PART TWO

Cloverleah

Chapter One

Raff tucked the last of the washing in the drawers and closed them with a satisfied sigh. He'd never had a home as pretty as the one Aelfric and Fafnir had made for them. It was a real house, with a front door, back door and everything in between. It was a far cry from the room Raff had been renting when Scott found him. *Was it only three weeks ago? Gods, how my life has changed.*

It was quieter in Cloverleah than it'd been in Texas. The pack kept pretty much to themselves, although the little township was full of friendly people who smiled and waved and said "good morning," even to strangers. Nereus had a car and had been pushing for Raff to learn how to drive. He magicked up, or zapped up, Raff wasn't sure which, a bright blue Pontiac Trans Am which looked like something built before Raff was born. It had amazing paintwork; the hood covered with a picture of crashing waves and dolphins leaping over the spray. Raff was terrified of scratching the lovely machine and kept making excuses, putting Nereus off.

It was causing a few problems.

The pack members were wonderful, couldn't have been more welcoming. Raff was thrilled Ollie found a real home with Luke, Kurt, and Tobias. Kurt was intimidating on a good day, but Luke was such a sweetheart despite his huge size. Tobias didn't seem to say a lot, but Raff could tell his mates worshiped the ground he walked on and they all doted on Ollie. The whole pack did. *But then all the mates are doting on each other too*, he thought. Sinking down onto the bed, Raff tried to work out why he was unsettled for the dozenth time.

Nereus was amazing. Sweet, kind, attentive in every way. So damn sexy, Raff's cock hardened just thinking about him. He couldn't think of one flaw in the man, and man, he'd tried. Often. Nereus knew the right things to say; he always looked like... a god. Even with his hair mussed and his scruff untrimmed, Nereus was picture perfect. And it was that perfection that was bothering Raff. No matter how hard he tried, in the face of that perfection, he didn't feel good enough.

That was why Raff loved his dogs. They didn't care if his hair was a mess, or if he looked like a blimp next to his model-perfect mate. Killer treated him like a normal person. Growled at him if there wasn't food on the plates, shoved his foot in Raff's face whenever he felt like it. Farted, burped and came home stinking of stuff Raff didn't want to think about. Raff could deal with that. He adored his little pup because of his flaws.

Nereus's perfection, not so much. Oh, he loved him. Raff admitted that to himself within a week of their mating. But he didn't, couldn't, say the words. It felt like offering… peanuts to a God. Raff felt unworthy and nothing he could do would change that. Raff sighed as the man in his thoughts came in.

"Hi sweetheart, have you seen Killer in the last half hour?"

Raff looked around. He hadn't been paying attention to his little friends. The quiet should have warned him something was wrong. Buddy, Buster, and Joey were sleeping by the window in the sun but Killer couldn't be seen or heard. He should have been worrying about that instead of his damn relationship with his mate. "No. I'm sorry, I thought he was with the others." He stood. He was going to have to look for him.

"I thought he was with Ollie, but I've just come from there and Ollie's fast asleep."

"Shoot. That means he's gone into the forest. Nereus, he could get lost. He's only a little dog." Raff mentally slapped himself. Killer didn't know the area; he could get distracted then lost....

"You have a fine nose that can track him down," Nereus broke into his worried thoughts. "You know, I haven't seen your wolf form yet. I wouldn't have a problem with you shifting and going for a run if that's easier on you."

"No, that's all right. I can't talk to you with fur on." Raff definitely did not want Nereus seeing his wolf form. Every wolf he'd seen since coming to Cloverleah had been huge, rugged and looked like he could take down an elephant single-handedly. Even the Fae's wolf forms were bigger than Raff's.

"We have a mind link. I know that works regardless of what form you are in," Nereus suggested quietly.

"I'll get my coat." Raff brushed past Nereus, not even stopping for a customary kiss. He felt bad enough already. Showing off his wolf form would only make him feel worse.

/~/~/~/~/

Teilo's ears snapped forward at the rustling in the bushes. He was running patrols, even though Kane said they were no longer necessary. Thanks to V, his brother's sexy mate, the whole territory was warded up the wazoo, but Teilo still liked to run on four feet, tracking down errant smells and enjoying the simple pleasures only a wolf could appreciate.

The rustle sounded again, closer this time. It could've been a rabbit, but the scent was all wrong. Teilo's wolf form wasn't worried; he was curious. Hunching slightly, his nose twitching, Teilo crept forward. There was something there, a very little something, but whatever it was, it wasn't doing a good job of hiding.

Teilo grinned; his wolf was always up for having some fun. He crept closer, his paws making no sound on the forest floor. *Come on, little whatever you are, come and play with the big bad wolf. I won't bite you, much.* He wasn't close enough to figure out what the scent was. He just needed to get a bit closer. *It smells like... like... DOG!?!*

Teilo scrambled back as a blur of apricot fur flew from the bushes. He felt a sharp nip on his hind leg and he snarled, but the little bundle of fur acted like he hadn't heard him. If Teilo hadn't been in wolf form, he'd have laughed. The little thing stood no more than four inches off the ground, six at best. But he was an energetic little guy, hopping around, barking and growling; for something so small, he had sharp teeth.

Snapping his teeth as the little sod leaped at him again, Teilo tried to back away. He remembered Adair saying, Raff, the red wolf, and his merman mate Nereus arrived a few days ago. He'd been more interested in the gorgeous wee bear cub Luke and his mates were looking after, so he hadn't met the other newcomers yet. It seemed he'd just met one of Raff's pack mates, a freaking teacup poodle of all things.

Looking around, Teilo knew they weren't far from the pack house. He'd lead the puppy back to the house. The poodle was far too small to be running around in the forest areas alone. Although they were the only predators, Teilo figured the little guy would get lost easily enough, and as much as his back leg still smarted from the bite, he wasn't heartless.

Come on little guy, let's go home, he barked, trying to move in the direction of the pack house. But the poodle bounded in front of him, snarling and barking back. *I don't speak canine, you silly mutt,* Teilo thought, leaping to one side. The puppy leaped with him—well, more like six leaps because he was so small, but he was fast. Teilo jumped to the other side, and the puppy followed.

Look, you silly mutt, I'm trying to get you home, he barked, but the puppy probably couldn't hear him over his own racket. Getting impatient, Teilo leaped over the poodle, only to get another bite to his leg for his troubles.

I've just about had enough of this, he snarled, whipping around, his lips curled back. His ears went back; he crouched down and growled as loud and low as he could. *Stand down puppy!*

"Oh my gods, don't hurt him, please don't hurt him. He doesn't mean anything."

Fucking brilliant, as if I would hurt something no bigger than a mouthful. But Teilo admitted he might be looking mean, so he sank down on his belly and put his head on his paws. The slender man coming through the trees had to be the red wolf, and he'd know Teilo was no threat.

Unfortunately, the apricot tornado didn't read things that way. Teilo felt sharp claws on his neck and then he howled as the little shit took a chunk out of his ear.

"Killer! That is not nice. Get back here." *Killer. Someone named an apricot mouthful Killer?* Teilo felt a trickle of blood on his ear and rethought his opinion.

"You're lucky this wolf's one of the good guys or Killer would've ended up lunch," another voice said, and Teilo looked up to see what could only be a god striding through the trees. Whereas Raff was slender, dark-haired with a gorgeously pretty face, this second man, who looked like he owned the forest, had brown hair that flared around his face and kindly blue eyes. They were the color of the sea. Nereus.

"Let me look at your ear, handsome wolf," Nereus said, coming closer. Teilo's nose was taunted with a delicious scent, salt spray on a stormy night. *Oh, my stars, my freaking cock's getting hard. No, no, I can't. This man's already mated.* He tightened his lips as strong hands stroked over his head and gently massaged his ear.

"Well, well, this is interesting," Nereus said, sniffing his finger. "Hey Raff, you'd better get over here. I think your Killer's just tried to eat our other mate."

Teilo was sure he wasn't the only one who squeaked although Killer didn't stop growling and barking. *Gods, did that little mutt ever shut up?*

Chapter Two

For the first time in his really long life, Nereus was flummoxed. *Two mates?* How was that even possible? Sure, Kurt, Luke, and Tobias were in a threesome, and then there were Jax and his two Fae mates. They were... *Fuck, it is possible.* But... but... things weren't going as well with Raff as he'd like. He'd been on his best behavior; he hadn't yelled when that little shit Killer kept biting him, which seemed like all the time. Kept his loving moves soft and gentle so his size didn't overwhelm his tiny mate... *At least I won't have that problem with this one,* he thought as Teilo strolled into their living room, dressed and on two feet this time. Teilo was only a couple of inches shorter than he was, and just as well built.

"Hey yup," Teilo held out his hand. "I'm Teilo. You must be Nereus."

"What gave it away?" Nereus curved his lips and quirked his eyebrow as he gave the offered hand a solid grip and a warm caress as they parted. Damn, his fingers were tingling. They were definitely mates.

Teilo blushed and then shrugged. "It's a pack, man; word gets around. My brother's mate reckons he might know you. Son of Poseidon. Reckons you're the slut, the academic or the goody-two-shoes and he discounted the academic because apparently, the guy doesn't go out much."

"That makes me the goody-two-shoes then. The slut's my brother, Baby, and clearly your brother's mate hasn't met my twin. He'd be known as the troublemaker." Nereus wasn't sure what to make of his moniker. "Sit down and tell me about yourself."

"I got coffee, tea, and soda," Raff said coming in from the kitchen with a large tray. "I wasn't sure what you liked. Oh, and I got some food too because I know shifting makes you hungry... oh, thank you."

Teilo had beaten Nereus in getting the tray and set it down on the table. "Don't need anyone to wait on me, little one," Teilo said quietly. "I'm Teilo. You must be Raff."

"Yes, I...." Raff didn't seem to know what to say to the larger wolf, and Nereus was ready to step in and help. Well, verbally. He was already sitting down. But it seems Teilo had an instinct about these things, because Raff was pulled into strong arms that weren't his, and Nereus could only stare. He wasn't jealous; it was kinda hot. It was the relaxed look Raff had on his face that worried him. Raff only looked like that with him when he'd climaxed.

"You don't have to worry about being around me, little one," Teilo said gravely. "I'm not perfect. I snore and fart with the best of them; I have a big mouth and a crude sense of humor at times. I often say the first thing that comes into my head, which means I'm bound to put my size 14s in my mouth more than once. But me and my wolf will never hurt you. You have my word on that."

Raff, if anything, snuggled closer. He seemed completely at ease with the rough and ready enforcer, and Nereus didn't know what to think. He coughed, and Teilo's eyes met his.

"I ain't ignoring you, big guy," he said in that same deep voice that sent tingles down Nereus's spine. "But this little one's strung tighter than a guitar string. When was the last time you went for a run in your fur?"

Raff shrugged and moved out of Teilo's arms and into the nearest single chair. "We've been busy," he said. "I haven't shifted since Scott saved me from being beaten up. But then I met our mate... and what with Ollie and the move...."

Teilo swung himself onto the couch next to Nereus and helped himself to some black coffee. "I imagine it's intimidating, the idea of running with our lot," he said casually. "They're all big buggers. You should see Diablo," he laughed and Nereus couldn't understand how come the guy was so comfortable in his skin. Couldn't he feel the tension in the room? "His shifted form has to be 400 pounds, and he is bigger than most of us. The only one bigger is Jax's natural form. He's a Dire Wolf and freaking huge."

Teilo shook his head. "Still, you have plenty of time to learn, no one will hurt you here. What's your story, big guy? I've heard rumors but seeing as we're bound to be getting intimately acquainted sometime in the near future, it would be nice to know a bit about you."

Teilo curled his leg on the couch and Nereus found himself the focus of amazing green eyes. He was a good-looking man; Nereus could see that at a glance. His mind flickered to Sebastian. His friend would think Teilo was the perfect "warrior" mate. His arms were huge; his face was hard enough for people to think twice about crossing him, and the way his clothes looked painted on left Nereus in no doubt as to the man's physique. He was stunning, in a very rugged warrior-type way.

"I'm the son of Poseidon," Nereus said, not sure how much Teilo had actually heard and how much of it was true. "I'm almost as old as the sea. I... I travel a lot and have houses all over the world. I like walks on the beach and when I swim, I develop a tail. What more did you want to know?" There were a lot of things Nereus could say, but he didn't want Raff to be any more uncomfortable around him than he was.

Teilo quirked an eyebrow at him. Nereus recognized the move for what it was. He'd been caught out. But Teilo seemed prepared to let it go for now. "What about you, Raff? Are you as closed off as our merman?"

Raff looked surprised to be spoken to at all. "What you see is what you get with me," he said quietly. "I don't have any money or possessions beyond what can fit in my backpack. My home pack kicked me out for refusing to bond with a female and have pups. Our kind is virtually extinct so they thought that was important. I couldn't do it. I'd been without a pack for about two years until Scott found me fighting for my life against some homophobic jerks and took me into the San Antonio pack where I met Nereus. Some serial killer thinks I can get pregnant, which is why I'm here, and yeah... I'm pretty insignificant when you think about it. My pups are about the most interesting thing about me, and I'm sure they rule the house, not me."

Roaring with laughter, Teilo shook his head. "You are anything but insignificant, little one. I can see you and I are going to get along famously."

"What can you tell us about you?" Nereus almost snarled. There was no point in jealousy between mates, but damn it, he wasn't used to being dismissed, or made to feel he was a liar. Why wasn't Teilo being nice to him?

"I'm a wolf shifter; we keep things simple. My dad roughed me and my younger brother up a lot as kids. Adair, my older brother, found out about it. Killed Dad, freed us. The three of us spent roughly forty, no," Teilo tilted his head, "more like sixty years working as mercenaries, helping other packs with rogues. I've killed people. A lot of people." Nereus noticed he was staring Raff straight in the eyes as he said that and the smaller man didn't even blink.

"Anyhow," Teilo continued, apparently satisfied with Raff's lack of reaction, "eventually Adair got sick of traveling around. I was too, you know, but I'd followed my brother for decades and it was a hard habit to break. He got the offer for us to move here as permanent enforcers, and here we are."

"No walks on the beach or love watching the sunrise type stuff to share," Nereus snarled, unsure why he was annoyed.

Teilo grinned. "Never been in a relationship. Fucked more men than I can count; no offense little one," he added as Raff growled. "Just telling it like it is. But as for beach walks and sunsets, can't say I've had the time or the inclination. I'm an expert with blowing shit up; I'm pretty proud of my hand-to-hand combat skills, and I can twirl a *rokushakubō* like you wouldn't believe."

"I'd like to learn that," Raff said suddenly.

"The bo?" Teilo asked. "I can teach you."

"I don't have a lot of muscles of my own and even my wolf's not much good in a fight. Maybe the bo staff will give me an edge."

"Put a bit of oomph behind it, and no one will be able to touch you. I'll be happy to teach you once we have our mating taken care of,"

Teilo smiled as he put his coffee cup down and stood up.

"You're leaving?" Nereus couldn't believe it. Even he could smell the arousal in the room, or maybe it was his, but still. He wanted Teilo in his bed; it'd been months since he'd had a rough romp and he thought the wolf shifter would've been onboard with it, too. The lump in his pants was big enough.

"I don't want to leave, okay?" Teilo wandered over and gave Raff a kiss on the cheek, stroking his face before he turned. Raff melted under the touch, but Nereus was struck by the resolve in those emerald eyes when they were focused on him.

"You two have issues; I can smell it," Teilo said bluntly. "Our Raff shouldn't be so uncomfortable around you, and I don't care how short a time you've been mated. You seem like a stand-up guy but you're hiding stuff. Stuff you don't want Raff or me to know. Until you can be honest with both of us, you're not someone I can claim or let claim me."

"Nereus has been nothing but good to me," Raff yelled, coming to his feet. "He saved me from the flood. He's kind and sweet and considerate."

"Just not honest," Teilo said, turning back to Raff and holding him close. "He's hiding stuff from you, little wolf, and your spirit knows it even if you don't want to face it. When a guy keeps a part of himself hidden, then he's not fully committed to the mating, no matter what words come out of his mouth. I'll be at the Enforcers' house if you need me for anything, okay? Just mention it to Griff or Diablo and they'll drop you there, anytime."

Nereus felt those eyes running over him once more before Teilo stalked out the door. Raff looked torn, his hands twisting, his gaze alternating between the door Teilo left through and the hallway to the bedroom.

"Raff, you mean everything to me. I've been nothing but good to you since we met. I'm not hiding stuff, please," Nereus said as Raff headed for the bedroom.

Raff tilted his head back and sniffed. "See, part of what you said was a lie. I can smell it now. I didn't know what that was before Teilo mentioned it."

"Check our mind link then," Nereus said urgently. "You'll know the truth then."

"Will I?" Raff asked. "Is that big-assed steel door you have in your mind opened at last?" He sounded so sad, but Nereus was too stunned to respond. He never thought for a second that his darling mate could see the blocks in his mind. Nereus closed his eyes as he felt Raff's presence in his head. But try as he might, he was too scared to let down his blocks.

"Guess I should have looked before I leaped," Raff said, tears running down his cheeks. "But you're not alone in hiding stuff. This isn't entirely your fault. I'll tell you what I've been hiding from you because I hate this; I hate not being honest with you and maybe, just maybe, my honesty might spur the same in you."

Nereus wasn't sure how many more shocks in a day he could take. Finding he had a second mate was one thing. But what had Raff been hiding from him? "Whatever you say won't make a difference to how I feel about you," he said, making sure every syllable was the honest truth.

Raff didn't look confident and the tears on his face tugged at Nereus so hard, but Nereus stayed on the couch, his calm mask firmly in place.

"Your utter perfection worries me; it makes me feel inadequate and I don't feel worthy of you. I know we're mates. I know the Fates chose me for you. But you never argue, you never get upset, you never even scratch your balls and I'm not used to someone being so... godlike. Every time you touch me you act as though I might break; I'm a lot stronger than you give me credit for, but you can't or won't see that. I could get past the lack of respect for my wolf side, but your perfections remind me of my own shortcomings and that's why I get uncomfortable around you. So, there, I've said it." Raff turned towards the door but then turned back. "One last thing. I love you. I have since before we moved here. Now you know I have no secrets left."

Nereus knew he should get up; he knew he should follow his mate, hold him in his arms and keep on holding him until all Raff's doubts disappeared. But he stayed frozen on the couch. He thought he'd been the perfect mate... but what was a demiGod to do when perfection was the one thing ruining his relationship? A waft of salt spray hit his nose, and he snarled. "Butt out Dad, I don't need your help." Knowing his irritating father was laughing at him didn't help his mood.

Chapter Three

Teilo was standing on the porch, watching the sun slowly climb the sky. He stared at the trees, knowing Raff and Nereus were about five miles away; his wolf was panting to be with them. Never in his whole life had he imagined he'd have one mate, let alone two. *And damn, they are some fine hunks of manhood,* he thought. It'd taken every single ounce of self-control and then some to leave them both the previous day.

"You'd better sort your shit out, merman, 'cause my wolf ain't going to wait much longer," he muttered as he took a sip of his coffee. He wrinkled his nose. Cold. Damn it. He headed inside the house as Marius came running out of it.

"There you are," Marius said, tugging his arm. "Come on, you can't miss this."

"What the hell's going on?" Teilo could see all the enforcers with Adair, and his mate were already in the living room, chatting excitedly among themselves. A couple of them were holding towels.

"That new pack member, the fish-man, merman, whatever," Marius said excitedly. "He's been burning up the phone lines since sparrow's fart, getting permission to put in a pool."

"At the pack house, or over at Griff's place?" Maybe he could take a peek and see Nereus's tail. He might have to stay in wolf form so he didn't inadvertently claim the sexy hunk and his gorgeously pretty sidekick, but he was sorely tempted.

"It's too big for the pack house grounds, man," Marius spread his arms wide. "That guy thinks big. Apparently, it's going to be a part of the sea, right here in Cloverleah. I can't wait to go swimming." He snatched a towel from the back of a chair. "Nereus in nothing but a tail. Damn, he might be mated to that little guy, but there's nothing to stop me from drooling."

Teilo slapped Marius around the head before he'd even thought about it. "What the fuck, man?" Marius rubbed his head and glared.

Teilo sighed. Every man and his dog were watching, but yeah. He didn't have the right to hit his younger brother, and it wasn't in Teilo's nature to hide anything from his brothers. "He's my mate, okay? Don't make a fuss, but he and Raff are my mates, too. I talked to them about it yesterday and we've got a few things to sort out before any claiming's done so let's not make a big deal out of this."

"Nereus is one of the good guys," Vassago said, as Adair strode forward and Teilo found his neck strangled by basketball-sized biceps.

"So pleased for you, little brother," Adair said in his hair, a catch in his voice. "So fucking pleased for you."

"Yeah, yeah," Teilo heard his own voice slipping. "It hasn't happened yet, okay. But you'll know about it when it's done."

"Honestly," Vassago stepped forward as Adair stepped back, clouting him on the back. Teilo was surprised by the hug he got from the much smaller djinn. "Nereus is a good guy. He might have issues, but try living forever and staying baggage free. Don't give up on him or the little one."

"Raff's about the same size as you," Teilo teased, not used to being the focus of so much attention.

"Pff, I can be bigger with a simple thought," and suddenly the tiny djinn was the same size as his mate.

"Cut it out," Marius said. "You know it freaks Adair out when you do crazy shit like that. I thought we were going swimming. I won't drool over your mate," he added to Teilo, "not in your presence, anyway."

"You do know it's cold as hell out there, don't you?" Teilo said as they all moved together in a huddle so Vassago could transport them all. "Your bits will shrink."

"Hey, even with shrinkage, I've got something worth looking at," Marius smirked. Teilo went to hit him again as Vassago whisked them all to the pool.

"Wow," Adair said as the men were stunned by the change in scenery. Teilo totally agreed. What had once been nothing but trees and grass as far as the eye could see, was now a water wonderland. He could smell the salt in the air, which was probably why there was a sand strip running between the water and the grass. But Nereus hadn't created a pool; it was as though he'd carved a piece of the beach and deposited it right in the middle of a landlocked space. There were waves and rocks and even a freaking island in the middle of the water.

Teilo could see baby Ollie playing on the edges of the water, being hovered over by a loving Luke. Kane, Shawn, Griff and Diablo were sitting in lounge chairs by the edge, wrapped up in coats and drinking beer even though it wasn't anywhere near lunchtime yet. Looking around, he could see other pack members doing the same. It was as if the sight of water had brought out a beach time vibe, even though everyone was wearing winter clothing.

Marius yet out a yell and a "whoop," as he went charging into the water, totally naked. One dive and he was covered in goosebumps big enough for Teilo to see at a distance. Shaking his head at his impetuous brother, Teilo looked around for Raff, who was sitting on his own, his pups huddled around his feet. Apparently, they weren't stupid enough to brave the water. His feet were moving in their direction before Teilo could even think about it. But then a flash of gold and silver stopped him.

"Nereus's tail," Teilo breathed out softly. He swore he'd never seen anything so beautiful in his life. The man's strong arm muscles cut through the water, dismissing the waves as if they were nothing. Teilo got flashes of the man's broad back and the swell of his butt cheeks. But from there on down there was nothing but the most beautiful, sparkling, huge fish tail. For the first time since he'd heard about him, and then realized they were mates, it hit Teilo hard that Nereus would always be so much more than a man. He was a freaking god. And he'd blown him off and essentially called him a liar. Oops. Teilo decided he'd go and sit with Raff. That was hopefully one mate he hadn't messed things up with. The welcoming smile the little wolf gave him as he sat down was a step in the right direction.

/~/~/~/~/

Nereus took another lap. The sea water soothed him. A little island had appeared in the center of the pool. He swam around it and shot off to the end of the pool and back again before starting another lap. When he reached the island, he pulled himself half out of the water and sighed, almost ignoring his tail which did gleam in the pale winter light. He didn't stretch his tail as often as he'd like.

"Well, I can see why you are hanging around with all these lovely males on tap. Look at that scenery. Yummy. I might have to join you for a few days." The voice from the rocks above him filled the space and meshed with the sound of the waves Nereus had created.

Nereus scowled. "What are you doing here? And knock off the voice shit."

"Now, now... is that any way to talk to me?"

The owner of the voice was beautiful, much to Nereus's chagrin. Silvery hair hung down to his butt; long muscular legs, broad well-defined chest. Exotic turquoise eyes and a leer as Poseidon took in the sight of so many muscular men on the shoreline. At least he was dressed although barely. His shiny pants were painted on and his bright blue shirt was opened to the waist.

"Damn it, Dad. What do you want?"

"You took my water for this... this paddling pool."

"You have plenty of water," Nereus sighed. It was a common enough argument. He wouldn't have been given rights to call the waters if he didn't have some sovereignty over them. Unfortunately, his Dad seemed to forget that. "This little pool isn't going to make any difference to the seas."

"You didn't ask me."

"I didn't have to." Nereus relinquished his tail and stood defiantly in front of his father, remembering to include pants in his shift.

"Hades, you did." Poseidon put both hands on his hips.

"Hades, I didn't." Nereus echoed his pose.

"I humored this silly mating nonsense..."

"It is not silly; the Fates chose my mates for me."

"Well, you've cocked that up. One of them uncomfortable around you, and one of them still unclaimed." The pools waves rose and lapped over the edges of the pool.

"Look who's talking. The man whose definition of relationship is I've come; close the door on your way out."

"I do *not* do relationships and you know that. Mermen don't have mates. I put the blame on your other father for this."

"You leave Abraxas out of this."

The earth started to tremble, as their angry voices melded with the roar of the earth and the crashing of the waves.

"Nereus! Nereus!"

He turned at the sound of Kane's voice to see his mates and the entire pack standing on the shoreline. Luke had a trembling Ollie in his arms. Nereus felt sick and spread his arms. The waves subsided, and the trembling stopped.

A thought and he was standing on the shoreline. Of course, his father had to be right next to him, a sexy smirk on the inhumanly beautiful face. "I'm sorry. I... We... I would like you all to meet my father."

He heard Diablo whisper to Griff, "Hell, I feel like the ugly duckling stepbrother."

Without thinking, Griff answered, "Yeah, he looks amazing". His comment was rewarded with Diablo pushing him into the pool.

Kane and Shawn were talking urgently, and when Shawn shook his head, saying, "I can't do shit. He's a force of nature," Nereus knew the only one capable of stopping his father wreaking havoc was him. Unfortunately, his father had a one-track mind.

"Hello, pretty wolves." Poseidon leered.

Vassago strode up and gave the beautiful man a push, sending him backward a couple steps. "Knock it off, Sei."

Poseidon's attention focused on the sexy djinn. Nereus noted he still favored leather pants which highlighted a spectacular ass. "Vassago, baby. Long time no see, beautiful. Is this where you've been hiding?"

"Forget the come on. You know it doesn't work with me." Vassago put his hands on his hips and Adair growled as he came to stand behind his mate.

The turquoise eyes surveyed Adair. "Oh, you do pick them nice. How about a three-way like that time we...."

That walk down memory lane was cut off as Vassago kicked Poseidon's shin. "I said knock it off. I'm mated and happy. Nereus is mated and happy."

Rubbing his leg, Poseidon grumbled, "We don't mate."

"Well apparently, the Fates didn't get the message," Nereus intervened. He could see Vassago spoiling for a fight and with his magic, things could get messy. "Raff and I have been mated three weeks, and we knew just from meeting him yesterday, Teilo is our mate too. There's no mistaking our bond, so why don't you just accept it?"

"Oh, those bitches have had it in for me ever since that party in Atlantis. How the hell was I supposed to know it would sink? I saved the population. It wasn't as though I let anyone drown."

"By turning them into dolphins," Nereus remembered. It hadn't been one of Poseidon's happier adventures and a lot of the gods were pissed off that day.

"I didn't know they couldn't change back like the rest of us." Poseidon's focus was diverted again as he suddenly noticed the Fae who were staring at him with fascination. "Oh my goodness. Fae... I haven't seen one of them in ages, and there are two of them here. Hello, Beautiful."

Jax stepped in front of them. "They are *my* mates."

"Well, four-ways are nice too, handsome."

Jax snarled and lifted his hands but before he could do anything, his mates grabbed his arms.

"No." Aelfric pleaded.

"You can't send him to the ice world. He's a force of nature here on earth." Fafnir finished the sentence. "It would fuck everything up faster than Global Warming if you get rid of him."

"Seriously?" Jax looked from one to the other as they both nodded.

It didn't stop Poseidon though. "Well, if he wants to be a stick in the mud, how about a three-way?"

"Dad. Just stop. They're mated. Almost all the men here are mated. They aren't interested. Mated wolves don't stray and once bitten, their partners couldn't stray even if tempted." Nereus folded his arms across his chest and glared at his father, who couldn't look repentant if his life depended on it.

"Don't start that, Junior. That's a bunch of hooey. We don't mate and any other mating restrictions like that are just a myth. I mean really. When I got the message about you and the little cutie here, I was shocked. Your brothers are just as surprised. Although considering how pretty your little wolf is, I would claim to be mated too." He waggled his eyebrows at Raff who blushed and looked away as Teilo growled.

"Although, I must admit, I don't blame you one bit for wanting to hang around here," Poseidon wasn't finished. "As I said before; a lovely group of men. Such variety. Oh, how lovely, a Shifter Guardian!" He beamed his smile at Shawn which set Kane growling. "I haven't got it on with one of you in at least two thousand years."

Kane yanked Shawn behind him. "And you aren't going to start."

"Oh, aren't we protective? I keep saying that I like three-ways. I wasn't excluding you. There's enough of me to go around."

Oh shit. Kane was getting distinctly furry. Nereus blocked his father as Shawn grabbed Kane's arm. "It's okay. He's not going to do anything without our consent."

"I leave that up to my brother, Hades." Poseidon poked his head around Nereus's shoulder and then stepped back into the limelight again. "Hades does that sort of thing. Carrying off the unwilling and having his way with them. Well, it wasn't like she was unwilling by then but he really pissed off Dee. And well, Zeus but then Ganymede was a bit of a horn dog, to begin with and he didn't complain one bit. Especially when he realized what went with the job. Eternal life and riches and all that. Who doesn't want to piss in a golden pot?" Poseidon gave them a sunny smile.

"Dad. Would you please stop? Nobody wants a walk in ancient history, especially not your version of it." Then something else clicked and his eyes widened. "Are my brothers coming to visit, too?" He hoped the shifters didn't pick up on his horror at the thought.

"Of course," Poseidon beamed, and Wesley and Thomas sighed. "Your twin, after he got over the shock, was totally delighted. He said something about a mating gift for your little one. I have no clue what he was rambling on about when he wandered off. I assume that he'll be along as soon as he finds whatever he's looking for. Your older brother will be here as soon as he gets his nose out of that dusty old book he's so fascinated with right now and realizes what I told him. And Baby's bound to bounce along sooner rather than later. He said something about wolves and stamina."

"Oh, Gods..." Nereus waved his arm and plopped down on the bench that appeared, covering his face with his hands. His family was going to ruin things. He just knew it. His mates were going to hate him and he'd be alone for freaking eternity.

Vassago shook his head and said to the rest of the pack, "I did warn you, Nereus is the normal one in this family."

Poseidon snorted. "He takes after his other father. Abraxas had no sense of humor either. Must have something to do with horse shifters. Or maybe it has something to do with being a Horse of the Sun?"

Nereus didn't want to listen. The last thing he wanted to think about was his other father. He heard splashing and turned to look. A beautiful white stallion waded out from the surf of the pool and wandered up to Poseidon, who had an apple in his hand suddenly. "I wasn't calling you. Missed me already?"

The stallion nickered and lipped the apple.

Raff moved from Teilo's side for the first time since Poseidon arrived. The look on his face was one of longing as though he just had to touch. Nereus tensed as Poseidon's prized stallion gazed at the small wolf and then stretched his neck to nuzzle the man's face. "He's not scared of me?" Raff's face lit up and not for the first time, Nereus wished it was he that drew Raff's smile.

Poseidon smiled indulgently. "Of course not. He's a seahorse. Wolves or other creatures of the land don't bother him. Would you like to ride him, little wolf?"

"Oh, yes."

Teilo and Nereus yelled at the same time. "No, don't, Raff! Come back here." They started toward him just as Poseidon swung up on the horse and pulled Raff up with him.

"Later, boys. The little one and I are going to have some fun."

Nereus screamed in fury as Poseidon and Raff disappeared into a huge wave, Teilo howling beside him.

Chapter Four

As their mate vanished in the pool surf, Teilo morphed into his wolf and tried to chase them. His only thought was he wanted Raff back where he could see his mate was safe. Unfortunately, he didn't get very far. Nereus caught him in surprisingly strong arms and dragged him back to shore. "Teilo, change back. My Dad won't hurt Raff. Raff is safe."

Teilo growled and struggled in his mate's arms.

"Dad doesn't force the unwilling. He'll try to seduce him but he's not going to force him. The bastard only took him because he wanted me to follow him. I'll go get him, Mate."

Teilo shifted and shook off Nereus's arms. He wasn't going to admit how wonderful they felt around him, not with Raff missing. "You're not going anywhere without me."

"Not without you." Nereus seemed shaken, and Teilo could understand. Well, sort of. Having a god for a father who looked more beautiful than anything mortal man could imagine had to be difficult.

"So long as we're agreed." Teilo shook the sand off his skin. Damn stuff really did get everywhere. "I need clothes."

In a blink, he was dressed. Teilo turned to the Fae, who nodded their heads. "Thank you."

Dean and Matthew stepped forward. "You should take us, too. Raff is going to be upset and I can help with that."

"And the rest of us." Troy shook off his mate's hand. "Anton, you know how I feel about this. Raff is pack. He might need us."

"Nereus is used to handling his father." Vassago patted Troy's arm and turned to Kane, who was frowning hard. "There's nothing the pack can do in Poseidon's world. He's not a predator, a sex addict maybe, but Raff won't come to any harm. Chances are he just wanted someone to show off his trinkets to. Honestly, I give you my word. Raff's my brother-in-law's mate. He won't come to any harm."

"It would be better if it was just me and my mate." Nereus said, "Although I appreciate the support. We'll bring Raff back, I promise."

Teilo looked at his mate long and hard. When they'd met, he'd been blown away by the man's good looks. This morning he'd been stunned by the beauty of his shifted form. Now he was impressed with the sheer resolve on Nereus's face. It was time to trust. When Nereus grabbed his arm and jumped into the wave he'd summoned, Teilo snapped his mouth shut and prayed his mate remembered he couldn't breathe underwater.

The water was cold, and Teilo could feel it seep into his bones. When the feeling receded, he and Nereus stood in a long marble hall and Teilo was completely dry, clothes and all. He was stunned although this wasn't his first experience with magic. What was amazing was the room they were in. Gold and silver ornaments inset with gems gleamed at them from various shelves around the hall. A full-sized ornamental chariot sat in front of them.

"Oh wow..." Teilo turned his head this way and that, trying to take it all in. He'd never seen so much wealth so blatantly displayed before.

"Yeah. This is Dad's idea of informal. You don't want to see the formal hall." Nereus strode past the chariot. "Mind the wheels. There are blades sticking out from them. Alexandros always did have overblown ideas about shit."

"Alexandros?" Teilo followed his mate, trying not to trip up. Everywhere he looked there were works of art, precious stones and vases that looked as though they'd come from ancient times.

"Yeah. You would know him from your history as Alexander the Great. He sacrificed the chariot and horses to Dad. Dad gave the horses to some guy he was having a fling with at the time in the British Isles, but he kept the chariot. That's how Sebastian and I met. You're bound to meet him later," Nereus added as Teilo wondered who Sebastian was. "Hopefully, Dad's through here."

/~/~/~/~/

Poseidon sighed with pleasure as he landed in his dining room. He put down the little wolf in his arms and leered at his son's mate. "There now, all safe and sound. How shall we entertain ourselves until my son shows up?"

He found himself talking to a small shivering Red Wolf standing among rags. Crystal amber eyes full of fear stared at him.

"Oh, dear, that wasn't supposed to happen. It's okay little one, I won't hurt you." Dropping to his knees, he stroked the soft fur of Raff's head. "Really, I won't. I told you, I don't force anyone. Could you change back? Please. I give you my word I'll treat you like an honored guest. It's okay. I'm so sorry I scared you. I just wanted to talk to the man my son's mated to."

Wolf bones and fur shimmered and stretched and within seconds Raff's human form came into view, although the little man was hunched over himself. "I need clothes," Raff said quietly.

"Indeed." Poseidon snapped his fingers and neatly folded deep green silken clothes appeared. He gestured to them, "Here you go."

He personally didn't think the lovely wolf shifter needed anything to wear at all. But he did promise Raff would be treated like a guest. Not that most of his guests wore clothes. But still. Having Raff naked when Nereus turned up would probably cause another scene.

"Turn around." Raff's face was bright red, but he had such a sweet determined little look on his face.

"I can't even enjoy the view? Fine." Facing away from Raff, Poseidon watched his guest get dressed in the polished silver shield that hung on the wall in front of him.

"What is this?"

Poseidon pressed his lips firmly together. Raff was struggling with the material and yet he wasn't supposed to be watching.

"It's a chiton. Do you need help with it?" *Oh please let me help, you delectable little morsel.*

"No!"

Poseidon couldn't help laughing. "Look, pull it on and I'll help you fasten the shoulders and you can figure out the belt. I promise I won't paw you."

After a long moment and more rustling of silk, Poseidon heard, "I think I might need some help, after all, you can turn around now if you like." Raff had pulled the chiton over most of his body, holding the edges over one shoulder.

"Ah. Just as lovely as I thought. I knew that color would suit you." Poseidon clicked his fingers and two pins appeared in his hand. The matching pair shimmered in the light. The jeweled tridents were bordered on one side by a jumping dolphin in platinum and on the other side a golden seahorse rearing back. "These are just a couple of trinkets which will help keep the material fastened."

The little wolf didn't need to know the sale of either one of the pins would keep him in luxury for life. Poseidon fastened the pins, keeping his twitching fingers away from the soft skin, and stepped back. "Now how about some food, little one? It must be lunchtime somewhere."

"No, it's all right. I don't need anything," Raff's eyes widened. "I... er... I heard about you. Isn't it true no one can leave here if they eat the food?"

Oh, this little one is delightful. Poseidon found himself laughing again. "You are thinking of my brother, Hades. Not me I'm afraid; otherwise, the hallways would be cluttered with people, and I like my peace and quiet most of the time. Now tell me what you'd like to eat?"

/~/~/~/~/

"I'm fine," Raff said firmly. The clothes were lovely if a little shiny for his tastes. He felt a lot more confident with his body covered up although with Poseidon being a god, the man could probably see through the green silk. Raff could eat. He'd had a horrible night. Nereus didn't come to bed at all and he realized he hadn't eaten since breakfast the day before. What was worse, his stomach growled as if calling him a liar.

"I'm familiar with wolves. You're always ready to eat." Raff let himself be guided into a room with a long table; food covered every inch of it and Raff's mouth started to water. "Please. Before your Nereus gets here, dig in. Enjoy."

The food did smell heavenly and Raff was really hungry. "You promise it won't keep me here?"

"I swear," Poseidon said firmly. He handed Raff a platter. "Please enjoy, but you'd better eat quickly.

315

Nereus is already in the building and he's brought another wolf."

"That will be our other mate, Teilo. He would have insisted on coming with Nereus. Wolf shifters are like that. Very possessive with their mates." Raff couldn't suppress the smile that thought gave him. That was the other reason for not being able to sleep. Thoughts of being claimed by the rugged enforcer warred with the sorrow at Nereus choosing not to share his bed. He'd had a rough night.

Poseidon studied him as though he was an exotic insect. "Yes. I've heard that before," he said. "Come, fill your plate and sit beside me. I need to make it up to you; I didn't mean to scare you. I'm sorry, Little Wolf."

"Raff. My name is Raff," he said, as he took the platter offered and started picking meats off the platters on the table. There was every type of meat Raff had ever imagined, and some he hadn't come across before. As he filled his plate, he said quietly, "We are mated, you know, me and Nereus. I'm sorry if you don't believe it, but I bit him. He carries my mating mark. I didn't mean to do it initially, but when he pulled me out of the flood, I just reacted to his smell. You were there the night he claimed me. I know you gave us the tattoos."

"Little Wolf... Raff, if you are my son's mate, I can think of no one I would rather have as another son. I gave you tattoos because the one thing my son has always wanted was a mate to love and cherish."

"Well, it isn't just me. Teilo is our other mate, and you might have given us tattoos, but my scar is on Nereus's neck and it's staying there." Raff sat in the chair Poseidon pulled out for him and picked up his fork. "We haven't completed the mating yet with

Teilo, but I know he wants us both. It's only a matter of time before he claims us." At least, that is what Raff was hoping. In fact, from the way Teilo didn't want to leave his side at the pool, Raff was hoping to be claimed before nightfall. If he hadn't been so overcome by the beautiful horse, he would have been.

"Ah. Two mates? Yes, well, that's not surprising. My son... My son tries to compensate for things that don't need compensating for. It's no wonder the Fates gave him two mates rather than one. I think it's the horse shifter genes Nereus has. Makes him need more of everything for some reason."

"He's half horse shifter?" Raff almost choked on some beef. Nereus told him he shifted into his merman form; Raff had seen it twice now. But....

"He didn't tell you?" Poseidon grinned. "He comes from two

fathers. His other father is Abraxas, one of the Sun's Horses. They were the original horse shifters. You must get him to show you his horse form someday." Raff was distracted from the idea of two fathers by a delicious smelling dish held under his nose. "Do try this," Poseidon said. "It's ambrosia. I stole the recipe from my brother, Zeus. His wife was furious I got it." *Real ambrosia? Wasn't that the food of the gods?* Raff wondered as he took a tiny bite. Listening to his father-in-law talk about names he'd only read about in history seemed so surreal and yet Poseidon continued to name-drop and share stories, all while keeping his plate filled. It was one of the nicest afternoons Raff spent in a long time.

Chapter Five

"Damn it. Dad, stop playing games!" Nereus roared as the next room took them to another long hallway. "He's rearranging the damn rooms."

He stormed through the hallway and slammed the door open at the end, startling the man in it who turned at the noise. Teilo could see the family resemblance. "Whatever are you screaming about, Nereus?" The other man pushed his glasses up his nose. "You are starting to sound like that idiot you call a twin." The man's eyes dropped to his book again, and he turned a page. From the tone he used, Nereus wasn't impressing him, whoever the guy was.

"Where the hell is Dad?" Nereus yelled. "And what in the hell are you doing here? You've got your own place."

The man in glasses sighed and marked his place on the page with a finger before looking up. "Dad's in the dining room; he's got a guest. I found this book in a bookshop and I needed some of the books from this library to verify the...."

"Yep. No. You start talking about whatever you're studying now and we'll never get out of here. I'll talk to you later, Brother."

The man in glasses didn't seem annoyed by Nereus's rudeness. His nose was buried back in the book before they'd left the room.

As they entered the next richly clad hallway, Teilo said, "Damn, we could buy all of Texas, Oklahoma, New Mexico and Arizona, with New Orleans thrown in for good measure, with this lot."

"Dad rules the sea, and anything that is in the sea or comes into the sea or is revealed in earthquakes is his. As humans started traveling the seas, as you can imagine, the stuff piled up after a while. He's always been a tad flashy."

"A tad?" Teilo mumbled. He'd never seen so much gold in one place before and *oh my gods, is that a diamond?*

"Yeah... well..." Nereus shrugged. Instead of going to the end, he yanked open a side door. "Finally. There you are!"

Raff's scent hit his nose and Teilo shot through the door before Nereus could stop him. A growl in his throat, he jumped the table and knocked the plate from Raff's hands, the food flying all over Poseidon. "Mine!" He managed to snarl between his fangs. He dragged Raff off the chair and retreated to what he considered a safe distance, holding Raff firmly against his chest.

Nereus seemed equally furious, glaring at his father. "How dare you take my mate?" His voice sounded like thunder.

Poseidon, on the other hand, looked perfectly relaxed. He leaned back from the table and brushed stray bits of what looked like beef from his shoulder. "I have no clue what your problem is. We're simply sitting here having a wonderful... well, we were having a wonderful meal and a chat. Then you come bursting in like a demented kraken. You can see there's nothing wrong with your precious wolf. You really must stop overreacting. I blame the horse shifter genes, personally. No one in my family acts like you do."

Teilo's mouth dropped open when Nereus screamed, "Stop with the fucking horse shifter comments! It's got nothing to do with my horse shifter genes. My only problems in life come from having a fucking sex addict for a father."

"I am not an addict. I like sex. I like a lot of sex. Everyone I've ever had sex with enjoyed every minute of it. Including your father." Poseidon threw a wink at Raff and Teilo wondered what that was about, but Nereus wasn't finished.

"It was like Grand Central Station during rush hour in this place. I never knew who was going to be sitting at this table. Hell, sometimes it was even Abraxas."

"Your father," Poseidon said quietly. "He did give birth to you, after all."

Bloody hell, can this day get any weirder, Teilo thought, but Nereus was still upset and suddenly his mate's closed off attitude was starting to make sense.

"His name is Abraxas. I will never call him Father. He left me."

"Nereus," Poseidon said patiently, "You're a Mer. You may be able to shift into a horse but you are a Merman who shifts into a horse. Had you got the Sun part of Abraxas's genetics, he would have kept you and your brother with him. We've been through this a million times. What on earth would a Mer do in the House of the Sun? You needed to be in the sea."

Nereus's voice was full of pain and Raff trembled in Teilo's arms. Teilo slowly put him down, his eyes glued to what was happening. "He could have tried," Nereus's voice broke. "He's a god of sorts. He could've done something. Instead, he leaves me and my brother here with nothing more than a kiss, telling us to be good little boys for a father we didn't know. He's all we fucking knew for five fucking years and he just dumped us like garbage."

Poseidon's voice became as still as a pond on a hot summer day, and just as soothing. "Nereus, my son. He tried. He tried to see you. He tried to visit you. You know that. You're the one who refused to see him. Your brother still sees him sometimes."

There was a very small frightened little boy's voice echoing in Nereus's deep one. "He left me."

Raff gave a small cry and ran to his mate, wrapping his arms around him. Nereus was crying openly now, even as he hung onto Raff like a lifeline. "I can't lose you, too. I just can't. I can't. I've tried so hard. I've been so good. I've done everything in my power to be perfect because I always knew if my own father would leave me, you will too. But my perfection is what's driving you away. I don't know what to do. I couldn't bear it if you left me."

"I'm not leaving you. I never will. Never." Raff was crying now, too, and Teilo was torn. Technically he had no business helping either one of them. He hadn't claimed them, nor they him. But watching Nereus in tears was tearing at his heart strings and he knew without any bond at all, Raff needed his support.

Teilo stared at Poseidon who answered him only by arching an eyebrow exactly like his mate. *The arrogant ass.* He took a faltering step toward his mates and then another; then he ran to them, wrapping them in his arms and hanging on tight. "Never. We will never leave you, Nereus," adding his deep voice to Raff's string of vows. Teilo felt the tingle of magic as Nereus transported them, and the last thing he saw as the palace of gold and silver disappeared was Poseidon grinning. The man looked so damned pleased with himself.

/~/~/~/~/

"Where the hell are we now?" Teilo's exasperated voice pulled Nereus from his thoughts and he looked around, his eyes still bleary.

"Oh, I'm sorry. This is my home. Italy, I think." Nereus shook his head. "Coming here was automatic for me. I'll take you back."

"No," Raff said quickly, and while Nereus was thrilled the little wolf was in his arms and didn't seem uncomfortable around him anymore, Nereus was beyond embarrassed at his breakdown and needed to pull himself together. "We're not going anywhere until we talk about what happened back at your dad's place. Teilo, you agree with me, right?" There was a thread of steel in Raff's voice Nereus hadn't heard before, and he wondered how Teilo would take it. But his bigger wolf mate agreed.

"We sit. We talk, and if you've got some food in this fancy place, it'd be welcome. I missed breakfast."

Food. Nereus could zap up food even if the thought of swallowing a mouthful made his stomach churn. A thought, a wave of his hand, and a table spread similar to Poseidon's but on a smaller scale appeared.

"Damn handy skill to have." Teilo's arms tightened around Nereus's waist briefly and then he was gone, pulling out a chair and filling a plate. "Come on, big guy. I know you ain't eaten today."

The words, "I'm not really hungry," were right on the tip of Nereus's tongue, but a gentle tug and a warm smile from Raff stopped them. "You've had an emotional day," he said quietly. "We wolves believe food can cure a multitude of ills, and you look like you could use some."

Nereus allowed himself to be led to a chair, and he sat down while Raff bustled about filling a plate for him. "I don't expect you guys to stay with me, you know," he said quietly when Raff finally sat down and sipped from a soda bottle. "What you saw back there. I swear my father's the only one who can make me angry simply by breathing, but my yelling... the crying ..." Nereus's voice dropped to a whisper. "How could you ever have any respect for me now?"

"Seems to me a good cry was long overdue," Teilo said casually, before taking a huge bite of a meat-crammed roll. He chewed for a few moments, and then Nereus was transfixed as the man swallowed. The Fates had done him proud. "Losing a loved one can be painful, regardless of the relationship. My mom died giving birth to my younger brother Marius. I was only two, but I still remember her like it was yesterday. I'll always miss her. At least your other dad's still alive."

Nereus thought he couldn't feel any worse, but Teilo's comment cut right through him. His big warrior had lost both parents and yet every five years, Abraxas had come to the sea, in a bid to see him. And Nereus had refused him for centuries, so upset by what he perceived as the man's betrayal.

"How did that happen?" Raff asked after a long silence. "Poseidon said Abraxas gave birth to you, but he's your father." A shocked look crossed his face. "I'm not going to get pregnant, am I?"

Teilo gasped and choked, and Nereus quickly thumped him on the back before soothing him as Teilo got his breath under control. "Please tell me it ain't so," he panted when he could finally speak. "If it is, you're using a condom, buddy."

"No, I can't get you pregnant." Nereus's lips twitched. "Not that I don't think it would be an amazing thing to happen. The only reason Abraxas got pregnant was because he's from a line of the gods. Poseidon is a god, and while I'm not sure if it was intentional or not, Abraxas could get pregnant with him. We can't impregnate male mortals, shifters or anyone else from the paranormal line."

"But you can women, right?" Teilo asked. "Do you have any kids?" It was Nereus who wanted to choke then, but he settled for shaking his head.

"It was a fair question," Raff said with a smile. "You're older than sin and have been with heaps of people. I imagine accidents were common in the Dark Ages."

The Dark Ages were nothing but a blur for Nereus, but he was sure he'd know if he had any accidents.

His father would have been crowing about it, for a start.

"Nope," he said firmly. "No kids. I always prayed for a mate. I didn't think much further than that."

"And now you have two," Raff said brightly. "And you will claim us now, won't you Teilo? Nereus doesn't have that steel door in his head anymore. He's not hiding stuff."

"If that's what he wants and you too, Raff," Teilo said, stuffing another bite of roll in his mouth. "I won't claim anyone who's unwilling and I won't have one of you saying yes and the other one saying no. It's all or nothing with me," he added around his mouthful. Nereus wondered why he thought his larger mate, who only yesterday seemed unafraid of anything, seemed like he was hiding something now.

Chapter Six

Okay, if I just keep eating then maybe that'll stop shit coming out of my mouth, Teilo thought as he chewed angrily. His wolf was giving him hell; his cock was threatening to split his pants and go on a rampage all by itself, and with two absolutely delicious men sitting at the table his only thought should have been *who do I fuck first?*

But Nereus's breakdown brought back memories of his own. Memories of him crying when his mother died, and then later when Adair left home; of when his father beat him senseless time and time again, determined to break him of his perceived weaknesses. Teilo had only ever trusted his brothers, no one else. His mates would expect him to trust them and Teilo wasn't sure... well, he was, but it was a scary thought. Teilo relied on Adair; he always had. He'd followed his brother blindly for

335

decades, never questioning the things his brother said or did. Nereus and Raff would expect to rely on him, and that switch in perspective, the thought of being responsible for two other people... It was scary... and so he hesitated, and maybe he hesitated and held himself back just a moment too long.

"You don't want us, do you?" Raff pushed away from the table and stood up. He was still wearing that ridiculous robe thing he must have gotten from Poseidon, and he looked like a mini Greek God. All he was missing was a laurel wreath in his hair. Teilo couldn't help but notice he had amazing legs. "You know as mates, you two are really trying my patience. Nereus wouldn't even sleep with me last night thanks to whatever upset him after your visit, Teilo. Neither one of you cares how much that hurt me. You, Teilo, you're a wolf shifter. Where're the fangs, rampant passion, and screaming MINE everyone talks about? Sitting there, stuffing your face like a mating's nothing more than an afternoon tea interruption. You know, forget trying my patience. Am I the only one who wants this mating? You guys piss me off big time. Both of you."

He stalked away from the table and Nereus yelled, "Where are you going?"

"To find a phone. I don't care if we're in Italy. You must have a phone," Raff didn't even stop. "I'm going to call Shawn and ask him if he can zap me home. I'm sick and tired of worrying if anyone wants me or not. I'm not leaving you; I'm just getting some space. At the moment, I'd far rather sleep with my puppies. At least I know where I stand with them."

Teilo knew his mate was talking about the four canines he looked after, but his wolf wasn't as understanding. All his wolf could hear was his mate was going to sleep with someone else, and he was furious about it. Teilo was on his feet and leaping for Raff before he realized what was happening.

"You're MINE," he snarled, his wolf flashing in his eyes as he took Raff to the ground. He managed to twist his body at the last moment, so Raff landed on top of him, saving his mate from the wicked thump his head made on the floor.

"That's more like it," Raff said, making no move to get away. In fact, the little man shimmied up Teilo's body, and the next thing he knew Raff's arms were around his neck and his mouth was on his, and Teilo thumped his head on the floor again. *You could have been doing this yesterday, you numbnuts.*

This close Raff's scent was overwhelmingly sweet, Jasmine and honeysuckle and some delicious musky undertone that smelled surprisingly like vanilla. Whatever it was, Teilo couldn't get enough of it. Raff's kisses were clumsy as if it was something he didn't do very often. The thought he might be inexperienced sent Teilo's blood boiling. He cupped Raff's neck and tilted him slightly, taking over and dominating his mate's luscious mouth. His other hand found satin, silky, warm satin that flowed over Raff's skin, and as his wandering hand went lower and skimmed the swell of Raff's pert ass, Teilo realized very quickly his mate wore nothing on under that robe. Skin became an imperative and Teilo's fingers scrabbled with the satin until he found the skin underneath. He cupped Raff's butt and his hips arched up, unable to help himself. His skin was so tight, his cock was making a mess in his jeans and he wanted with an urgency he'd never felt before. When he felt hands on his boots, tugging them off, his senses went into overdrive, as he realized both of his mates were with him and one of them was keen on getting him naked. He could handle that.

/~/~/~/~/

Nereus was stunned at the speed with which Teilo moved. One moment he was sitting at the table, the next he was on the floor, Raff pulled over him like a blanket. Not that his little mate seemed to mind. Raff's visit with his father seemed to have given him a backbone, and when he and Teilo kissed, it was Nereus's heart that soared. He knew his next decision was critical to their mating. He could either join in or walk away. If he joined in, he faced possible rejection. If he walked away, rejection was guaranteed.

Teilo's large hands exposed Raff's buttocks to the air and Nereus groaned. He wasn't a shifter, but the sexual tension in the room was building fast and that sexy tattoo got to him every time. *I'd be an idiot if I let them go,* he told himself firmly, forcing himself to his feet. The urge to magic them to his bedroom was strong, but Nereus needed to be sure of his welcome first. A few steps and he was kneeling at Teilo's feet, making sure the warrior wolf wouldn't kick him as he removed the huge boots, setting them aside.

Jeans. Slightly more difficult with Raff wiggling his pert behind in the air, two groins almost glued together and Teilo determined to keep the two of them as close together as physically possible. Nereus pushed Teilo's legs apart so he could get closer to Raff, encouraging the man's legs to straddle his future mate.

"Help me with his jeans, sweetness," he whispered in Raff's ear, and then oomph, Raff's arm was around his neck and Nereus found himself face to face with Teilo.

"Your turn," Raff said, slipping off Teilo's body and pushing Nereus's head down. He barely had time to pucker up when Teilo grabbed him with a growl. This time it was Nereus with his back on the floor, his body covered by a lust-filled wolf that devoured his mouth like a rare steak. *Gods, has anyone ever wanted me with so much passion before?*

Nereus couldn't remember, but then remembering his name was difficult at that point. Teilo was everywhere, his hands tugging at his pants, Nereus's chest hair getting caught in the fibers of Teilo's shirt. He wanted his bed; he wanted fewer clothes. Nereus flailed out with his arm, hoping to find Raff. The moment hot skin hit his, he focused his will.

So much better, Nereus thought as his back hit the comfort of his mattress and his body was now covered by a naked wolf. *Now lube. Where's the lube?*

/~/~/~/~/

Raff couldn't have moved his eyes if someone held a gun to his head. He'd been the recipient of Nereus's cock a fair few times in the weeks before they came to Cloverleah but he'd never even dreamed of his mate being on the receiving end. And that was going to happen; Teilo's dominance over Nereus was... fuck, his own private porn show. Raff curled his arms around his legs, ignoring his own cock which throbbed in time to his heartbeat. His lovely robe had disappeared along with everything else Nereus and Teilo'd been wearing but he wasn't cold. He didn't have a problem with sitting and watching. Teilo was a wolf on a mission. He'd get his turn.

Chapter Seven

Teilo had one aim, one goal and that's all he needed. Get his cock in Nereus's ass, his teeth in the sexy fucker's neck and then do the same thing to Raff. And okay, that might have been two goals, but Teilo was beyond reasonable thought. Everything about Nereus was right for him, the heat, the scent, the feel of his hard muscles straining under his. Even the body and facial hair, not something Teilo contended with very often provided an extra tweak on his senses. He tried to lift Nereus's legs up, but the man snarled at him and rolled over onto his hands and knees instead.

"Ready," Nereus snapped, but Teilo was stumped momentarily by the tramp stamp glaring at him from atop a perfectly formed behind.

"You might want to think about another visit to the tattooist," he said, checking with fingers to make sure his mate was as ready as he claimed. *Fuck, these guys with magic cut out all the good bits*, but yep, his fingers slid in with next to no resistance and Teilo was keen to see if his cock would go in as easily.

"The tattoos were a gift from Daaaad," Nereus's voice rose on a wail as Teilo slid home. *Oh my god, it's been too long since I've done this*, was Teilo's last conscious thought before his wolf took over. Nereus was strong, his spirit wild and untamed, and for some reason that excited Teilo's wolf to the point of madness. No matter how hard he pounded, Nereus took it. A tinge of blood hit the air and Teilo thought he heard a whimper but it wasn't coming from Nereus. The big man took everything he had to give and begged for more.

"Touch me," Nereus yelled and Teilo would've been happy to oblige but he was using Nereus's hips for leverage and it was a two-handed job. Not to mention his claws were out. Nereus groaned, the sound long, loud and beautiful, and looking down, Teilo could see Raff's behind sticking out from beneath Nereus's bulk. Their little sweetheart was giving his mate a blowjob. Teilo wished he could see it, but his wolf was getting impatient. Teilo's balls tightened, his spine arched, and he howled before his teeth dropped and he sank them into Nereus's neck. Waves and waves of pleasure rocked through his body; searing heat hit his lower back and his groan joined Nereus's as his balls emptied and he slowly swallowed a mouthful of Nereus's blood. Nereus muttered some words, but with the blood pounding in his ears, Teilo didn't catch them.

"Holy fucking God," he panted once his teeth were free, and he'd carefully licked Nereus's neck to seal the wound. It was already healing, the shades of the silver scar showing through. "Is it always like this?"

"Pretty much," Raff said as he came out from under Nereus, who collapsed with a groan face first on the mattress. Raff's face was flushed and his lips were puffy and wet. Teilo's cock pulsed in anticipation. "Did you feel any heat on your back when you came?"

"Yeah. Why? Does that mean something?" Teilo carefully pulled out and collapsed beside Nereus.

"You've been tattooed. I said the words and took you as a mate," Nereus mumbled. His hair was a sweat-streaked mess, and the merman seemed to be having trouble keeping his eyes open.

Teilo looked down and sure enough, he had a matching symbol to Nereus and Raff, the trident with a wave and a dolphin jumping through the prongs. "Cool," he said, his wolf quietly cocky they'd been marked by their mate. "How come I felt it on my back, though?"

"This tattoo comes from Nereus," Raff said, climbing over Nereus's back and placing a hand on his mating mark. "If you felt heat on your back, I'll bet you have one there as well from Poseidon."

"A tramp stamp?" Teilo craned his neck, trying to see behind him.

"Not necessarily," Raff said, as he leaned over Teilo's torso, clearly trying to get a look at his back. "I got a wave on my ass." He waggled said body part in front of Teilo, causing his cock to stand to attention. The waves crashing towards the tight crack were giving Teilo all sorts of ideas. Like claiming his little wolf as soon as he'd gotten something to dampen his dry throat.

"Oh my god, turn on your stomach, quick," Raff said, his voice all excited. Teilo didn't have a lot of modesty and his butt was one of his attractive parts so he turned on his front, wondering what had his mate so het up.

"You're amazing," Nereus rumbled, his mouth stretched in a smile. "You switch at all?"

"For you guys, I will, but I'm guessing you haven't let Raff top you yet, and for his wolf's sake it would be a good idea," Teilo said seriously.

"Really?" Nereus quirked an eyebrow, and Teilo could see why his brother thought the merman was drool worthy.

"It's a wolf thing and I'm betting he's never done it before." Teilo leaned over and rubbed his nose with Nereus before tilting his head over his shoulder. "What are you doing back there?"

"Oh my god, you should see this. I wish I had a phone or a camera or something," Raff squealed excitedly. "Scott would just love to see what I'm looking at right now."

"Should I be worried?" Teilo asked Nereus.

Nereus shrugged. "It's my dad. Worst case, you've got the same tramp stamp I did."

"He did, he did;" Raff clapped his hands. "You've both got 'Property of Raff' stamped on your lower backs."

Teilo groaned and made a silent vow to wear waist high pants from now on. Marius would have a field day if he saw that. "I'm pleased for you little wolf, but from the smell of things you still haven't come and I'm in the mood to claim you, too especially seeing as I have your name on my ass. How about you go and get us some water and we can get round two underway?"

Raff squeaked and Teilo felt the bed bounce as he jumped off.

"Down the hallway, right to the end you'll find the fridge in the kitchen," Nereus called out.

"You could've zapped a couple here," Teilo whispered.

"I needed to talk to you first. I want you to be careful when you claim Raff," Nereus hissed, no sign of being sleepy now. "He was a complete virgin when we met and while I'm built to take your sort of pounding, in fact, I'll scream for more, he isn't."

Teilo snapped his mouth shut against his automatic response; that he would never hurt his mate. Instead, he considered his mate carefully. "You're probably not going to realize you just insulted me because you're not a shifter," he said slowly. "And believe me, I like this version of you, being a real person instead of an untouchable god, a lot better than the guy I met yesterday."

"I think we've proven how touchable I can be," Nereus said with a wink. But Teilo could scent the worry Nereus was feeling.

"Stick to being honest and we'll all be fine. But as far as Raff goes, he may look slim, he may seem fragile, but my wolf tells me his animal spirit is extremely strong. I think you're underestimating him, big time."

"I just worry. I damn near drowned him because of my own stupid temper when we met. It would devastate me to see him hurt."

Teilo shook his head. Nereus had all the right instincts; he just needed more confidence in trusting them. "Hopefully we'll be able to argue like normal people without the water being drained from the pipes, waves appearing in the sink and the foundations being shaken by earthquakes. None of us are perfect, babe and arguments are a fact of life. But it doesn't mean we'll ever leave you. Wolves never leave their mates. But as for arguing, you should hear me and my brothers."

"You should see me and mine," Nereus said ruefully. Then Teilo felt a strong hand cupping his cheek. "I'm sorry I insulted you and your wolf."

"Bound to happen a few times until we all get to know each other," Teilo could tell for all his being a demigod, Nereus had a lot to learn about human interaction. "Now, given I have offered to switch, you feel up to fucking me while I claim our other mate?"

"Oh Hades, yes." Nereus leaned forward and Teilo closed his eyes. Kissing Nereus was like riding the waves and Teilo clung on, every sense in his body coming alive.

"Hey, I thought it was my turn?" Raff's voice came from the door and Nereus leaned back.

"It is, sweetheart, I am just getting him warmed up for you. Come and join us," Nereus said as he patted the space between him and Teilo. Teilo cast a quick glance at Nereus's cock which was already hitting his navel and suppressed a gulp. He was a wolf shifter and if Raff could handle him, so could he. But anyone who saw that and didn't have a twinge of doubt was a fool. Hopefully claiming Raff's sexy body would help take the edge off his first-time nerves.

/~/~/~/~/

It hadn't taken Raff long to find the kitchen. He grabbed the water, and turning to find Poseidon sitting on the kitchen counter almost caused him to drop them again. "Did you like my gift, little wolf," Poseidon grinned.

"I did," Raff nodded. "But I am guessing you are talking about the tattoos, but you set this whole thing up didn't you? You wanted

Nereus to lose it; you wanted him to admit he was scared of us leaving him?"

Poseidon shrugged. "You have to admit it worked, and all of you are getting down to the proper claiming side of things now, so it all worked out well."

"I should be mad at you for upsetting my mate," Raff said firmly.

"Or you could say thank you and agree to do me a little favor," Poseidon said with a leer, as he took in Raff's lack of clothes. Raff forced himself to keep his hands firmly around the water bottles.

"I'm not giving you a blowjob."

Heaving a sigh, Poseidon rearranged the muscles of his face so the leer was completely gone. "Sorry, force of habit. You're naked and looking positively edible, but I promise to behave. No, I want you to encourage Nereus to see Abraxas."

"I'm not going to force him to do something that will upset him," Raff said, torn between wanting Nereus to make up with his other father because he believed all families should be together, and wanting to stop Nereus from being hurt by the mere thought of the man who left him as a child.

"Abraxas didn't have any choice but to leave Nereus with me. Nereus would've died in the House of the Sun if he'd stayed much longer. It broke Abraxas apart when he had to give him and Lasse up. He's allowed to visit once every five years for one twenty-four-hour period; you don't want to know what favors I had to pull in to allow that dispensation. He's due again next month. Please say you'll try."

"I'll try but I'm not promising anything." Raff would try because if he had a chance to see his family again, he'd grab it with both hands.

"That's all I ask, my sweet little wolf. Now I suggest you run along. Your mates seem to be getting hot and steamy again and it would be a shame for you to miss it. I might go and find some fun of my own. Adios." Poseidon disappeared.

Raff shook his head; his wolf still thought the whole 'there one minute, gone the next' was weird, although his animal side wasn't scared of Poseidon after their shared luncheon, and Raff trusted his wolf. But for now, he needed to focus on his mates. He ran down the long hallway again and stopped just inside the bedroom door. Sure enough, Teilo and Nereus were tangled in each other's arms, their kissing hard and heavy. Raff jumped on the bed when invited to do so, trying to calm his breathing. He was sure his cock was going to burst if anyone so much as touched him, and when Teilo rolled across his body, pinning him down, Raff bit the inside of his mouth to distract himself.

"Nereus tells me he's been real gentle with you so far;" Teilo's voice had a thread of growl in it when he was horny. "Did you want me to do the same, or do you want something more energetic?" Teilo's grin was sinful and Raff's wolf went belly up, panting with excitement.

"I don't care," he said quickly. "Whatever you want, but please, I've wanted to come since I kissed you."

"And I think that's where we should start again." Oh, Raff wanted the promised heat in Teilo's eyes to come true and the sooner the better, but Teilo's kiss was slow and decidedly thorough. Raff forced his naughty thoughts of being slammed into the mattress far into the back reaches of his mind and tried to focus on the moment.

Teilo's mouth was different from Nereus's. For a start, there was no scruff scraping his cheeks and chin. Teilo's lips were a soft relief from the hardness of his face and the tight grip Teilo had in his hair. Raff hoped he'd be forgiven for making comparisons, but Teilo was only the second man to touch him so intimately, and damn he needed more.

Just as with Nereus, the moment Teilo tasted him, Raff felt a surge of confidence that came from knowing he was wanted. His senses, always highly attuned to others, picked up the slight tremor under Teilo's strength as he held himself back. Raff wasn't having that. It was bad enough Nereus treated him like someone breakable. He pulled back and growled as low and mean as he was able; the wolf in Teilo's eyes flashed.

"You're playing with fire, little wolf."

"I'm reminding you I'm no pup," Raff snapped back, and he nipped the side of Teilo's neck; not enough to draw blood, but it definitely got the bigger wolf's attention. Raff's wrists were caught in just one of Teilo's chunky hands and he felt his excitement soar.

"You do like that," Teilo purred. "Oh, we're going to have fun, you and me. But for now, this is more important." Raff felt lubed fingers fumbling at his hole and he spread his legs wide and closed his eyes. The mixed scents of his two mates had him primed and leaking. It wasn't going to take much to push him over the edge.

The fingers were rough, harder than Nereus's but just as accurate. Keeping his eyes firmly shut, Raff wallowed in the sensations, his mind filled with sensuous thoughts, not all his own. He could sense Nereus through their mind link, but it was different somehow. *Teilo and Nereus share a mind link too. Oh wow.* Raff wasn't sure if he'd be able to take it with both mates in his head.

And it was going to happen. Teilo's fingers left his body and Raff suppressed a whimper. He knew what was coming and hopefully it was him. No nudge, nudge, push in, pull out with the wolf in control. Teilo surged over his body, his cock sliding home like it was made to and the weight on Raff's wrists increased.

"Tell me when," Teilo growled. Raff's eyes flew open, and he saw Nereus slathered against Teilo's back. *What did I miss?* But Teilo was looking at him so intently, and Raff wasn't going to make him wait.

"Move."

That's all it took. Nereus thrust; Teilo thrust and as Raff watched, it was like being fucked by two people at the same time. Nereus's hair was mussed but the grim determination on his face had Raff biting his lips to stop from grinning. Teilo was in no better state. His eyes were closed, his head thrown back, but the hands holding Raff's hip and wrist were warm and solid and his cock couldn't be ignored as it plundered Raff's insides. Raff could only imagine what Teilo was feeling—taking and being taken at the same time. He added that to his sexual experiences bucket list as he fought to stop from hitting his climax. Teilo's cock found his prostate and was teasing it mercilessly.

The sensations overwhelmed him and his eyes dropped closed as Raff pushed his head back on the bed, riding the power of Teilo's wolf and the surge of the sea. He could feel it coursing through his body; damn, he could almost taste it and when he heard Nereus grunt, "Now," his cock went off without a touch. Strong abs mashed his release into his stomach as strong sharp teeth sliced the skin of his neck. His wolf howling in his head, Raff could only manage a groan as his cock pulsed through another wicked orgasm, leaving him boneless and breathless. He just hoped his mates remembered he was the little guy in their relationship and didn't fall asleep on him. He was ready for a nap.

Chapter Eight

"He's not a wolf; he's a demigod and bigger than me physically. In your eyes that should make a difference." Teilo slammed a pile of tee shirts into his duffle bag and reached for his jeans. Nereus had transported them back to Cloverleah after three long days "getting acquainted", and after a week of running back and forth getting clean clothes, Teilo was in the Enforcer House, packing his bag for the last time. Raff made a very sexy case for them all to live together, and as Teilo knew his wolf would pine if he wasn't with his mates anyway, he readily agreed. Although the blowjob Raff and Nereus collaborated to give him as an effective argument didn't hurt. He'd only been putting off the actual packing because he knew Marius would be upset.

And Marius wasn't making the packing process easy. "We were

raised taking it up the ass makes us weak. I never dreamed you'd do something like that," he hissed and Teilo automatically looked towards the door which was shut.

"We were raised to be killers. Sex never came into the things our father taught us. Look, you don't have a mate yet; you can't presume to know what it's like, so just back off a minute and let me explain," he said, determined not to lose his temper at his younger brother.

Out of all of them impacted by their father, Marius suffered the most being the youngest, and despite the decades their father had been dead, some teachings still came through in the things he said. Piling his jeans into the bag, Teilo flipped over the cover and hooked it shut before turning to face his brother, who was lounging against the headboard.

"There are three of us in my relationship, yeah? Two wolves and a merman. Why should Raff or Nereus always bottom for me when we're equals in our mating?"

"You're not equals," Marius glared. "Raff's a tiny man, and I bet his wolf can't fight his way out of a paper bag. Nereus isn't even a wolf. How could you let either one of them dominate your wolf like that?"

"If my wolf had a problem with what I do in bed, he'd let me know about it, and please don't insult my mates." Teilo sat on the bed and threw his arm over Marius's shoulder. "I don't even know why you're talking to me about this. Since when do you care what I'm doing in bed with someone else?"

"You still smell of spunk. Nereus's is my guess and as your hair is wet, it wasn't hard to work out where that spunk is hiding."

"Just as well I brushed my teeth, then isn't it, or you'd smell Raff too."

Marius's mouth dropped open. "You didn't... you... both at the same time? But... how could you?"

"Marius, we're mates," Teilo sighed. "When you find yours, you'll understand. Nothing is taboo between mates. Believe me; I like everything the three of us do together. Absolutely everything."

"I've never been on the receiving end before," Marius said in a whisper. "Dad... you know... just the thought of it makes my balls run and hide."

"You are keeping those ideas to yourself, I hope," Teilo said with a grin. "Because I bet there're a lot of big men here who happily bottom behind closed doors. I know Griff does and I've caught Shawn going at it with Kane once too."

"He's the Alpha." The look on Marius's face was priceless.

"A mated alpha, and if Adair hasn't been topped by Vassago, I'll braid my hair with pink ribbons and wear them for a week," Teilo said. "Honestly, bro, you have no idea who your mate will be. If he ain't wolf, then structure and hierarchy don't count. Hell, they don't count even if your mate is a wolf. You heard Matthew let Dean claim him and I bet that wasn't the only time. He's a bigger alpha than Kane."

"Did you, with Raff?" Marius asked and Teilo knew he was looking at the scar he wore on the side of his neck.

"Not that time, no. But," he added when he saw Marius was ready with another question, "I intend to and so does Nereus. Raff hasn't done that before and never expected to, so we're giving him time to process the fact we're willing. He was a virgin when

Nereus met him, so we're not rushing things."

"I still don't get it," Marius sighed. "If being mated means, we have to do stuff we've been taught we shouldn't do, then I don't think I want to find mine."

"You'll feel a lot different when you catch a whiff of that special scent. Believe me, I didn't have time to think of Dad when things were getting hot and heavy, and given that he's dead, he's not bothering me now. Tell me what's really wrong? You did not follow me in here to rag on me about my sex life."

"You're moving out." Marius's voice went quiet.

"I'm mated. Mates live together and Raff and Nereus have their own house so it makes sense to move in there. It's only five miles away, even less through the forest, and I'll be here regularly to patrol with you, just like always."

"But Adair's mated and I barely see him on his own anymore even though he lives here, and now you're going too. He said he'd always have time for me, but he's always got Vassago around. And you have two freaking mates."

"It's been just the three of us for a long time," Teilo agreed. "But having mates simply means our family got bigger, that's all. You didn't seem too worried when Adair mated."

"I had you." Marius wouldn't meet his eyes, and Teilo knew his brother's insecurities were showing.

"And we have a pack now. Surely that's got to count for something?"

"Yeah, you're right," Marius bounded off the bed. "Don't worry about me. You have two very fine men probably waiting naked at home."

"I was thinking we could do some sparring, go for a run or something before I head home. Raff was talking about taking his pups out to explore the area and Nereus said he needed time in the pool; something about Mermen and sea water, so I'm free for a bit."

"We could run to the pool and do a spot of training there?" Marius's eyes gleamed and Teilo growled.

"We'll head over to the west quadrant and you can work off your urges there," he said firmly, climbing off the bed and heading out of the door. "Seriously, it's time you got laid. You're not drooling over my mate."

"Spoilsport," but Marius laughed and some of Teilo's inner tension eased. He'd actually planned to stalk Raff. He hadn't seen his mate's wolf half yet, and he was keen to see how pretty a red wolf could be. If he could convince him to shift with others around; Raff always seemed to have an excuse. But Teilo didn't want to leave Marius upset either and the fact the man was now smiling was a step in the right direction. Making a mental note to chat to Adair as well, Teilo shifted and together the two wolves slipped through the trees.

/~/~/~/~/

Nereus strode into the water, ignoring the goosebumps on his skin. He was glad of the cold; it meant none of the other pack members were around. They seemed to love the novelty of having a pool so close to their living space, and he imagined in the summer it would be a busy place. The Cloverleah pack was a lot different than Damien's, more like a giant family group than a pack. It was definitely the sort of place where everyone thought they had the right to stick their nose into anyone else's business.

But for now, he didn't want the pack's help. Hell, he even begged off from his mates, which was a shitty thing to do. But after the communication he had from dear old Dad this morning; he needed some alone time. Time to process. Stretching his arms forward he leaped into an effortless dive, his form changing as he was completely submerged in water. He dove; his pool was deliberately deep for this very reason. He didn't want to hear or see the world above.

When he finally reached the bottom, he turned and curled his tail behind him as he lay on the sand. Being in the sea for him was like having an all-over massage. Nereus missed being in the water; not that he'd ever share that with his mates. For some reason, the

Fates saw fit to bring him two mates who were land-based shifters, and after wanting someone to call his own for so long, Nereus wasn't going to complain.

Is that why Abraxas went out and mated with a human? Nereus snorted, the air bubbles rising in front of his face. He didn't know anything about the man who gave birth to him. Only snatches of memory from a time so far back in history it was uncountable in years. He thought Abraxas was in love with Poseidon and had assumed his sea-dwelling father engaged in casual fucks because as godly beings from two different realms, he and Abraxas couldn't be together. But from the missive he got that morning, it would seem Poseidon never had any romantic feelings for his sire at all.

The note had been sitting by his head when he woke up. After an initial flash of annoyance at Poseidon for barging in where he wasn't wanted, Nereus scanned the note's contents hurriedly. If Dad had taken the time to write, then the message must be important.

My dearest son; that phrase on its own made the hairs on the back of Nereus's neck stand up. His father was never one for showing affection.

It seems the mating bug is contagious. Your father, sorry, Abraxas, let me know this morning that he has found and claimed his true mate. A sweet little human known as Jordan, who is now residing in the House of the Sun with him. Apparently, they are both so sweet on each other it's gag-worthy material. But, nevertheless, he asked me to let you and Lasse know and that he will still be visiting on the 14th of the month as expected. Jordan is accompanying him, and is keen to meet his new stepsons although he turned down my offer of a threesome. Tiresome boy. It sounds like they are so well suited for each other.

I am sure this will be the perfect opportunity for you to show off your own mates. This will be important to them, as wolves are all about family and bonding. Abraxas is happy for the first time since, well... you don't like to hear about that, but I am happy for him. I do think this is the perfect time to make amends–you have held onto your grudge for long enough.

So come and make nice for a change. Do. Not. Let. Me. Down. I will see you then if not before.

P.

Snippets from Poseidon's letter rolled around Nereus's head all morning. He hadn't told his mates; he didn't know what to say. He knew if he mentioned Abraxas and this Jordan person, Raff would be all for him going. His gorgeous amber eyes would be soft and sweet and fill with tears if Nereus said no. What's worse, if he refused, Poseidon would hound him as well. Nereus blew out a long sigh, idly watching the bubbles as they rose to the surface.

He remembered the pain from Abraxas leaving like it was yesterday. Even at five, he knew who Poseidon was, of course. It wasn't as though the man was a stranger. But it wasn't until Abraxas led him to a room he hadn't seen before and told him it was his that Nereus started to worry.

That worry got worse when he saw Abraxas unpack his sea dragon stuffed toy; it was the one toy he couldn't sleep without. He'd watched in silence as all his clothes, toys and belongings were stashed away, and when Abraxas came and brushed a kiss over his forehead and told him to be a good boy, Nereus bit his lip. He wouldn't cry. But when Abraxas closed the door behind him and Nereus was alone, he cried buckets. To this day, he never understood why Abraxas had left him and Lasse with Poseidon.

Your father tried to explain a million times. Mers couldn't live in the House of the Sun... Lasse was getting sick and he was only two years older than you... you would have gotten sick, too. Nereus knew all that; his logical brain told him Abraxas didn't have a choice, especially when he got older and learned about being a man of the sea. But in his heart, Nereus was still five years old watching his father walk out the door, and every time he heard that name since, he'd wanted to run away and hide.

Is it finally time to see him again? Nereus wanted to. He'd missed the man who gave birth to him. *Teilo and Raff would make things all right.* Nereus knew they would. They were a mated ménage and his mates would stick by him no matter what.

Meditation. That's what I need to do. Meditate on this, clear my mind, sharpen my energies and then face what has to be done. Closing his eyes, turning off his mind link, Nereus laid his head on his arms and emptied his mind. All he knew were the soothing sensations of the water around him and silence. Brilliant, calming silence.

Chapter Nine

Resting his nose on his paws, Raff stretched out as he lay on the brittle grass. The air was chilly, and the grass crackled under his body, but in his fur, he barely felt it. He'd never had the opportunity to run with his dogs in wolf form; that sort of thing would be frowned upon in the city, but here in Cloverleah Raff felt free to be who he was. With his puppies sprawled out beside him, he took a welcome moment to think how much his life had changed.

Where to start? Everything in my life has changed. Raff huffed, startling Joey who looked at him as though expecting another game. He shook his head and Joey settled down with a sigh of his own. He hadn't run in his wolf form for weeks so he was tired and glad no one was around. He'd always had a solid bond with his wolf, but his animal was shy around others. *And it doesn't help the others are so freaking big.*

Lying in the forest and listening to the water babbling nearby reminded Raff of Ollie. He hadn't been to see the little cub since they'd gotten back from Italy, although Nereus had taken the pups over a few times for a play date. Luke absolutely adored Killer and the mini pack. It was handy that the bears and Tobias had a home of their own too, though. Killer seemed to delight in antagonizing the alphas in the pack with everything from peeing in boots he found lying around, to cuddling up to the mates and growling possessively. The mates, like Shawn, Troy, Dean and the Fae thought it was funny. The alphas, not so much.

I should go and see them. I need to talk to Kane about a job. Jax told him the house was theirs outright, and no rent was needed.

Nereus summoned food with a wave of his hand and didn't seem to care about money. Teilo earned a wage as an enforcer and paid for him to have lunch in town the last time they went, without a second thought, but Raff wanted money of his own. Christmas was only two months away and even though he hadn't got a clue what to get either of his mates, at the moment he could only dream of affording anything.

A snapping twig in the trees made him look up. Killer growled and Raff tensed. Killer snarled at the alphas all the time, but this was a far more sinister sound and the little dog's hackles were raised. Raff raised his nose and sniffed, hard. Earth. Trees. Birds. The faint scent of other wolves. Nothing out of the ordinary. Nothing unexpected but Raff's own hackles started to rise. He knew he was being watched.

Another snap. Closer this time and Raff got to his feet. He wasn't big enough to take on any threat and the sensible thing to do would be to run. But his pups were short-legged and Killer would blindly attack anyone he thought a threat. Raff couldn't stand the thought of his dogs in danger. He growled, as low and mean as a small Red Wolf could get.

There was laughter, mocking laughter coming from the trees. There should be a scent; some indication of who was there, but there was nothing. Raff didn't know what to do. If he howled and called the pack and it turned out to be a pack mate having a joke, then he'd look like an idiot. But Killer was angry and had riled up the other pups too. Even Joey's hackles were raised.

He lifted his snout, ready to howl when he heard a voice. "I knew I'd find you alone, eventually, and those pills worked just as well as he said they would. You didn't smell me coming. But look at you protecting those mutts like a good little mommy. If you come willingly I won't be forced to kill the noisy little mutts."

No! It couldn't be. Raff knew that voice and his whole body trembled. As a dark shape ran out of the trees, heading straight for him, he howled. He was still howling when he was knocked to the ground; his dogs were all barking and snapping around him.

/~/~/~/~/

Teilo grunted as Marius hit him and then swirled and delivered his own kick; pulling it short so as not to do too much damage. Although he longed to get back to his little wolf, the run had been fun, and the workout was doing him good. Marius was laughing and joking and all thoughts of his packed bag by the enforcers' front door were forgotten.

Marius stepped back, shaking his head, his braids flying. "Come on then big guy, show me what you've...." He stopped and tilted his head. Teilo did the same. They could both hear a howl.

"It's coming from behind Griff's place," Teilo yelled, falling to the ground on all fours. He didn't know the howl; it wasn't one of the pack, which could only mean it was Raff. His sweet innocent Raff who would not use their mind link, claiming it was an invasion of privacy.

I'm coming, babe, he thought frantically as he shifted. He could run much faster on four legs. His wolf was pissed off; he knew it was Raff in trouble and if Teilo hadn't been laughing and goofing off with his brother, he'd have known it too.

Another black wolf ran effortlessly by his side. No matter his misgivings, Marius would never leave him to face trouble alone. The howls had stopped, but that just made Teilo run faster. Raff must be in his wolf form but he wouldn't howl unless he was in trouble. *Why hadn't I taught him to fight with the bo? Too busy munching his sexy ass and now... fuck it.* Teilo's anger spurred his feet and as he caught a trace of blood in the air, he snarled. They were getting close and now the sounds of the puppies' high-pitched barking drowned out anything else.

Bursting into a clearing he saw a black shape. Not a wolf, human, maybe, but whatever it was it was tugging the prettiest wolf Teilo'd ever seen away from the dogs; or he was trying to. All four pups worked in tandem pairs. Nipping, biting, growling and then retreating quickly when a boot got too close. Killer and Joey were jumping as if they knew their bites were useless through boots. The attacker was annoyed; swinging at them with one arm, then another; trying to kick them out of the way. But the bastard never let go of Raff's leg and Raff... he wasn't moving.

Without thinking of the consequences, Teilo leaped, knocking the man to the ground. His wolf was incensed. Raff was hurt. It wasn't much but there was blood in the air and their smaller wolf wasn't capable of defending himself. He bit down on the nearest arm and then spat it out as the most disgusting taste flooded his mouth. He went for the throat, but the man was strong, knocking him back. Sinking slightly on his haunches, Teilo snarled. This man was going down.

"Teilo, Teilo." Teilo turned. Marius had shifted, dragging Raff back to the grassy area, but the wolf was unconscious. He turned back, and the attacker was gone. Fuck!

Shifting in one fluid movement, Teilo was by his mate's side in seconds.

"He's so small," Marius whispered. "Pretty. Really pretty, but he's so tiny compared to us."

"I don't know if this guy's injected him with something, hit him or what," Teilo said, carefully running his hands through the fur. The blood was from a long gash on Raff's back leg. Otherwise, there was no visible sign of injury. The pups quieted down, although Killer ran into the trees a few times, and then looked back at Raff. His distress was obvious and Teilo clicked his fingers hoping the poodle would come to him.

"We need the Fae, Dean, Shawn, someone." Marius's face was twisted with concern.

"They should be here; it's not that far from the pack house." Teilo tilted his head; hearing the faint sounds of wolves pounding their way across the forest floor. "They're coming. The whole lot of them by the sounds of it, but they're coming."

"Bit fucking late," Marius muttered under his breath, but Teilo knew the feeling. Raff moved to Cloverleah to be safe. Until today, Teilo would swear Cloverleah was the safest place on earth. It was part of his job to make sure of things like that. But the man he'd bitten wasn't a mirage. The bastard was flesh and blood. Foul tasting blood, but it was real. Teilo could still feel traces of it in his mouth.

Adair was on the scene first, pulling him into a one-armed hug. "What the fuck, brother? Is this Raff?"

"Can't you smell him? Of course, it's Raff."

"Er… actually, bro," Marius said from the other side of him, "I can't smell him either."

Teilo bent his head and sniffed. Shit. If it wasn't for the fur under his fingers, he wouldn't have known Raff was there. "The puppies wouldn't have protected anyone else," he said sharply, nodding at Killer and the others who were now cuddled around Luke's bear form.

"I know it's Raff; his spirit is still the same," Shawn appeared in front of him. "He's been drugged. I'd say it's the same sort of stuff used on Madison and Scott."

"So the killer tracked him here?" Hair flying, naked as the day he was born, Kane looked ready to kill someone. "How the hell did he get through the wards? Why didn't those fancy electronics warn us, this asshole was in the area? Jax, Anton, track him."

"They won't be able to," Marius said quickly. "T and me both saw the guy, but he's got no scent either. I already checked."

"I bit him," Teilo snarled. "Raff was already unconscious and hurt. Marius called me back to help him, which is what mates do." He leveled his best glare at Kane, who nodded although he didn't look happy. "But before that happened my wolf took a chunk out of his arm. There was something wrong with his blood. It tasted of ash and decay." He looked at Shawn. "Did he inject my mate with something? Is Raff dying?"

"I doubt it, but I don't dare transport him; he'll have to be walked back," Shawn said. He looked up at Kane. "Hon, can you call Damien? We need to know more about this guy in case we are dealing with the same man, and I want to see if Elijah can come and take blood samples. He and Miles might be able to work out what is going on in that lab of his."

"Let's do it," Kane huffed. "Enforcers spread out. If this guy is bleeding, we might be able to find traces of it. Everyone else, back to the pack house. I want to know how the hell someone like that was walking around our land and no one knew anything about it."

Teilo stood up and scooped Raff's limp form into his arms. Surrounded by wolves, bears and even Diablo in his panther form, he started making the slow walk back to the pack house. Only Marius and Adair stayed in their human form and from the hunch of his shoulders, Teilo knew Adair was taking the breach of security as a personal insult. He could have made some soothing comment; security was the responsibility of all the enforcers as well as key members of the inner circle. This wasn't Adair's fault. But with Raff so unresponsive in his arms, he just couldn't bring himself to do it.

Nereus, you bastard, where the hell are you?

Chapter Ten

"Hi honeys; I'm home," Nereus called out as he appeared in their living room, his arms outstretched to get the hugs he was sure his wolves had been missing. Silence greeted him and he slowly lowered his arms and frowned. It'd just turned dark; Nereus had been gone longer than he thought. Raff and Teilo should both be home; Raff said he was going to cook dinner tonight. *So, where the hell are they?*

It didn't take him long to check out the house, but it was clear no one had been there since he left that morning. His shirt was still slung over the dining room chair, and Teilo's half empty coffee mug was still on the table from breakfast. The pups' food bowls were standing empty and waiting under the kitchen counter. Nereus checked the coat rack by the door. Teilo's leather jacket was gone;

Raff's threadbare jacket was still there.

I must get my little honey a warmer jacket, Nereus thought, wondering why he couldn't feel his mates in his head. Raff never used the mind link, but Nereus could always sense him there in the back of his brain. Teilo was like a force of nature sometimes; his thoughts hitting Nereus with the finesse of a gale force wind. But he couldn't sense either of them. Nereus's alarm grew, and he paced the floor.

Where... you fucking idiot! Nereus remembered he'd turned off their mind link so he wouldn't be distracted while meditating. He closed his eyes and blew out a long breath as he removed the blocks from his mind. He still couldn't sense Raff, but Teilo was there loud and mean.

I swear Nereus you bastard when I find you I'm going to kick your ass to kingdom come. Making me go through this alone; Never around.... Nereus didn't bother listening anymore. His mate was angry with him and there was no sign of Raff in their link. Calling on the bond he had with Teilo's life force, Nereus closed his eyes and materialized in the pack house. It was a full house, but all Nereus could focus on was his mates.

"What the fuck happened?" He yelled as soon as he saw a limp wolf with his head on Teilo's lap. "My mates were supposed to be safe here; what's happened to Raff?"

"Where the hell were you?" Adair shouldered his way through the others to stand front and center. Not that Nereus had a problem staring him down. He was mad enough to take down anybody. "While you were busy communing with the sea or whatever the fuck you want to call it, Raff was attacked; someone tried to take him."

"Why did he leave the territory on his own?" Nereus was just as capable of snarling as the wolf in front of him. He tried to see past Adair's shoulder, wanting to look at Teilo, but the big asshole was as effective as a brick wall. "Were one of you mean to him? Did anyone upset him?"

"He didn't leave the territory." Dean appeared beside him and Nereus felt a hand on his arm. He felt a tingle that notched down his anger a bit, but not enough. "He was attacked on our land."

"And you're head enforcer." Yep. As soon as Dean was pulled back Nereus's fury returned, and he shoved Adair back. "It's your job to see this doesn't happen. Your job to see everyone here is safe. Where were you? Fucking your djinn, I suppose."

Adair ducked his head, ready to charge and Nereus was ready for him. Yes, he was feeling guilty, but none of these men needed to know that. The burning accusations in Teilo's eyes and Raff's fragile form were enough to scar him for life. But this... fighting Adair. *Bring it on.* He tensed slightly as Adair charged, but just as suddenly the big man froze, the grimace still etched on his face. Shawn winked from his place by Kane's side.

"Enough," Kane yelled from the corner of the room. "Fighting among ourselves isn't helping anyone. Nereus, get your ass over to your mates. You don't have to explain your whereabouts to us, but I'm sure Teilo will have a bone to pick with you later. In a pack, mates stay together. If there're problems in your mating, fucking fix them, because we've got enough on our plate as it is, right now."

Nereus scowled at Adair as he went past the frozen figure. The urge to kick him was strong. He also wanted to stick his tongue out at Kane and tell him in no uncertain terms there was nothing wrong with their mating. But the guilt he was feeling was riding him harder. Kane was right in that respect. He should have been with his mates. He slipped onto the couch beside Teilo and draped his arm over Teilo's shoulder.

Sorry.

We'll discuss this later. Teilo's part of the mind link snapped shut.

Yep. He was in the dog house. Nereus stroked his hand over Raff's soft fur. At least the little wolf was warm and breathing.

"Luke managed to track the blood spots to about fifty meters from where the attack took place," Kane said in a calmer voice. The whole pack was crowded into the main living room, even the paid enforcers. "The asshole must have realized he was bleeding, and either shifted or bound the wound tight. He doesn't have any scent and now he's gotten past the wards there's no way of tracking where he is. Diablo, what have you found from the surveillance system?"

"Not a lot," the cat shifter looked worried. "We've, that is, none of us have been paying much attention to the cameras and alarms because we all thought the magic wards would be enough to keep anyone out. The only thing Griff and I could find was a glimpse of a gray wolf on the edge of our territory from four days ago."

"The wolf would have had to be a natural wolf, not a shifter," Fafnir said. "The wards pick up any shifter activity."

"Or the shifter part of his ability was suppressed by drugs," Shawn said, looking at his phone. "Elijah text back. Raff's definitely been drugged but they won't know anything else until tomorrow, if then." Teilo swallowed hard and Nereus's arm tightened around his mate's shoulder. "Miles is running tests using Raff's blood against his mate's blood samples to see if it might impact shifting." He looked up from his phone. "This isn't an exact science. We still don't know if there's anything in our blood to denote shifter ability. That's something Miles and Elijah have been working on for months. But without knowing what he's been drugged with, we've got no antidote."

"Can you enhance the picture of the wolf you saw, Diablo?" Jax growled. "Teilo, you said the attacker was wearing clothing; if the guy's managed to suppress his shifter ability to get through the wards, then he had to have something to change into when the drug wore off. Unless he's a magic user."

"He's not," Vassago said. He was standing by an unfrozen Adair who was glaring at Nereus. Nereus ignored him, still trying to work out what happened to Raff. "Anyone with a tinge of magic would set off the wards."

"Unless they're djinn or demon," Vadim broke in quietly.

Vassago nodded. "Agreed, but I'd sense it the moment a djinn got within ten miles of this place and a demon has no reason to be messing with Raff."

"We don't know that the guy in the woods was after Raff specifically," Matthew said, cradling Dean on his lap. "Maybe he was targeting a small shifter and Raff just happened to be on his own."

"He wasn't on his own," Luke said quickly and Nereus noticed he had Killer cradled in his arms. Tobias was holding a sleeping Ollie and Kurt was scowling at the other pups at his feet. "Killer fought bravely to protect his wolf, and so did the other pups. They really care about Raff and they're upset he won't wake up." Kurt barely restrained rolling his eyes and Nereus wondered why the big guy had so much attitude. He never seemed to mind the pups when they were playing with Ollie.

"Why don't you guys take the pups and Ollie up to bed; I don't think there's much more we can do tonight," Shawn said to Luke kindly. "I'm sure Teilo and Nereus would appreciate you taking such good care of them when they have been so brave. Until Raff wakes up, he has to be their number one concern; but Raff will be so pleased if he knows his pups are being cared for so well. You must be tired too, with all that excellent tracking you did today."

Luke preened and his smile was so bright. It seemed the loving bear took a lot of pride in being given what he considered an important job. Tobias had a smile as well as he left the room with Ollie asleep on his shoulder although Kurt still looked like he wanted to complain. Nereus's lips twitched when he thought about how much bed those puppies could take up. He'd insisted they sleep in the spare room since he'd been mated to Raff.

Raff. Fuck. How could he have been thinking about anything else with his mate lying lifeless on the couch? Nereus's heart ached as he focused on his smaller mate. Raff's wolf form was slender, nothing like Teilo's bulk. Where Teilo's fur was long and black, Raff's was shorter and a mixture of reds, ginger, and whites on the sides and undersides, with blacks and browns darkening his back. There was a long line down his back leg that looked like a scar. "He was badly scratched," Teilo muttered. "Shawn could heal that, but he can't do anything to wake him up. Neither can the Fae or Vassago."

"Can't he be made to shift? Wouldn't that clear the drug from his system?" Nereus thought he'd remembered hearing how an Alpha could compel another wolf to shift forms.

"Nope, not while he's unconscious," Teilo shook his head. "We just have to wait until the drugs wear off and hopefully he'll shift by himself."

"Do you want to take him home?" Nereus asked. Everyone else had separated into small groups, probably going over security measures. There was a heavy air of tension in the room and any positive Zen Nereus got from his swim was completely gone. "I can zap us if you like."

But Teilo shook his head again. "Shawn said it's too risky. He can sense Raff's been given more than a sedative. The Fae and Vassago don't think there's magic involved, but it's too risky to try. We don't need him to get any worse. But I wouldn't mind getting out of here, though," he added. "Do you know how to drive?"

It can't be much harder than riding a motorbike. Nereus nodded. Their home was only five miles away. If he took it slow, he could keep the car on the road at least. Hopefully.

Chapter Eleven

"I thought you said you could drive," Teilo hissed as he dragged Nereus into the kitchen. Raff was still unconscious; Teilo put him on their bed and left him reluctantly. Kane had ordered protection for them and he knew Marius and Adair were patrolling the grounds outside the house. He didn't need either of his brothers deciding to stick their noses in where they weren't wanted, but there were things he and his merman mate needed to sort out.

"I didn't do too badly for my first time with a manual," Nereus said quietly. "I can ride a motorbike and an automatic. It's not that different."

"Except for the little matter of the middle peddle being the brake not the clutch, you did fine." Teilo stalked over and refilled the coffee pot. He was determined not to sleep until Raff regained consciousness.

"Look, I'm sorry. I was just trying to help." Teilo steeled himself against the hurt in Nereus's voice. He had every right to be angry. Fuck it. They had to have this conversation and if his brothers heard, well to hell with them too. He spun around and glared. "Where the hell were you?"

"I told you, I went to the pool. I'm like shifters. I need to be in my Mer form sometimes."

"Vadim went there; he couldn't see you and he went around the fucking thing twice." And damn it if the hurt didn't flood his system like it had when Vadim told him. The thought his mate couldn't be trusted to be where he was supposed to be… Teilo rubbed his chest.

"I was under water," Nereus said. He was sitting at the kitchen table, his head in his hands. Teilo knew he should be comforting his mate; they should be comforting each other, but he was still angry. "I had things I needed to think about. I can meditate underwater. It helps."

"There is so much wrong with that statement I don't know where to start," Teilo snapped. "One," he held up one finger, "if you have stuff that's worrying you, you are supposed to talk to us about it. Two," yep, he'd count them off as he raised a second finger, "you turned off our mind link so when our sweet baby was attacked you had no fucking idea and three," stuff the fingers; Teilo threw up both hands. "Trust. Trust mate. Where's the trust you're supposed to have for us; how can I trust you when I can't even get you half the time?"

Teilo was exaggerating about that last bit. He and Nereus used their mind link quite often, especially when teasing their little wolf. Their little wolf who was currently lying in their bed totally oblivious to life. Teilo's heart broke. He quickly made two mugs of coffee and went over to the table, placing one in front of his mate before slumping in the chair opposite. "Talk to me," he said in a softer tone that had Nereus raising his head.

"It seems so stupid now after what's happened to Raff. I... er... I got a note from my father this morning telling me Abraxas has found his true mate."

"I thought him and your dad were mates but didn't want to acknowledge it because they lived in different realms or something." Why else would that Abraxas fellow give birth to two kids to the same guy?

Nereus shook his head. "Poseidon doesn't believe in mates; he'll fuck anything that moves. Abraxas, well, I guess I'd always thought he'd remained faithful to my dad."

Teilo bit back the "Abraxas is your dad too," comment and said instead, "I still don't know why this is upsetting you. You refuse to see Abraxas; why is news of his mating enough to send you pouting under the deep for fucking hours?"

"Because Abraxas visits the deep every five years for twenty-four hours; his next visit is due in less than a month and Poseidon," Nereus heaved a huge sigh, "Poseidon thinks I should take you down there to meet him and his new mate. Jordan's a human. He's probably never met a true shifter before. My brothers will probably be there too. I know Lasse will be."

"Aren't you allowed to go and see Abraxas at his place? Can you only see him during his once every five-year visit?"

Nereus frowned as if it was something he'd never considered before. "I suppose I could. I am not only a Mer; I can shift into a horse like Abraxas as well. But look," he added, putting his elbows on the table. "I'd decided if you two thought it was a good idea, then I would go. It's just, my brothers can be a bit much sometimes, but once they've met you, they will probably leave us alone."

"You didn't want to face Raff's sad puppy dog eyes if you told him you weren't going to meet with Abraxas at last." Teilo could understand the sentiment. Raff's eyes were so expressive.

"That too." At least they agreed on something. "But look, with what you said about trust. I didn't think of it that way, no." Teilo growled. "Wait. Hear me out."

Damn it, Teilo thought. *I'm a pushover for my mates*, but he put his listening face on.

"Honestly, it was sheer carelessness on my part today," Nereus sounded so formal. "I moved here expecting Raff to always be safe with the pack and as for talking about Abraxas, I just wanted time to think about it. That's all. I planned on telling you both." Nereus cast a longing look in the direction of the bedroom. "I know you're angry with me and you have every right. I turned off my mind link because I needed to meditate. It calms me and helps me get my thoughts in order."

"You just sit under the water and think about stuff?" If that's the worst thing Nereus ever did, it wasn't that bad. "You were gone for hours."

Nereus sighed. "I told you, I simply didn't think. The water, I go so deep I can't even see the passing of the sun in the sky. I know Abraxas can see me when I'm outside in the sun and usually I just forget about it and go about my business. But today I needed to be under the water where even he couldn't see me. It never crossed my mind anything would go wrong. You have to believe me."

Teilo did. He could scent deception and he had a feeling he was going to have to just chalk this whole incident up as one of those things. The idea about Abraxas being able to see him–yeah, Teilo would talk about that another day. Perhaps after he'd met the man. But for now, he needed to get Nereus to understand a few facts about wolf mates.

"I do believe you," he said softly, reaching over the table and taking hold of Nereus's hands. "I also know you're not a shifter, and this triad arrangement is something we're all getting used to. But today, when I knew Raff was in trouble, I needed you with me. I've only relied on my brothers before now, and most of the time I don't need anyone to help me get through shit. But today I *needed* you. Raff howled for help. I was sparring with Marius. We got there as quickly as we could, but fuck...." Teilo would never forget seeing that man's stinking hand gripped around Raff's leg, dragging his mate's body as though he was a hunting prize.

Nereus patted his hand and suddenly the table between them was nothing but a nuisance. He let Nereus pull him across the polished surface and draped his body over the merman's form. "I can't smell him," he whispered into Nereus's neck. "The drugs, whatever's been done to him. I can't smell him. It's killing my wolf."

"Then we need to hold him," Nereus said firmly. "Your wolves love that too, right? His spirit will know we're there. I'll zap us up some food, and we'll stay with him and with any luck, he'll be awake in the morning and can tell us if this guy said anything before he tried to drag him away. I'm worried sick it's that guy from San Antonio."

"Why are you worried it's him?" Teilo heard snippets about the man who abducted Scott and Madison, but he hadn't paid much attention.

"Because the man's got some deluded idea that because Raff is a red wolf shifter, he can get pregnant. He wants to build his own pack, and he plans on using Raff to do it. He's already tortured and killed one of the subs from Damien's pack and he told Madison he'd do the same to him before he was rescued. He's sick," Nereus shivered. "He's fucking sick in the head and if it is him, then Raff won't be safe until that asshole's dead."

Teilo was all for killing someone if it kept either of his mates safe. His wretched father's training might come in useful for something for a change. But for now, he needed Raff to wake up and if Nereus was offering comfort, he'd take all he could get.

Chapter Twelve

"No, no… NO!" Raff clawed himself out of the darkness, his lungs bursting, his heart pounding out of his chest. His mates, his pups. Some bastard was trying to take him from his mates and was threatening his dogs. He remembered howling, fighting and then the prick of a needle. He sat up wildly looking around, unsure if what he was seeing was real or just a dream.

"It's okay, babe, it's okay. You're safe. The pups are safe. You're home." Oh, my god, Teilo was there, and Nereus, their warm bodies blanketing him. Raff felt his eyes watering and his hands gripped the closest flesh and he hung on tight.

"I thought… I thought… it was *him*." Raff stared into Nereus's eyes willing him to understand and he could see from the furrowed brow and the look of anger that flashed across Nereus's face, his mate got the message.

"We need to get you fed and cleaned up. The pack's been waiting, searching, praying for you to wake up. Anything you can tell us might help," Teilo said from behind him, his breath warm on Raff's neck.

"How long have I been out of it?" Raff arched instinctively into Teilo's touch and then moaned as he felt the fuzz from Nereus's beard run along his shoulder.

"Five days, baby. Five very, very long days." Teilo said behind him burying his nose in Raff's hair.

"Five…. But…." Raff gave a discreet sniff. He smelled of soap. He didn't feel overly hungry although he could eat. He felt as if he'd just had a long sleep.

Gentle hands cupped his cheeks and Raff could see tiredness etched on Nereus's face. "Shawn put you in some sort of stasis for the first three days, so your body didn't suffer. For the last two mornings, Aelfric and Fafnir have been popping in giving you some zap of their super juice to keep you hydrated. They've only just left which is why you're probably feeling so good."

"Did they give any to you?" Raff stroked the lines on Nereus's face which weren't there the last time they were together.

"Nereus and I have been taking turns, watching over you and sleeping. We're fine," Teilo said and Raff twisted his head so he could see his other mate properly. Teilo's hair was a mess and the lines around his eyes were as bad as Nereus's.

"Liars, the both of you," he said with a rueful grin. It was heartwarming to know his mates cared about him so much even if they didn't say so in words. "Let's get this meeting with the Alpha done and then I think you two need a solid meal and a decent sleep."

"I just want to keep holding you so my wolf can bathe in your scent," Teilo said with a chuckle.

"You can do that at the meeting, so long as I get my turn too," Nereus agreed. "Come on, sweetheart; let's get you dressed before I forget how tired I am."

Raff blushed. His mind had been going in the same direction but he didn't have it in him to keep the Alpha waiting. "Did they get the guy? Is he dead?"

Teilo and Nereus shared a look and Raff wondered who'd rescued him and what state he'd been in when he was found. All he could remember was that hot hand grasping his leg like a vice. It was Nereus who shook his head. "Not yet," he said, "but every single person in this pack is working on finding him."

"I don't think I'm going to be a lot of help," Raff said quietly, dropping his head.

"Then the meeting won't take long at all," Teilo said firmly. "Now come on, get some clothes on. I don't want anyone else knowing what a sexy ass my sweet mate has."

Raff grinned because it was expected of him, but inside his stomach churned. The man who tried to take him was still out there somewhere... waiting. He prayed his mates wouldn't pick up on how scared he was. They both looked like they could do with a shift and a sleep and they wouldn't get that if they thought he needed protecting again.

/~/~/~/~/

Nereus had a strong urge to kill someone. It wasn't his normal

425

state of mind; in fact, if asked, he'd say he only took someone's life if it was necessary. But watching Raff's pale, haggard face, the tightness in his shoulders and the way he strived for invisibility in a room full of people who all wanted something from him he couldn't give, it was making Nereus rethink his moral stance.

"Raff's already told you all he knows," Nereus punctuated his words with a thump on the table. "The guy is the same one from San Antonio. Raff recognized the voice. That bastard still wants to doo the physically impossible and breed from my mate and you want specifics like hair and eye color? What difference does that make? How many other bastards are roaming around Cloverleah territory trying to kidnap people?"

Jax growled and Nereus felt Teilo bristle beside him. Raff's face flushed bright red and his eyes were far too bright. Taking a deep breath, Nereus said more calmly, "I know this is hard on all of you, but badgering my mate who's only just regained consciousness isn't going to help."

"Raff and Teilo are the only two people here who've seen this guy, Nereus," Kane snapped back. "We don't know what we're dealing with here."

"You saw him?" Raff's voice was almost a whisper and his face ashen as he stared at Teilo. "You stopped him from taking me?"

"Your pups did that," Teilo said gruffly. "I bit him but... I wasn't fast enough to kill him. You have no idea how sorry I am."

Kane cut off anything else Raff or Teilo might have said, but Nereus noticed Raff creeping closer, his hand firm on Teilo's knee. Nereus added an arm around Teilo's broad shoulder and could feel the added weight as Teilo leaned into the touch. Nereus probably knew more than Raff how devastated Teilo was that the asshole was still running free. They'd talked about it often enough, Teilo browbeating himself every time the topic came up.

"You mentioned the man who tried to take you said something about someone else giving him drugs which he clearly used on himself and on you. We're assuming that's what got him through our wards."

"Something like that," Raff shook his head sadly. "Look, I don't want to bring trouble to this pack and I'll leave if that's what you want. I just need to know how come this man knew where I'd gone in the first place."

"Damien's investigating that. Apparently, your stalker is a wolf shifter by the name of Larson Birch." Shawn's voice was a lot softer than Kane's. "At least, that's what he thinks based on a process of elimination. Damien barely remembers him but once Scott heard the name, he confirmed it was the same guy who kidnapped him and Madison. Larson was a Dom at the club these past four months but no one has seen him since the young sub was killed."

"Someone from the pack could have told him about you moving packs and as the enforcers have orders to kill him on sight if he turns up there again, it makes sense he'd get out of town. Cody confirmed Larson was the last one seen with Joel," Kane added.

More than a few pack members bowed their heads at the thought of a young wolf killed before his twenty-fifth birthday. Nereus was all for taking Raff as far away from the wretched place as possible. But he couldn't take Teilo from his brothers. Teilo spoke often of the closeness he shared with Adair and Marius. Their bond was formed amid violence and mayhem and it would kill his strong wolf to be parted from them.

Griff broke the silence, his gruff voice abrasive as always. "You're not leaving Raff. Let's not hear anymore about that. Yes, you were the one attacked and you do seem to be this maniac's main target, but while someone is wandering around in our territory, none of us are safe. We need to find him so we can find out where he got those damned drugs."

"And then kill him," Nereus's voice blended perfectly with Teilo's.

"And then kill him," Kane agreed. "And Griff is right, Raff. You belong here. Larson isn't just a threat to you; he's threatening all of us." He looked lovingly at Shawn and then slowly ran his eyes around the men in the room. "We've never run from a threat before and we aren't starting now. We need to find this guy and find him fast." Everyone straightened in their seats.

"Tonight, everyone will participate in a pack run. The whole pack, no exceptions," Kane said when Matthew looked like he was going to argue. "Every one of us, on four legs or two, I don't care; we're going to run over every inch of our territory as a pack and we are going to find this guy and run him down. Am I clear?"

"Alpha, what about Ollie?" Kurt asked. "He's too young to run all that way at night."

"Shit. You're right." Kane ran a hand over his face. "My apologies. It's going to take some time to get used to thinking about children." He sighed. "I need Luke with us; Luke's our best tracker. I'm sure you and Tobias can care for Ollie and the pups on your own if you don't mind. They may get hurt when we find this guy."

"I'll help Kurt and Tobias," Raff said. "That is... I presumed you would need Teilo and Nereus running with the pack, and I can help look after Ollie."

"I need you on the run tonight," Kane's bright blue eyes hardened. "If anything is going to get Larson to come out of hiding, it's going to be the sight of you. You'll be in the middle of the pack, but you are coming and I'll make it an order if I have to."

"Like fucking hell," Nereus flew from his chair, his fists hard on the table. "Five days; five fucking days we've waited for Raff to wake up and now the very same night you want him running over a thousand acres of territory? As bait?"

"That's exactly what I said," Kane was standing now too. He was shorter than Nereus by a good three inches and Nereus knew he could take him. A rumble sounded under the house and he could feel the waters of his pool start to surge, waiting on his command.

"You are pack, Nereus," Kane enunciated slowly. "Pack obeys their Alpha. I am the fucking Alpha and I have given you a direct order. Now stand down or fuck off and stop rumbling the foundations of my house. Ollie's sleeping in the spare room."

"Oh so now you decide to remember the wee cub," Nereus snarled right back. He wanted to bury the house so deep underwater and their thoughtless alpha with it. "You are not using my mate as BAIT." On the last word, his voice rose and he could feel the power from the moisture in the air to the waters of the creek and his pool; all of it his to command.

Nereus STOP. Just stop damn it. There are innocent people here. Teilo's voice came through his mind like a slap in the face, but it was Raff's voice in his head that had Nereus pulling his power back. Raff hadn't used their mind link since they'd mated with Teilo.

This is pack, my love. Raff's sweet, hesitant voice blasted away his righteous anger. *Pack. It's more than keeping me safe. Bigger than any single person here. This man threatens our security, our way of life. Think of Ollie, Dean, the Fae and Vassago. They are all in danger here not to mention my fellow wolves. Kane trusts my mates to keep me safe, don't you get that? He trusts you to do what a wolf shifter would do.*

Nereus closed his eyes, the urge to slump in his chair strong enough to weaken his knees. He focused on the bonds he could feel from his mates; Teilo's strength, his focus; his willingness to stand by Nereus even if it meant going against his brothers. And Raff. Dear, sweet Raff who'd already gone through so much in his short life. The man strong enough to use the word love without hesitation.

Letting out a long breath, he opened his eyes; Kane and the rest of the pack were watching him closely.

"It seems I have been overruled," he said quietly. "But if we are going to do this effectively, then all three of us need to rest. The last five days have been *difficult*."

Kane nodded, hopefully understanding how hard it was for Nereus to back down. "Go. Rest. Do whatever. We will meet back here at eight o'clock. That goes for all of you. It's going to be a long night."

Chapter Thirteen

Teilo knew he needed to sleep but his wolf was already in protective mode. Raff was in his arms, his lithe body twitching now and then. Nereus's rumbling snores rang around the bedroom and his arm was heavy on Teilo's hip. None of that was keeping Teilo from his sleep; his mind churned over all that had happened, and what was to come. He knew from experience any type of drug user was unpredictable and this guy couldn't be scented. The whole situation was a shitfest waiting to happen.

When Nereus stared down Kane, Teilo was in hearty agreement with his mate's anger. His wolf spent five days mourning Raff as though he was dead, the smaller wolf's spirit so muted and his smell nonexistent. Half the time Teilo had been trying to prop up his wolf; the other half he wondered if his wolf was right. To know Raff was going into possible danger again, neither he nor his wolf could handle that.

But Teilo heard Raff through their mind link at that pivotal moment and although pack was a new concept for him, an ancestral memory of pack stirred and he understood. Having a pack, an Alpha, it was all instinct for his wolf and his wolf respected the alpha's command, even if he didn't like it. Only Adair's imploring gaze and the slight shake of his head kept his mouth closed and his claws sheathed.

Now his sweetness was in danger. Teilo never had sweetness in his life. He didn't even know he missed it until he held Raff in his arms. But now… He looked down at Raff's face and saw those amber eyes were open.

"You're worrying when you should be sleeping." Raff's smile was warm and sleepy, but his eyes were bright. Teilo was seized with an urge; he had to know if the endearment Raff used for Nereus applied to him. He didn't know why it was important, but somehow it was vital. He racked his brains, trying to think of how to ask when Raff beat him to it.

"I love both of you; I'm sorry if you thought otherwise," Raff said, keeping his voice low. "I feel as though my life has become a whirlwind in so many ways, but you two form the rock I cling to. I can cope with anything with you in my life."

"I love you too, sweetness," Teilo pulled Raff closer, his body heating as skin met skin. "You and our mermate are equally important to me, but you…." Teilo stopped unsure if he could actually say the words causing a lump in his throat. Raff's eyes twinkled and Teilo dug deep. "You bring something special no one's ever given me before. A sense of sweetness, light. I want to be a better person because of you."

Raff's lips twitched and then his face bloomed into a full-sized grin. "My mercenary can be sweet," Teilo leaned into the hand stroking his face. "That sort of thing makes my cock hard."

Teilo grinned; then the last part of Raff's endearment hit his brain and sent a direct jolt to his dick. "Oh babe, I was trying to be romantic." He went to pull Raff closer, but Raff was already there, his length leaving a trail on Teilo's leg as he surged upwards, his mouth searching for friction.

"It worked," Raff said against his lips, and then his sweetness moaned and Teilo lost it. Five days without; five days of celibacy. Not something Teilo or Nereus discussed. It was simply understood. When Raff was lost to the world, only staying by his side mattered. But celibacy combined with approaching danger. Teilo ached.

A deeper moan and Nereus's tousled head appeared over Raff's shoulder. "Looks good, can I get in on that?"

Teilo wasn't ready to give up on Raff's lips, but it seemed Nereus didn't expect him to. The demigod had no problems leaning over Raff's slimmer body and mashing his face into theirs. It took a bit of searching through facial hair, but soon enough Nereus's lips were there. Raff moaned and did a little thrust and bump and Teilo didn't need to be a genius to know why.

/~/~/~/~/

This is h-e-a-v-e-n. Raff couldn't stop the moans from falling out of his throat. Teilo's crisp autumn air with mulled wine smell combined with Nereus's sea air scent. Home. So much like the North Carolina sea coast. But for once, Raff noticed homesickness didn't hit him. He was horny, and yes that was one reason, but it was more than that. His mates were home. The feel of Teilo's skin against him comforted and aroused him. Nereus pressed against his side touching them both. So right. So... mates. Home. His wolf agreed. *Home*.

Both men were hard yet so different. Nereus's skin was the sea. Warm, smooth, comforting and enveloping, threatening a storm Raff would happily lose himself in. Teilo's was soft and hard at the same time. Satiny. But Raff would never tell him that. Not his warrior who prided himself on strength and his ability to protect. Both completed him and that was enough.

Teilo rolled to his other side; *when did I end up on my back?* But then fingers trailed over his body. Raff wasn't sure whose were where but it didn't matter. His wolf and his body were in hearty agreement; four hands were better than two. Petting, stroking, exploring. Raff tangled his hand in Nereus's hair drawing him back for a kiss. The other pulled Teilo in and their tongues battled and explored until he wasn't sure where one started and the other ended. None of that mattered.

Gifts. His men were magic. Wonderful, beautiful gifts worth waiting a lifetime for. *How did I get so lucky?* Nereus kissed down his throat and Teilo joined him. Both found a nipple to tease, lick and gently nibble. Raff arched his body, demanded more, and they delivered. Hands stroked down his stomach. *Oh yes, closer.* Then a hand was on his cock and fingers were tracing his hole. Both men had a fascination with that part of his anatomy and again Raff was too inflamed to care. When a finger penetrated him, he arched again, pushing back into the finger with a growl.

Nereus chuckled against his neck. Teilo raised his head, his lips swollen, his eyes heated. "Feels good?"

"Gods, yes. Oh my yes. Don't stop." Raff couldn't have told anyone who was doing what, but damn it, he loved every minute. Another finger pushed its way inside him as someone teased the tip of his penis, brushing the glans with feather soft strokes. He wanted to howl. He wanted to burst. Holy fucking Zeus. His moans were a constant stream falling from his mouth.

But wait, through the lust haze Raff was almost sure he heard a chuckle that wasn't his mates. *If Poseidon's playing voyeur, I'm going to kick his ass. Hard.* But Raff wasn't going to bring it to his mates' attentions. For one thing, he couldn't talk and secondly he felt too damn good, and it'd been so long. *Oh, fuck yes. There...* He thrust back on the fingers in time to the strokes on his dick. His hands sought his mates and found them, hot, hard and ready. Their precome coated his hands, making his movements slick. The smell of sex and lust mixed with the scents of his mates. It was intoxicating. Right. "Love you," he muttered, caressing the heat in his hands.

Nereus licked his ear and then whispered, "I love you. My soul. My sweet soul."

Teilo's eyes clouded with tears and Raff felt the urge to comfort him. Words stuck in his throat, so he opened his mind to them both.

Mates. My mates. My soul and my strength.

Nereus's voice joined Teilo's, answering him in kind. *My Psyche. My Thymoeides*. Raff watched as

Nereus stroked Teilo's cheek. *My Logistikon*. Then those same fingers were warm on Raff's face. Somehow Raff knew his wonderful demigod was referring to them as parts of his soul; Teilo, the strength, the force; he was the love, the goodness, the thought. How... his mind blanked as the feelings overtook him when a hand cupped his balls and the one from his dick slipped down to join the one working on him. "Gods..."

Nereus laughed a deep throaty sound full of light and passion. "Yes?"

Raff grinned. His mates leaned across him and kissed; a soul devouring kiss. He didn't move; he barely breathed. So perfect. He just wanted to watch. So very perfect. Lost in the moment he gave a yip as the hand on his balls, slithered up a bit and grasped his dick, working it in earnest.

Shit. He hadn't been doing anything to his mates…. Raff's hands moved, exploring the soft velvety balls he held in each hand, reaching for the one spot he knew would… damn it. He couldn't reach. He slid down impaling himself deeper on the fingers. How many did they have in him? Oh, who the fuck cared? It felt amazing. Now he could reach. Raff stroked that special spot under the balls and was rewarded when his mates broke their kiss to gasp. Hands vanished from him.

Teilo slid down, lifting Raff's hips, turning them to one side; his dick brushing the tender hole readied by those thick fingers.

Nereus straddled his chest.

Oh yes.

As Teilo pressed in, Raff closed his lips, making Nereus push in echoing Teilo's movement. Both of them. His mates. Nereus suddenly jerked and pushed forward into his mouth. Teilo. It had to be Teilo. Oh, fuck this respecting privacy shit. He was tired of blocking his mates and face it, they couldn't be more intimate than they were in that moment. Raff let down the walls in his mind and Nereus and Teilo flooded in. Warm and comforting and arousing. Their passion fueled his; it was an ever-increasing circle. Oh yes. Teilo's hands were busy. Raff knew Teilo was a butt man and their mate's was exquisite. A glow of gratitude from Nereus and a flush of agreement from Teilo brushed his mind. Raff closed his eyes and focused on the feelings; they were completely joined, body, mind, and soul. His, theirs. There was no separation.

A strange voice echoed in Raff's head, *"And the three shall become one. The little one shall be safe."*

His eyes flew open, and he stared at Nereus who shook his head. Then Teilo hit his prostate just right, forcing him to focus. Raff raised his head and deep-throated his mate as far as he could with his head bent. Nereus fell forward bracing himself on his arms. Raff tilted his head back and opened his throat so Nereus could thrust into him. The voice forgotten, all three focused on the physical, their feelings building as their bodies pushed to their inevitable conclusion.

Lust, love, heat, and scents all combined into one huge bubble... until suddenly it burst. Raff came, his inner muscles clenching around Teilo, while he scraped the underside of Nereus's dick with his teeth, just enough to send Nereus over the edge. He was flooded; Nereus's come filling his throat, while Teilo pumped into his ass. With a groan, Nereus collapsed to the side, Teilo to the other, the two of them ignoring the mess and simply holding Raff tight. Contentment. He felt the utmost contentment, and it was a hard feeling for him to get used to.

Conscious that their intimacy was over, at least for now, Raff's concern about invading his mates' privacy returned. He knew it was silly to feel that way about something so precious. But none of his pack had a mind link; none of them were true mates and Raff was always scared he might think something he shouldn't, or worse, hear something he didn't want to know. He tried to put his walls back up. He couldn't. It was if his and his mates' minds were joined as firmly as their bodies had been just moments before. There were no doors, no walls he could erect. His mind was an open book and so were his mates'. "Teilo?"

"What?" Teilo answered, sleep rasping his voice.

"Can you close our link?"

"Nope, never really liked to anyway. My wolf likes to feel you. Why? Can't you?"

"No. Nereus?"

"What? Wait, a second. No. I can't. I'm sorry little wolf." Nereus's voice took on a strident quality. "Dad! Damn it! What did you do?"

"You called, oh son of mine?" Poseidon's silky voice sounded clear as a bell.

Oh shit, Father-in-law. Raff hissed at Teilo through their link. *I don't care if he's staring at your butt. Cover me.*

He's what? Teilo jerked and Raff's body was completely covered.

Do. Not. Move. Raff trembled. Maybe Poseidon heard what he thought earlier. He was too young to die.

You both have lovely butts and really, little wolf, I wouldn't kill you. Wait, why can I hear that? Nereus?

The sensation of Poseidon being there vanished.

"Well, I can shut Dad out," Nereus's voice sounded smug even smothered by a pillow.

"Your father has a mind link with you?" Raff wasn't feeling so contented now.

"Well, it's a Mer thing. We don't talk when we're swimming. All Mer can link with others of their kind."

Raff almost shrieked, "Were all of them listening in when we talked?"

"No, little wolf. My son does know how to block the rest of us. But for some reason, he was broadcasting and so were you. I don't understand it." The shimmery shape that was Poseidon vanished.

"Wait!" Raff was too late. Damn it. Now he'd never know how much

Poseidon saw or heard. Was that earlier chuckle him?

"Can I roll off you now? My butt feels exposed." Teilo said with a quiet thrust of his hips. Raff stroked Teilo's shoulder as the bigger man slid back onto the mattress.

"Nereus...?" Raff asked timidly.

"I know. It's not going away. I'm sorry. I..." Nereus started to apologize.

Oh, his demigod should not feel bad about himself. "Now stop that. I can feel you're sorry. It's not only thoughts. It's... it is actually nice." Raff decided he was going to accept their continual mind link as the gift it was meant to be. He wasn't going to let Nereus beat himself up about it. "We won't ever be alone anymore. I was just curious how it happened?"

"No fucking clue sweetheart. No fucking clue," Nereus said heavily.

"But that weird voice said you'd be safe now, and that's got to count for something."

"I agree," Teilo said. "Keeping you safe... hell, we'll all be safer because of this. And I can tempt you both with sexy thoughts on the pack run."

Raff started to laugh and Nereus joined in, the echoes of it running through their permanent bond. It really was a nice feeling.

Chapter Fourteen

Nereus wasn't sure if going for a pack run was something he would do on a regular basis. As they gathered at the pack house, prior to taking off, Teilo pulled him aside and told him his horse form would be welcome. Wolves were predators, but shifter wolves were cognizant. Nereus was forced to whisper that his horse form tended to glow, a side effect of being Abraxas's offspring. Somehow, when Kane called for stealth, Nereus didn't think the light coming off his hair would be appreciated and it wasn't as though it was something he could turn off.

So he ran in his human form; Vadim was the only other one on two legs. The Fae and Vassago magicked an animal form; Nereus was shocked to see Vassago's wolf appear. Shifting into animals was an extremely rare gift in the djinn realm and he resolved to pull the djinn aside later and find out what else had changed for his magical friend. Vassago was more powerful than he remembered.

The run itself was a quiet and focused affair. The wolves spread out, covering every inch of the ground with their noses. Diablo took to the trees; his massive panther form almost invisible in the darkness as he bounded from branch to branch. The soft glow warning the sun was coming up was just coloring the sky as Kane led them back to the pack house.

"Well, that was a fucking waste of time," Kane snarled as soon as his human form appeared. "Did we miss that guy slipping out of our territory again?"

"We couldn't have," Adair shook his head. "There's been someone watching those cameras every fucking minute of the day since Raff was attacked."

Nereus wasn't sure where to look. There was naked flesh everywhere, and no one seemed bothered about it.

"Maybe we should get some breakfast," Shawn said, clothing him and Kane with a flick of his fingers. "We're all... Luke! Hold up. You have to shift before you go into the house."

The big grizzly Nereus knew as Luke, keened and shook his head. Kane and Shawn frowned. "Luke, you have to shift. What's wrong?"

Luke banged his head with his huge front feet and pointed to the house. When no one said anything, he banged his head again and then spread out his paws. "You can't hear Kurt or Tobias in your head?" Shawn guessed.

Luke stood on his hind feet and roared. "I guess that's a yes," Kane growled. "Fuck, Reef brothers... you know what, fuck it, two of you are mated now too. Everyone search the house. Luke, oh fuck, you stay here. I can't have you in the house in your fur. You're too big."

And there's a good chance Luke will lose his mind if something's happened to his mates and cubs. Come on, stay with me. Teilo's words were firm in Nereus's head and with a sinking feeling in his stomach he followed his mate into the pack house.

None of them had to go far.

"Don't come any closer." A tall dark-haired man was standing in the middle of the living room floor. Kurt and Tobias were hogtied; their ropes looped around their necks stopping them from shifting, two darts on the floor by their heads. But that wasn't the worst of it. The man had Ollie trussed up, swinging from his arm like a handbag. Raff gasped and Nereus quickly pulled him under his arm, flicking his fingers so at least his mates had sweatpants on.

Kane stepped forward, his expression far more arrogant than Nereus had ever seen. "I'm Kane, the Alpha of Cloverleah," Kane said. "Let my cub go."

"Aww, is he yours? I don't think so," The dark-haired man said with a sneer. "After all, you're wolf and this little darling clearly isn't. I'm amazed he can shift so young, but then you do have an unusual pack, don't you."

Shawn flicked his fingers. Nothing happened. Out of the corner of his eye, Nereus saw Fafnir and Aelfric do the same. Still nothing, although the dark-haired man laughed. "Magic doesn't work on me at the moment," he said, the sneer still etched on his face. "And if any of you come closer, this little one dies." He rested a hand on the back of Ollie's neck. Nereus saw Vassago appear behind the man, but suddenly the little djinn yelled and was thrown back against the wall; Adair hurried to his side.

The dark-haired man tilted his head. "Oh, good. The shock field works too. Now, I won't take up any more of your valuable time. I see you've all been out hunting. Find anything interesting?" The man laughed.

Can you do anything? Teilo asked through their link.

Not unless you want to endanger the pack, Nereus answered grimly.

Don't let anyone else get hurt, Raff implored. *It's him. It's the man from Damien's pack. Larson.*

"You clearly want something, tell us what it is and then get the hell out of my territory," Kane said firmly.

"I had thought to take over your territory, but no. There are no towns nearby. You have far too many others in your pack for my liking. I don't know how you can stand the stench of bear, magic, and fish." Nereus felt the man's eyes on him and curled the side of his lip. "I only want one thing, anyway; actually, I want two things. I definitely need the red wolf for breeding purposes, but you have an omega too. How precious. I'll take him as well."

"NO!" Almost all the men in the pack yelled, but the stranger lifted Ollie, both hands wrapped around his neck.

"I'll go with you," Raff wriggled out from under Nereus's arm and ran forward, Teilo growling behind him. "Promise me you won't hurt anyone and I'll go. Just leave this pack alone."

"Your pups might need some medical attention, but that can be taken care of after we're gone. You won't need them when you're taking care of our pups now, will you?"

"Whatever you want; just please put the cub down."

What the fuck is he doing? Teilo's snarls rang loud and clear.

Trusting us to save him, Nereus replied, hearing Raff's agreement through their bond.

"I'll go too," Dean stepped forward; Matthew's face like thunder behind him. "Just, what Raff said. Put Ollie down and step away from him and the others." He grabbed hold of Raff's hand and Nereus's heart ached at the braveness of their actions. The two smallest men in the pack were willing to put their life on the line for one tiny cub.

"You know we can't track you, once you go," Shawn said, his eyes full of tears.

"No, you can't," the stranger said with a horrible grin. "Oh dear, how sad, never mind. Say goodbye." It was over in the blink of an eye. One minute Raff and Dean were standing in the living room and the next, Ollie was thrown in the air and the stranger, Raff and Dean disappeared in a cloud of smoke.

"Catch Ollie," Kane yelled. But there was no need. Nereus zapped himself, catching Ollie one-handed as he landed with a tiny thump on the couch.

"Do you want to explain what you meant by that last statement, mate? Because I have to tell you, seeing one of my mates disappear before breakfast was not on my list of things to do today. We just got sweetness to share his mind with us and now it's gone!" Teilo was furious, his brothers bristling beside him and Matthew looking like he was ready to tear someone limb from limb.

"You know we can't trace them; we have no idea what magic Larson possesses or how the hell we're going to get our pack mates back," Great. Now Kane was in his face. Nereus ran his hands over Ollie's ropes, letting them fall to the ground.

"He's sleeping. I don't think he's been drugged," he said to Shawn as he handed the cub over. "You might want to let Luke see him; it might help him calm down enough to shift so he can see to his mates. If someone could find out what happened to Killer and the others, I'd appreciate that too."

"Thank you." Shawn didn't look happy either, but he carefully took the sleeping furball and went outside.

"Teilo, my love," Nereus ignored Kane and turned to his mate. "When we were in San Antonio, the killer, this Larson, who Raff assures me is the same guy in here today; he wanted Raff then in exchange for Scott's and Madison's lives. Raff wanted to go, and I was furious with him. We'd only been mated a matter of hours/days. I thought he believed the lives of Scott and Madison were more important than his and I was determined to get him to see things from my point of view."

"You had every right to be angry about it. I'd have tied him to the bed." At least Teilo was listening.

"Yes, well, we all feel like that about our mates. But my reasoning was wrong, and I had to apologize," Nereus turned and faced the others. "You see, Raff told me the only reason why he was willing to sacrifice himself for two men he'd barely known a week was because he trusted me to save him."

"I understand that and the whole pack will go in and save them if necessary," Kane said soberly, "but we have one small problem. We'll never be able to find them. Shawn is blocked when he tries to follow their scent. Fafnir, Aelfric, Vassago; none of them can trace the magical signature. It's as though it just disappears. Can you still trace Raff through your link?"

"Nope," Nereus lost Raff as soon as the men disappeared from the house.

"Then how are we meant to save them?" Matthew snarled.

"By doing something I never thought I'd do. Call on my family connections."

"Poseidon can help us find them? But I thought he was the God of the Sea," Teilo looked hopeful for a moment.

"He is, and if Raff and Dean were lost on a boat, or underground, I would call him in an instant. In fact, given how much Poseidon cares for Raff, I imagine our mates would be back already," Nereus said. "But no, not Poseidon this time. There's one man; one being who knows where all souls are at all times."

"Who is that? Can you get in touch with him? Will he help?" Kane asked.

"He should, although he'll probably want a favor. I'll probably have to go to dinner or something once all this is over; offer to spend Christmas with him or something," Nereus sighed. "It's my uncle, Thanatos; you probably know him as Death."

There was a collective gasp around the room. "The angel of death is your uncle?" Teilo asked.

"Meh, he's no angel," Nereus grinned. "But yep, if I agree to dinner, I'm sure he will."

"If Thanatos knows where all souls are, why didn't you ask him to find Larson before our mates were taken? We could have saved all this bother when Raff was attacked," Matthew's anger was understandable. It didn't bother Nereus. He'd been brought up with gods and they all had volatile tempers.

"Because Thanatos is not allowed to interfere in affairs on earth unless there is a danger of a soul being taken before its time," Nereus explained calmly. "Until our mates were in physical danger, I didn't have the right to call him. Teilo thwarted the last attack, so the intervention wasn't necessary. But this time, with us not being able to track them and wolves dying if they're separated from their mates, then yes, I can ask him."

"And he can bring them back?" Teilo asked and Nereus felt a large hand on his arm.

"Provided the Fates agree, yes," Nereus said firmly. He looked Matthew in the eye. "But you have to realize that if Dean or Raff were meant to die from this, in accordance with the threads of Fate, there is nothing Thanatos can do but deliver their souls to Hades. Gods are bound by rules, just as we are."

"I guess it would take more than a promise of dinner to get them back from Hades," Matthew said grimly.

"Yeah, for that I might have to go and spend a week swimming with the dolphins at Atlantis," Nereus sighed. He laughed when Teilo looked at him in astonishment. The other men in the pack looked equally surprised. "What? Hades has a weird sense of humor. It could be worse. He could make me clean out the snake pit or stoke the fires in Dante's inferno. You never know what he's going to ask if you need a favor."

"You're related to Hades, God of the Underworld?" Kane asked with a quirked brow. The normally tanned alpha looked a little pale.

"Another uncle," Nereus shrugged. "I come from a big family."

I'll do dinner with Hades and Thanatos if you can get our sweetness back. Nereus grinned at Teilo's suggestion. He wondered how his mates would like visiting the Underworld. Maybe Vassago could give them some pointers. The little djinn had been down there often enough. But first, he had to hope his Uncle Thanatos would answer his call.

Chapter Fifteen

"Are you okay?" Raff heard Dean's whisper through the gloom. He was tied, not drugged, and he figured that was a good thing. He needed to keep his wits about him before Nereus and the others came.

"Yes," he whispered back. "Did he hurt you?"

"No, I'm fine," Dean laughed. "I've been in worse situations than this before, believe me. At least this time I have a friend to keep me company."

"Is that why you stepped forward? Because we're friends?" Raff felt his eyes well up. "I thought you came because of Ollie."

"We both came because of Ollie, but I wasn't going to let you do this by yourself. You're too special and we are friends." Raff heard some shuffling around and he felt someone touching his hand. He twisted his wrist so he could hold on. "There you are. Now you listen, Raff. Our mates are going to save us. My Matthew," Dean sighed. "He came for me last time, when my ex-home pack stole me from the pack. He was magnificent. In fact, the whole pack came, Damien and some of the Denver pack, too. I've never been so proud."

"I'm not sure they will be able to do that this time," Raff held back his whimper with effort. "I trust my mates, believe in them absolutely. But if they can't find us, then it's going to be a little hard to save us. You probably should have stayed with Matthew."

"Nah," Raff felt a warm presence at his back and was comforted by it. "You're mated to a demigod. We might not get the whole pack invasion type rescue like I got last time, but someone will come."

"Hopefully not in a flood of water," Raff giggled and then was immediately embarrassed. "I mean, Nereus made a mess of Damien's club and I can't swim in human form."

"Nah, I'm sure it will be a lot more subtle this time. Shush," Dean's back stiffened against Raff's. "Sounds like the asshole's coming. Be strong and have faith."

Strong? Faith? Raff was tired of being strong. Two years he'd spent on the street and no asshole wanted him then. No, just him and his pups against the world until Scott saved him. Then Nereus and Teilo. Yeah, that's where he'd get his strength from. His mates, his friends. This guy wouldn't win.

"Well, well, well, don't you two look cozy," A harsh light came on overhead and Raff blinked rapidly. "Now I thought," Larson picked up a beer crate, turned it over and sat on it, his leather coat swirling on the floor. "I thought I'd go over a few rules; after all, I am your alpha now and I can't just let you two run amuck. I'll explain the rules and then we can work out where we go from here. First rule; you will both be naked and kneel in my presence unless told otherwise."

"Our hands and ankles are tied; we can't kneel," Dean said spiritedly. Larson glared.

"I'll untie you after I've explained the rules, and that's rule number two. No one speaks unless spoken to."

"But you were speaking to us," Raff said. "I thought we were having a conversation."

"I'm giving you orders, boy; shut up." Dean's fingers tickled Raff's hand, and he stroked Dean's thumb.

"Now, where was I? Rule three. Butt plugs. I expect you to wear them at all times. I can't be bothered with this prep shit. And cock cages. You will not orgasm unless on my say so. No rubbing each other off."

"We won't orgasm, anyway. We can't even get a hard on," Dean said. "We both have true mates and the claim marks to prove it. You touch us and we'll be sick."

"There's no such thing as true mates. Your heads are full of nonsense." Larson stood up and for a moment, Raff was sure they'd be hit, but he decided to pace the floor instead. "Now stop interrupting me. I keep losing my place."

Larson paced a bit more, muttering under his breath and ticking things off his fingers. "Five."

"Four," Raff piped up. "I thought the rule about butt plugs and cock cages was the same rule."

"Will you shut up! I'll fucking gag you in a minute."

"Good. I don't want your cock down my throat, thank you very much. I'm likely to spew all over you," Dean said.

"Grr," Larson stomped over, looming over them, his fist raised. Raff refused to flinch. Larson stood there for a long moment, but the hit never came and after huffing for about thirty seconds, Larson moved away. "Your pack members. You'll find I am not an abusive man, but you have to follow the rules."

"Not abusive?" Raff couldn't let that comment go. "You killed Joel; you were going to do the same thing to Madison. You're a killer and there's no other word for it. How is that not abusive?"

Larson took a long breath in, clenching his fists and then opening them again as he exhaled. "Joel and Madison were never meant to be part of my pack. They were toys. Sex toys. Toys break.

It's a fact of life. An alpha rules his pack fairly, only dishing out punishments when absolutely necessary." Larson looked at them both, probably expecting another comment, but when it didn't come, he continued.

"Now then. Rule five. Your jobs are to serve me. Once you are pregnant, red wolf, then the omega will see to your comfort and will take care of my needs until you are ready to breed again." He frowned. "Father didn't tell me how long a red wolf pregnancy was. Is it different than females?"

"I have no idea," Raff said honestly. "To my knowledge, I can't get pregnant. I don't have the right parts."

"Your family must have said something? You can't have been the only male in your generation."

"I have a brother and male cousins." Raff felt a pang of

homesickness then, but he missed his mates more. "None of them got pregnant, and our parents were all male-female couples."

"Hmm, how strange." Larson definitely looked confused, but then his face cleared. "Never mind. My father never lied to me and it was he who shared the secrets with me. Maybe your pack was protecting you."

Or maybe you're batshit crazy, Raff thought.

"Right, so obviously, you will both service my sexual needs until red wolf gets pregnant. I don't want either of you getting jealous about it. It's what happens in a pack. I have more than enough stamina to fill you both on a daily basis."

Dean coughed loudly. Larson frowned, but then said, "and there will be times when I will bring in toys. I don't want you two getting pouty about that either. I have needs beyond sex. It will take too long to train either of you in a sub role and I can't have you damaged. Although, did Damien train you at all, red wolf?"

"No."

"Such a lazy alpha," Larson shook his head. "Never mind. Okay, well that's it. That's all the rules. Now, which one of you shall I have first?" He cupped the lump in his leather pants. "Hmm, I have a fair bit of spunk saved up. I'll do you first Red Wolf and with any luck, you'll get pregnant right away. I want this pack growing as fast as possible. Don't worry, Omega. I'll still have enough for you."

There was staying strong and then there was the sheer terror Raff felt as Larson picked him up by the shoulders as if he weighed nothing. He tensed, promising himself he would fight as soon as his hands and legs were free. But all he heard was the sound of ripping cloth as the sweats Nereus magicked for him after the run were torn from his body. *The bastard's not even going to untie me first. Nereus!* Raff screamed in his mind. *Teilo! Somebody!* He was slung over the crate, his arms and legs still held by ropes. A hot hand smacked his ass, and he screamed out loud this time. "Don't touch me!"

"You will like this!"

"NO!" Raff felt something hot and thick trying to push its way past his butt cheeks. He clenched as hard as he could, trying to wriggle his way off the crate. "NO!" He screamed again as Larson persisted. Tears poured down Raff's face as the terror of what was about to happen hit him hard.

"UNHAND THAT BOY!" A deep powerful voice rang around the room. Raff whimpered as he felt Larson step away.

"Who the hell are you? This is pack territory. You have no rights here. Get out of here before I am forced to kill you." Larson hurriedly shoved his cock back in his pants.

Raff twisted his head. Standing in the corner of the room was a dark-clothed figure. As the man stepped out into the light, Raff gulped.

"You can't kill me for I am DEATH. I have come for you."

"Me, no." Larson backed away. "I'm not doing anything. I'm nowhere near close to death. You must have your dates wrong."

"I am never wrong," Death promised, "But you're right. It isn't your time just yet. You have one hour left."

"Then come back in an hour," Larson's panicked eyes swept the room. "An hour. Yes. I'll be ready then."

"I know you will be," Death laughed and Raff shivered. It was as though every horror movie had come to life. "But your last hour is going to be busy. We have to return these two wolves to their mates before I take you."

"They're my pack." Larson was almost whimpering. "You can't take them. They belong to me. They came willingly."

"Oh, yes I can take them and I will." Death glided across the floor, his black robes barely skimming the surface. "You took two men from their true mates, which is a death sentence for a wolf. They sacrificed themselves to save a cub. It's not their time. Raff and Dean still have a lot of living to do. With their mates!"

"No. I. Mates. There's no such thing. You've been misinformed." Larson was babbling now.

"Tell that to my nephew Nereus!" Death roared. Raff sighed with relief. It wasn't the rescue he thought would happen, but hey, he'd take an Uncle Death any day of the week if it meant he could be back with his mates.

"Er, excuse me, Uncle Death, sir? Do you think you could untie me and Dean? I feel a bit exposed here."

Death whirled around, a smile on what was now a handsome face. "Of course, little one, and you can call me Uncle Thanatos. I prefer that."

"Thanatos," Dean whispered as Death flicked his fingers and both men were free and clothed. "You saved Madison."

"I did indeed. Such a lovely boy mated to my son Sebastian you know. Oh, that silly boy of mine had some foolish ideas, but Madison got him groveling in the end." Now Death looked exactly like someone's favorite handsome uncle. Raff smiled, but then he noticed Larson trying to slip out of the room.

"He's getting away," he yelled.

"No, he's not." Death smiled and without even looking at Larson, the killer wolf was suddenly entangled in a black web. "No one gets away from Death." He winked and Raff laughed, suddenly feeling better than he had in hours. He ran over to Dean, hugging him tightly.

"You have a pretty amazing family," Dean whispered as Death swirled his robes and all four of them landed in the Cloverleah pack house living room.

Chapter Sixteen

"Raff, thank the Fates. Are you okay? Did he hurt you?" In that moment, Teilo didn't care about anyone or anything else. As soon as his mate appeared he grabbed him, hugging him tight. "Are you sure you're okay? You've been crying. What did he do to you?"

"It's over now," Raff said quietly, leaning against Teilo's chest. "The whole thing is over now. Look."

Death, at least Teilo assumed that's who the robed man was, had Larson tightly encased in a black net and was arguing with Nereus.

"I spoke to the Fates," Death said firmly. "You can't cut this man's thread."

"Why the hell not?" Nereus roared and Teilo pushed through the crowd of men and stood by his mate's side, Raff tucked firmly under his arm. "I've taken lives before; hell, there's not many in this room that haven't. What right does this man have to keep breathing when he killed that poor sub back in Texas and probably a dozen more besides?"

"The Fates have a different path for him. You can't go against the Fates."

"No disrespect, Death... er... Sir," Kane came forward. "But Matthew, Teilo, and Nereus all have the right to kill this man for taking Raff and Dean. It's pack law."

"Call me Thanatos."

"Raff's been crying, look! You can't expect me to do nothing," Nereus implored his Uncle.

"I'm okay," Raff said but Teilo caught a glimpse of what Death had saved him from and he snarled.

"I won't allow this man to breathe another minute. Not after what he tried to do to Raff."

"The operative word is tried," Thanatos said in a voice that was hard to disobey. "I got there in time; Raff and the delightful Dean are unharmed. And don't you dare go talking to me about poor Joel. It was his time, and that sucks for him. But he'll come back to a better life than the one he had. I've been promised that although it's up to the Fates, not me, not Hades, not anyone."

"Thanatos, surely you can see... are you just going to let him go? You have to know Raff and Dean will always be in danger if Larson stays alive." Shawn was always the voice of reason, but Teilo was tempted to just kill Larson and apologize afterward.

The Fates will enact a punishment if you do, Nereus warned. *They can cut your thread without blinking.*

I won't have Raff in danger.

What if it was his threads they cut?

That stopped Teilo in his tracks. He wasn't a philosophical soul. He was a mercenary. He gave no thought to the idea that others manipulated the way his life progressed. But losing Raff or Nereus for that matter to take revenge on Larson....

"Warrior." Death, Teilo found it hard to think of him as Thanatos, stood right in front of him. "Your heart has always been pure, despite the lives you've taken. Every kill you made was guided by Fate's hand. For you to kill Larson... for any of you to kill this scourge on the shifter nation would be totally unfair to the other young souls who cry for justice. This man has cut too many threads prematurely. It is the Fates who've decided his punishment."

"Will Raff and Dean be safe?" Teilo pushed his wolf down and met Death's eyes squarely. He'd never feared the grim reaper.

"You have my solemn vow, as do you all," Thanatos turned and looked over the silent men standing guard on the ones they loved. "The Fates have a message for this pack. You are where you are supposed to be. You are with the ones you will spend a long lifetime with. Do not hesitate. Do not lose faith. This pack will shine as a beacon when the time comes."

"What will happen to Larson?" Shawn asked. "Are we allowed to know that at least?"

"The Fates have granted him immortality. Wait. Let me finish." Thanatos held up his hand as the room erupted in a chorus of snarls. A quick order from Kane and everyone settled down, although Teilo was seething and through their link, Nereus wasn't feeling any better.

"Larson has been granted immortality, but he will no longer be able to walk on earth. He is to be transported to the Underworld where he will spend eternity suffering the torture he's spent his mortal life inflicting on others. While some souls are granted the right to be reborn after their lessons are learned, Larson will never have that opportunity because he cannot and will not die."

"The Fates found a loophole," Nereus beamed. Teilo was still confused.

"Actually, that was your Uncle Hades's idea," Death said with a wink. "Joel was my mate's best friend and comes from the same pack."

"You have a wolf shifter mate, Uncle Thanatos?" Raff asked, his eyes gleaming.

"I certainly do, little one," Thanatos looked at his watch. "Now, I'd better deliver Larson to Hades, who is waiting with gleeful anticipation. He has all sorts of things planned for this one, and then I'd better get home. My little mate can get very upset if I'm late for dinner."

"Hey wait, I'd rather take my punishment from the pack if it's all the same to you," Larson yelled as Thanatos grabbed hold of the ropes binding him.

"You've been outvoted," Kane snarled as Thanatos and Larson disappeared. The whole pack seemed to heave a sigh of relief.

"Dinner," Kane said with a smile. "I think a huge dinner and then we can all go and get some well-earned rest. It's been a long twenty-four hours."

The scent of magic hit the air as Aelfric, Fafnir and Shawn all threw up their hands. Nereus turned and stroked Teilo's cheek before cupping his hands around Raff's face. "Did I do okay?"

"You've both been brilliant," Raff smiled, but his eyes were still red-rimmed and Teilo swallowed the urge to chase Thanatos and kill Larson before he got to Hades. He hated that he hadn't been able to save his ray of sweetness.

"You're the one who's going to teach me how to use the bo," Raff said and Teilo realized he was talking to him. "I think it's time I had self-defense lessons."

"We'll start tomorrow," Teilo's wolf preened at having something important to do.

"The day after tomorrow," Nereus interrupted sweeping them both into a hug. "Tomorrow, we're all staying in bed."

That sounded like a good plan to Teilo, but as he ate his meal with the rest of the pack, Raff tucked between him and Nereus, he wondered how Raff might take any type of sexual overtures, given

what he'd seen through their mind
link when Raff returned.

Chapter Seventeen

Raff loved being in his mates' arms. It was his favorite place on earth. But as Nereus rested his cock against his ass, Raff flinched and immediately wished he could have hidden it. His mates were quick to notice anything like that. In seconds, he was face down on Teilo's body, with Nereus inspecting his behind and not in a sexy way.

"You've been bruised. Hit by a hand that's not ours," Nereus rumbled.

"It's nothing; it's all good. Uncle got there in time to stop anything major happening." Raff shivered as the memories assaulted him. He'd never felt so helpless in his life: the ropes cutting into him, the churning of his stomach at being touched by the killer's hands; the threat of that horrible bulge trying to force its way into Raff's most private part.

What he'd forgotten was thanks to their permanent mind link, his mates were hit with the full force of what he went through. Teilo's growls rumbled through his chest while Nereus's were shaking the bed. "Please," Raff cried out. "I'm sorry. That wasn't meant to be shared. It's not fair to either of you. You weren't there, and yes it was horrifying, but Thanatos stopped Larson before he actually did anything."

"He did enough," Teilo's hands were soothing on his skin. "That feeling of helplessness; I haven't felt anything like that since I was a boy and I've never been threatened sexually."

"It happens to a lot of people," Raff said. "I'm luckier than most. I have you two and I just need you to hold me. Both of you," he added, reaching his arm out for Nereus who settled on his side, holding them both.

"At least you're not totally against the idea of sex," Teilo said after a long moment where Raff was soaking up his mates' scents, their differences and how strong they were around him. "You're leaving a bit of a mess on my abs there, sweet one."

"I know," Raff buried his face in Teilo's chest. "I smell you, I want you. Your smooth chest muscles are crying out for me to lick them; the hair around your cock, Nereus, reminds me of how much I love to bury my nose in them and sniff." Nereus groaned and both men's arms tightened around him.

"I just don't know if I can bottom for you today," Raff whispered. It was one thing to know his mates would never hurt him, but it'd been a horrible day. He couldn't help his body's automatic response to his mates; he just didn't know if he could follow through and do something about it. "You know I love it, no matter which one of you is filling me, but tonight. I don't know that I can."

"Hey," Nereus tilted his head so Raff could lose himself in those bright blue eyes. "We're mates. Equals. I love how your cute little ass holds us tight; making us so horny we burst inside of you. You'll let us know when you're ready for that again. But we've always said you can top anytime you like. Why not tonight? I'd be happy to have you inside of me."

"You got his first kiss, his first blowjob and his first go at bottoming," Teilo objected. "I think this first belongs to me."

Nereus grinned and through their mind link Raff knew there was no real jealousy from his wolf mate. Teilo was just staking his own claim. But a larger wolf, an alpha wolf at that, submitting to him. Now was not the time to die from an attack of the vapors.

"I'll prep him for you," Nereus said helpfully. "I know how you love to watch."

Oh, Raff did. He definitely had a voyeur streak; not something he was aware of until they met Teilo, but now. He pressed a soft kiss on Teilo's lips and managed to snag Nereus's in passing. Hmm, their three-way kisses were getting better all the time. Raff pulled himself away with reluctance when Nereus's hands went south. The urge to join in warred with his love of watching two fine men together.

Teilo didn't often take the role of bottom but when he did, he threw himself into it with enthusiasm. His grunts and moans were worthy of any porn and by the time Nereus's beard was tickling his butt cheeks, Teilo was swearing up a storm. Teilo loved being rimmed and Nereus was an expert at it, at least in Raff's eyes. It wasn't something he got to do very often, but watching Nereus's sweeping red tongue against the brown of his beard, working at bringing Teilo to the point of madness, set something burning in Raff. He loved his men, loved them with everything he was. Nothing and no one could take that away from him.

"I think he's ready," Nereus's eyes gleamed above his spit coated mouth. "Let's get you into position."

Raff looked down at his cock. It was eager; his wolf was panting.

"You won't hurt me, I promise," Teilo growled. "Now you get in there and Nereus get your ass up here. I fancy something long and hard down my throat."

Raff and Nereus shuffled around, Nereus watching him as he held out his cock for Teilo to taste. Raff was between Teilo's thighs; his mate's hole still looked small.

"You just feed it in, just like this." Nereus leaned forward, rocking on his knees as Raff watched the head of his cock push its way into Teilo's mouth. Teilo let out a muffled moan and his hips jerked. "You can do it."

Raff looked down again. A trickle of precome ran down his cock and he smoothed it over his length. Biting his lip, he carefully pushed the head against Teilo's opening. "Now thrust," Nereus said with a grin, doing exactly that. Raff pushed forward with his hips... he was in and *oh my fucking god this is incredible.* Teilo grunted his approval as Raff slowly went deeper. He'd never felt anything like it. Not even the wonderful blowjobs he got on a daily basis were as good as the feeling of Teilo's ass around his cock.

"I won't last," he gasped.

"None of us will," Nereus moaned, his head back, his hair streaming like a waterfall down his back. "Move. Just go with your instincts."

Nereus's words were echoed by Teilo through their link and Raff threw caution to the winds. He leaned over Teilo's torso, his abs brushing the head of Teilo's cock. Supporting himself with his hands on the bed, Raff pulled out a bit and thrust back in. He was a bit jerky at first; it was almost a foreign feeling, but as Raff's lust grew, so did his confidence.

Feelings not his own flew through Raff's body. Nereus was close, Teilo not far behind. Both men shared their pleasure, not only through their bond but in grunts, moans and the occasional, "hell yes," from Nereus. Teilo had got his arm bent, his fingers playing with Nereus's hole; the other hand brushed against Raff's abs as he worked his cock. Raff got caught in the whirlwind and before he knew what was happening, his hips jerked and his balls tightened.

"Oh fuck, that's so amazing," Raff yelled as he shoved himself deep inside Teilo's body. His teeth dropped and Raff bent his head, his fangs piercing Teilo just above his heart. Teilo's yell was muffled, but Raff felt him climax through their link, his come soaking the pair of them. Raff felt a splash on his back and then on his cheek and he looked up to see Nereus finishing in spectacular fashion. He looked up at Teilo who was slumped on the pillows, his eyes closed.

"Are you okay?" Raff asked, reaching up and stroking Teilo's face.

"You did perfect, sweetness," Teilo gave a lazy smile. "Now because you topped, it's your turn to get the washcloth."

"I might need a shower," Raff said, tugging at some spunk in his hair.

"We'll all shower, rest up a bit and then I get to take Teilo's place while you fuck me," Nereus said gruffly.

Hot damn. Raff wasn't sure where he'd find the energy, but he was sure he'd dredge some up from somewhere. He wanted to know what Nereus's fine furry butt would feel like against his groin.

Chapter Eighteen

Nereus slipped away from his mates while they were training. Raff was working hard with Teilo, trying to mimic Teilo's moves. Nereus had to admit his larger mate sure looked fine, twirling his long staff, rippling muscles snapping to attention. Killer and the other pups were panting under a tree. It seemed even the most audacious of pups knew to stay away from an expertly wielded stick. Unwilling to be a distraction, because Raff did need to know how to defend himself, Nereus headed for the pack house. He had an idea, but he needed some help with it.

Kane and Shawn were curled up on the couch together; both were looking more rested than they had been the week before.

"Nereus. What a nice surprise. Come in, sit down. Is everything okay?" Kane got a small furrow between his eyebrows and Nereus was quick to reassure him.

"Everything is fine," he said smoothly, sitting down in the nearest chair. Thank goodness Kane believed in big solid furniture. But then with the size of the pack members, it wasn't surprising although Nereus stood a good couple of inches taller than everyone else. "Raff is busy with Teilo learning some self-defense moves. Teilo ordered him a custom-made bo stick and he's showing real promise."

"Teilo and his brothers have excellent fighting skills," Shawn said with a soft smile. "Those boys have been a blessing to this pack more than once. I'm glad Teilo's passing a few of those lessons along. But what have you come to talk about? I guess this isn't a social call."

Nereus felt a twinge of guilt. It wasn't that he was uncomfortable around Kane and the others. It's just, he wasn't used to living in a pack. "Yeah, sorry about that. It's just tricky learning to bond with two people instead of one. But we're doing well," Nereus's cheeks heated at the thought of how well he and his mates were getting on. Reminding himself wolves could smell arousal he quickly got to the purpose of his visit. "As you know I've decided to take my mates to Poseidon's next week. I've... er... I want to introduce my mates to my other father, Abraxas. He'll be there with his new mate and it will give me a chance to introduce my mates to my brothers."

"You're not looking forward to it?" Kane asked. Nereus knew Kane wasn't being nosy. It was just the pack's way.

"I haven't spoken to Abraxas since I was five," he admitted. "And my brothers? None of them are mated and they tend to be a bit boisterous when they get together. It will be *interesting*."

"Did you want some of the enforcers to go with you as back up?" Kane asked and Nereus grinned. The alpha was always safety conscious.

"No, I am sure that side of the visit will be fine. It'll be noisy, and I may have to apologize to my mates afterward, but we won't be in any danger. No, what I wanted to talk to you about was Raff's family."

"His home pack? Don't they live in North Carolina somewhere?" Shawn sat forward showing his interest.

"Yes. From what Raff could tell us, originally, they were a huge pack that pretty much ran Roanoke Island. But once the Spanish arrived, they got driven out because of their association with the local Indian tribe. The tribe was shifters too and a lot of the families intermarried which could explain why the pack was so big. With the arrival of the Spanish, Raff's pack moved in with the Tuscarora tribe in the mountains; this was way back in the 1700's, and when the tribe got moved out, they stayed on. They've always passed well as white despite the marriages between the two cultures."

"There's so much we don't know about those times," Shawn said wistfully. "The horrors that caused the tribes to move out, the Lost Colony of Roanoke. I've always wanted to know more about that. I never imagined there were shifters in the area."

"Well, then you might be interested in my plan," Nereus said. "Look, as a shifter guardian you are all about helping shifters, right?"

Shawn nodded. "Of course, if there's anything we can do to help Raff's pack, then we will. There's a good chance Raff's pack is the only pack of red wolf shifters left in the country. I've never heard of any others."

"Well from what I can gather, Raff's pack is in trouble because they've tried to keep the family lines pure. The woman he was supposed to mate with was his cousin, several times removed. Barely any babies are born and those that survive are pretty much forced into mating with pack members. There were fewer than thirty left when Raff got kicked out; the lack of breeding was the reason he was kicked out in the first place."

"Because he's gay and couldn't mate with a female." Kane's face looked grim. "He's not the first or the last that will happen to. Damien's pack is full of cases like that and Claude's has more than a few too. But with the red wolves being so rare, you'd have thought

Raff's pack might have tried to come up with something else. Artificial insemination or something."

"They don't hold with that sort of thing," Nereus grimaced. "His pack is mountain men, through and through. They can trace their roots to well back before the Spanish arrived and they all carry family names. Raff's older brother was named Dare and his mother's name is Virginia, both old family names. Ring any bells?"

"The Lost Colony of Roanoke? Could Raff's pack be descendants?" Shawn certainly looked excited about it and Nereus was quietly confident his plan would succeed.

"I'm not sure, but you have to admit it's one hell of a coincidence with those names." Nereus had been reading up on the area. "What I was thinking was, I was going to take Raff to his pack lands for a visit. But they did throw him out and they're not likely to listen to him if he suggests they'd be safer in a bigger pack."

"You're thinking about San Antonio. Have you spoken to Damien about this?" Kane asked. "We just don't have the room or the manpower to secure women and children at the moment. Especially not rare wolves like that."

"I mentioned it to him. Damien's more than happy to take in anyone who wants to move there. But I was hoping you two would consider coming with me and my mates. Adair and Marius would probably come as back up. They won't want Teilo going somewhere without them, especially if the locals are a bit unfriendly."

"We could take Dean and Matthew too. Dean's great at keeping the peace if tempers flare," Shawn said. "Oh Kane, if there's a chance we can help an entire sub-species of shifter. You know we have to."

"I know," Kane's smile was indulgent, but that was something Nereus enjoyed about the Cloverleah men. They were never ashamed or afraid to show their love for each other. He had a sudden urge to have his men in his arms.

"I was thinking of going tomorrow if that suits Alpha," he said, standing and smoothing down his pants.

"So formal," Kane laughed. "Tomorrow is fine; make it about ten o'clock. We can all meet here. Can you transport us all? Shawn might be able to, but with you not being a shifter...."

"I can take all of us. I'd better go and find a map and get Raff to pinpoint where his pack is."

"Yep, some of those mountains are pretty rugged from memory,"

Shawn said. "The people can be a bit clannish too, so it would pay to get the place right first time."

Nereus left Kane and Shawn canoodling on the couch and headed out into the winter sun. He hadn't bought Raff his winter coat yet. A snap of his fingers took care of that. It was going to be chilly in those mountains and the snow on the ground wasn't the only chill Nereus was worried about. *Gods, I hope I am doing the right thing. If his pack upsets my sweet mate, there'll be an earthquake the size of which has never been seen. That's without the damage Teilo and his brothers will do.*

Chapter Nineteen

Raff twisted his hands nervously as he stood between Teilo and Nereus. Beside them Adair and Marius stood with Dean and Matthew; Kane and Shawn stood on the other side. Vassago was leaning on Adair but looking just as alert. Aelfric, Fafnir, and Jax stood by the pack house door.

"We'll monitor everything and yank you back if anything happens, and you get stuck," Jax said gruffly. Kane was still being over protective, but Raff understood the need for concern. No wolf shifter willingly went into another's territory without permission. He couldn't believe Kane and Shawn agreed to Nereus's plan, especially when he had to explain his old pack didn't even have access to a phone. They lived totally off the grid.

"In that case, everyone ready?" Kane asked.

Raff grabbed the backpack Luke insisted on packing for the pups. Candy, toys and all sorts of unknown goodies Luke insisted were necessary. Since becoming a father, Luke had developed a soft spot for anything to do with children and when Kane had made a passing joke about Raff and his mates adopting, Raff couldn't hide the unfurling hope in his heart. He'd been raised to be a father, even if he couldn't lie with a woman to have kids of his own. But the Cloverleah pack was still in danger from some dark unknown force and any of the men who wanted to have children had opted to wait. Ollie was a special case and while Raff have children of his own just yet, he could do something for the children in his home pack.

"Okay, Nereus lets..." Kane didn't get the chance to finish the sentence before they were standing in the middle of a highway Raff remembered well. The road stretched out in a straight line; houses were in clearings cut from the woods bordering both sides of the road. "Fan out everyone. Be friendly," Kane ordered.

Raff glanced around. The hair on the back of his neck prickled. Something was deathly wrong. His backpack dropped to the ground unheeded as he stared at the silent houses. He couldn't keep the panic from his voice as he whispered, "Where are they? There should be people on the porches, children playing on the road."

The lawns were overgrown and the grass surrounded dust-covered vehicles. From the length of the grass, it hadn't been mowed since summer. There was a cold breeze, but no snow yet. But as hard as Raff strained his ears, he couldn't hear anything. Raff focused on the pack house and started running.

His alpha would be there; Fridolf never left the area. His mates were hot on his heels as he banged on the packhouse door. The door creaked open from the force of his blows and stale air greeted them.

"Alpha! Alpha Fridolf, are you here?" Raff yelled for his pack leader and enforcers. "Liulfr! Lyall! Hemming! Kenyon." No one answered his call.

Kane glanced around. "Adair, Marius, look through the house."

Nereus held onto Raff, Teilo holding them both close. Raff stood frozen in fear until Adair and Marius came back shaking their heads. "Nothing," Adair said, his arm wrapped snugly around his mate. "No bodies, no blood, no signs of a struggle. Just dust. Nothing's been packed. Everything seems to be all here; just no people. There hasn't been anyone here for a long time."

"Go check the rest of the town," Kane said sharply.

"There's a communal dining hall and kitchen. Maybe they're having a meal or a meeting," Raff said, hoping it was true. Shawn cast him a look so full of pity, Raff's knees almost gave out on him, but holding tight to his mates, he led the way to the dining hall across the road. The table was set as if waiting for a meal. The water pitchers on the table were dry. In the kitchen, the pots on the stove were full of food that had never been served. It was covered in rot and ants. The ovens held the remains of what had been cooking before the stoves burned out.

"The fire in the stoves burned out. They were never allowed to burn out. Alpha Fridolf always used wood stoves and ovens. Said the food tasted better." Raff sat heavily on a chair. "What happened? Oh gods, what happened to them?"

He could feel the tears threatening his eyes. Two years he'd been gone. He'd never expected to hear from his family; his father turned his back on him the day he was banished. Raff would've done anything to see his father's unyielding back now.

"I don't understand. Where could they have gone?" Raff stared at the table set for a meal, covered in dust. "No one is here."

"They haven't been here for a long time." Shawn's quiet voice rumbled through the still house.

"What the devil could happen to a whole pack? It's a village. It wasn't just a couple people." Kane looked from the table to Shawn, eyes searching.

Shawn shook his head.

Adair and Marius came back in. "Every house looks exactly like this. Some show preparations for meals. No signs of a struggle and they have been gone for a very long time from the level of dust around."

Matthew put his arms around Dean who was openly crying. "Shawn? Can you send us back? No disrespect to Raff, but this is bringing up bad memories."

Shawn nodded. "I'll send you to the pack house. Tell Jax to call in the others. Stay with them until we get back."

Matthew and Dean vanished with a flick of Shawn's fingers although Raff barely noticed. He was staring at the dust, trying to make sense of what had happened.

"I am not getting anything," Shawn said. "It's as if they didn't exist. They've simply vanished."

Vanished. Raff couldn't stand it. His heart broke at the thought that he'd never see his mother baking cookies, his father reading his book at the table, or that his brother would never pull his curls and tease him again. He ran outside, shrugging off the beautifully warm coat Nereus had gotten for him. He had to shift. His wolf demanded he find his family. As soon as he was in fur, Raff howled, calling his pack. The howl echoed off the valley and died. He howled again. The echo was a mockery of the sound that wasn't answered. Raff's next howl was of pain and loss. His pack couldn't answer him because they weren't there. They were gone and while it'd been years since Raff's wolf had run with his family, the loss was acute, painful. Sharp.

Beside him, Teilo stripped and shifted. The large wolf nuzzled his mate and when Raff howled again, the deeper voice of Teilo joined him in mourning the missing pack. Nereus sat on the ground oblivious to the cold, his hands wrapped in his mates' fur as Raff mourned and Teilo comforted him. One by one, Kane, Shawn, Adair and Marius, even Vassago, all shifted and joined in the painful chorus. The Cloverleah pack raising their heads and mourning the loss of a fellow pack; possibly the end of the Red Wolves as a species.

/~/~/~/~/

"What do you mean, you can't tell me what happened?" Nereus pulled his Uncle Thanatos outside. The wind had turned bitter, but Nereus didn't feel it. He was seething. The one being who could give him answers apparently couldn't or wouldn't.

"I mean, I wasn't called to take their souls," Thanatos said patiently. If he was surprised at being summoned by his nephew, he gave no sign of it.

"So, they're not dead. You can help me find them," Nereus persisted. It was his stupid idea to try to help Raff's pack and now his mate was exhausted from crying and Teilo was trying to help him sleep.

"You know that's not how it works and I didn't say that. But," Thanatos held out his hands, "I'm saying I don't know what happened to them."

"You know where every soul is. Every soul from angels to demons, human to paranormal, you know where they are. I need to tell my mate something that will give him comfort."

Thanatos sighed and ran his hand over his face. "I can't tell you anything because I don't know. All I know, all I can say, is that this is the Fates doing and no one else has been told what happened to that pack."

"I'll go to them. I'll plead my case with them then." Nereus would have to get both his fathers' permission to approach the Fates, but he'd do it.

"You can't," Thanatos hissed, looking around as though worried someone would hear him. "If your shifter guardian doesn't know, then you're not meant to. Not yet. If you go to the Fates, they could see you as someone unfit to care for the one red wolf left. Do you want that?"

"They'd do that?" Nereus was shocked. He knew Poseidon had problems with the Fates in the past but that was only because Poseidon was a god who liked to piss people off. Atlantis was just one example where Poseidon had upset the holders of the threads.

"I don't know," Thanatos said, "but honestly, do you want to take the risk? If you upset the Fates, there's no telling what could happen to

Raff or Teilo. They're wolves. They will die without you."

"You didn't see him, him and Teilo, Kane and the others. Howling into the forest with no one answering," Nereus felt tears running down his face. "What's the point of being born to the gods if I can't fix this?"

Thanatos's hand felt clumsy on his shoulder. "One of the biggest burdens to being a god is realizing that some things are not in our control," he said softly. "Red Wolves have been hunted their entire existence. Their small size and beautiful fur have made them prized by human and paranormal hunters alike. I'm not saying this is what happened to young Raff's pack. I don't know. But what I am saying is that sometimes you just must learn to accept and move on. You can't change what has happened; you can only make a difference going forward. Protect the wolves that are left."

"There's more danger coming?" Nereus hadn't even considered that.

"The men attracted to Cloverleah, those find their mates here? They are all here for a reason, just like you are. The dark times aren't over yet, which is why you need to leave the Fates to their business and be vigilant with your mates."

Nereus was desperate to ask more, but he knew it was unfair. Thanatos had come at his demand, even though he didn't have to. None of the gods were answerable to anybody, except the Fates. He patted the hand on his shoulder and said gruffly, "I'd better get inside. Raff will need me. I just wish I knew what I could tell him."

"Tell him to keep the faith and trust in love," Thanatos said cryptically. "After all, when times are at their darkest, love is the greatest power of all. Don't ever forget that."

Nereus nodded and giving Thanatos a quick hug, he watched as his uncle shimmered and disappeared. His steps were heavy as he made his way into the house he shared with his mates. So much laughter and love shared already in their tiny house. Nereus hurried into the bedroom. Raff was asleep in Teilo's arms, the tear tracks still evident on his cheeks. Teilo raised his head. "Anything?" He whispered.

"Trust in love," Nereus said softly as he climbed into bed and pulled Teilo close, Raff caught between them. "We have to trust in love."

Chapter Twenty

"Stop fussing with your clothes. You're like an old woman," Teilo laughed and pushed Nereus's hands away from straightening his jacket. "You look very godlike. I'm sure your fathers will be very proud."

"I look like a biker. Maybe I should wear a business suit or something." Nereus's face was a picture of nerves and Teilo sighed.

"You do biker beautifully. Now, where's Raff? Let's get this circus on the road or Abraxas will be gone and we'll have to go through this shit again in another five years."

"I've been baking all morning," Raff said coming into the bedroom holding two large plastic containers. "I'm not sure what to take."

Nereus opened his mouth and was probably going to say something stupid like they didn't need to take anything to Poseidon's domain, and Teilo intercepted quickly. "Whatever they are, they smell delicious. We'll take both and if the guys down there don't like them, then there'll be more for us. Have you got your coat?" Raff flashed a quick smile and disappeared from the room again.

"I've never taken anything down to my father's place before," Nereus whispered.

"Remember what Shawn said. Baking is Raff's way of coping with his grief and his nerves at meeting your brothers. Be supportive."

"I'm going to get fat," Nereus said, rubbing his stomach. Teilo knew exactly how he felt. Raff had taken to baking like a pro and after some lessons from Dean on how to use the internet for recipes; he spent at least two hours every day baking one delicious treat after another.

Raff had wanted to get a job and had even spoken to Kane and Shawn about it. But after Kane gave a long lecture on pack safety and Teilo and Nereus spent an equal amount of time explaining how Raff didn't need to pull his weight financially, Raff had decided baking was going to be his way of contributing to their household. Thankfully, he was as keen on making savory pies and pastries as he was on making delicious sweet cakes otherwise Teilo was sure he'd end up the only diabetic wolf shifter in existence.

"Today is about you," he said, pinching Nereus's butt and making him jump. "Meet Abraxas; show off a bit of fur for the human. Thump your brothers the first chance I get. That's how today is going to go, isn't it?"

"Probably," Nereus sighed. "Am I doing the right thing, T?"

"Raff thinks so."

"Raff thinks what?" The sexy little wolf came in complete with coat and boots. Teilo thought he looked adorable with his flushed cheeks and hair that stuck out all over the place.

"Nereus is nervous about meeting the man who gave birth to him," Teilo said with a grin.

"Serves him right for holding a grudge for thousands of years," Raff said pertly. "Family is family, Nereus. Be glad you have yours."

"You have us, sweetness," Teilo said quickly folding Raff into a hug. "You have me, Nereus, Adair, Vassago, and Marius. We're all family."

"Not to mention Poseidon who thinks you're wonderful, Thanatos who can't stop singing your praises and I'm sure my brothers will be kicking themselves I got to you first," Nereus said, joining the group hug. "Let's get going before

I have this urge to rush you back to bed and we'll meet Abraxas another day."

"Oh no. You're not getting out of this meeting," Raff said hotly, wiggling out of the arms that held him and reaching for his containers. "I have four dozen cakes and biscuits here. Unless you want to eat them yourself, get zapping."

"Yes sir," Nereus said with a grin, and it was that grin Teilo held onto as his demigod of the sea zapped them to Poseidon's home so he could meet his Horse of the Sun father. *Who'd have believed it?*

The last time Teilo had been in Poseidon's home beneath the waves, he'd been worried sick about Raff and wanting to stake his claim on his mates. Not that he had a lot of time to look around this time either. Raff's gasp and comment, "Heavens, you could be

532

twins," had Teilo paying attention to the men in the room.

Poseidon was always easy to pick out of a crowd. His long silver-white hair shone in the light glinting from various lights staged around the room. Next to him was an equally tall well-built man who glowed. There was no other word for it. The newcomer's hair was a similar shade to Nereus's although streaked with gold and his eyes were orange... yellow... definitely light-colored, Teilo decided.

But the man who could only be Abraxas wasn't the only stranger in the room. Abraxas had a tiny blond tucked under his arm. The man was pretty, really pretty with a mass of bright blond curls and pure blue eyes. His red lips were half open, and he was staring at Raff. The other man Teilo didn't know was a blond version of Nereus, right down to the beard, although his eyes were a warm brown. He was slung over a chair as though he really didn't care about anyone else. Although he bounded out of his chair as soon as he knew Nereus was in the room.

"Brother," the blond boomed as he strode over to meet them. "You brought sweet things."

"I brought some cakes and biscuits I made this morning," Raff said, looking up at Nereus.

"I meant you, sweet thing," the blond said, "although these look good too." He tugged the plastic containers from Raff's hands and set them on the table. "Did you know we're a very huggy family?" He held out his arms.

"Knock it off, Lasse," Nereus snapped, slapping his brother in the chest. "These are my mates, Raff and Teilo. They're both wolf shifters and are likely to bite if you get too close."

"Oh, that sounds like fun," Lasse bowed. "Lasse, son of Poseidon and Abraxas at your service."

"They don't need your type of service," Nereus looked as though he was going to have a fit and Teilo let himself be led to where Poseidon and the others were standing.

"Poseidon, you've already met my mates. Abraxas, these are my mates, Teilo Reef and Raff. We are living with the Cloverleah pack." It was Nereus's turn to bow. Teilo looked across at Raff who shook his head but then Poseidon swept forward, grabbing his hand and shaking it vigorously.

"Teilo Reef. We really didn't have a chance to chat last time you were here. You and Raff simply must say hello to this little darling Abraxas has claimed. This is Jordan. He's human. Isn't he adorable?"

"They're not an oddity, Poseidon, even if you think so, stuck down here all the time. You need to get out more. I lived among them for two years," Raff said as Poseidon laughed. Teilo watched as Raff stepped forward and held out his hand to Jordan. "Nice to meet you. I'm a small red wolf. This is Teilo, he shares his spirit with a huge black wolf."

"Oh wow," Jordan was cute with his mouth open and pre-mating days, Teilo would have been all over the sweet looking man. "Can you shift? I mean, is it okay to ask? I don't want to cause offense or anything."

Teilo looked over to where Abraxas and Nereus were just staring at each other. "We have to get naked to shift, otherwise it's hell on clothes. Why don't we go into that side room over there and we'll show you?"

Jordan must have seen something in the way his mate was watching his son. Even Teilo could see the sheer joy and happiness on Abraxas's handsome face. "Yeah, let's give these guys some alone time. Come on Poseidon, you'd never turn down the chance at a free show. You too, Lasse."

"Yes, Dad," Lasse said with a huge grin. "Oh, I do love having a curious stepfather. Naked shifters are my favorite kind." Teilo made a point of keeping himself between Lasse and Raff as they went into the other room.

/~/~/~/~/

"You haven't changed," Nereus said quietly. "Well, you have. You seem happier. Lighter than other times I've seen you down here. But in outward appearance, you seem the same."

"You've changed. You were only this tall the last time I saw you,"

Abraxas smiled as he indicated a point by his knee. "You've grown into such a fine young man. I am so proud of you."

Nereus felt his cheeks heat and a flood of supportive warmth came through his mating bond. "I owe you an apology," he said, struggling to get the words out. "I... all this time I thought you'd abandoned me, even though Poseidon kept saying you had no choice. I was wrong to keep hating you."

"I did abandon you," Abraxas said. "Choice. Rules. I should've known none of that would mean anything to a five-year-old. But with Lasse already sick, I knew it'd only be a matter of time before you would be too. I wasn't going to lose you after all the hassle I had carrying you."

"I can't imagine how hard that would be," Nereus said. "It worried my mates a bit, knowing I'd come from two fathers."

"You are using condoms, aren't you?" Abraxas laughed as Nereus's eyes widened. "I'm kidding. Unless one of your mates' ancestors tangled with a god, I'm sure you'll be fine."

"Yeah, I might have to double check on that," Nereus said managing a grin of his own. "But I'm fairly sure they're pure wolf shifters."

"You've done really well." Abraxas looked across at the room the others had disappeared into. Someone was laughing and Nereus guessed it was Jordan from the smile on his father's face. "A fine warrior and a gorgeous young man with a heart of gold. Two mates to hold dear for eternity."

"You believe in mates then?" Nereus was surprised. Abraxas wasn't a god like Poseidon, but he thought all higher beings thought the same. Although Thanatos mentioned having a wolf shifter mate, too.

"As soon as I touched Jordan's hand, Helios's voice rang through my head demanding I claim him and bring him home." Abraxas's face beamed and Nereus relaxed.

"Poseidon tattooed all of us. I have a feeling he was in the room when we claimed each other," he said ruefully. "I have a tramp stamp on my ass and so does Teilo. Raff has waves crashing over his butt. It looks good, but every time I see them on my mates, I think of Dad. Not exactly who I want to be thinking of when my mates are naked."

Abraxas laughed and Nereus could see the family resemblance. He and Lasse both took after their Horse of the Sun father in looks, yet they got their Mer genes from Poseidon. He felt a warmth, as though his heart was full for the first time in his life and he stepped forward, giving Abraxas a hug.

"I'm so sorry, Dad," he whispered into Abraxas's hair.

"You were always the stubborn one," Abraxas said fondly. "Just come and see us sometimes, please. Helios says you're always welcome; you and your mates."

"I will. I promise," Nereus vowed. Raff and Teilo were right. Family was important. Cutting Abraxas from his life was like cutting off a limb; a really stupid thing to do when it wasn't necessary. Teilo had his brothers, but no parents. Raff lost his whole pack and may never know what happened to them. But Nereus had two fathers who had always loved him, not to mention three annoying brothers. He was the lucky one.

"Come on," Abraxas stepped back, at last, blinking rapidly. "We'd better go and rescue our mates from Poseidon and Lasse. Those two are cut from the same cloth that's for sure."

"Will you watch out for us?" Nereus asked as they walked arm in arm. Nereus liked to think neither one of them were ready to lose contact just yet. "While you're up there dragging the sun, I mean."

"I always have; I always will," Abraxas promised. "Although, from what I've seen, you've always managed to look out for yourself. Tell me, that time in Turkey, probably a couple of hundred years ago, now. You and Sebastian were fighting bandits or something. You disappeared into a big stone building and I didn't see you again for weeks. What happened?"

Nereus racked his brains, trying to think. "Oh, I remember. Yes. Well, it turns out…." Heads together, Nereus filled his father in on the bits of his life Abraxas had missed.

In turn, Abraxas told him about the antics the Horses of the Sun got up to and how Jordan had finally convinced Helios to try contact lenses. With his mates by his side, eating Raff's delicious home baking, Nereus didn't think he'd ever had such a fun, family-orientated afternoon.

Chapter Twenty-One

Raff relaxed, getting into the zone as Teilo called it, flicking, twirling and running the bo stick over his arms, neck, chest and... yes, a flip between the legs and he caught it. "I did it," he beamed at his mate who was sitting in a lawn chair by the pond.

"You sure did sweetness. Your lunges make your ass look cute too." Teilo winked and Raff felt his cheeks heat.

"You're supposed to be helping me with my stance and form," he huffed dropping down into the nearest chair.

"I can multi-task." Teilo laughed. Raff looked around. Kane and Shawn set up a grill and were debating BBQ fuels. Adair and Marius were sparring, their chests gleaming in the pale winter sun. The other pack members were sitting around, beers in hand, just enjoying an unusually fine day.

"Where're Killer and the others?" They'd been playing with Ollie down by the water's edge last time Raff saw them. Killer seemed overly protective of the cub although he also tended to lead the precious child into the smelliest of situations at times. As Ollie wasn't fond of bath time and still preferred to be furry around other pack members, Raff always felt responsible when he turned up smelly.

"Luke made doggy treats," Teilo nodded to the far end of the pool. "And it seems like they're all gone," he added as Killer raced towards them, his pack and Ollie lumbering behind them.

"Hey Killer, did you have fun, boy?" Raff slipped onto the ground, suddenly covered in pups. "Hmm, you're getting fat. I'm going to have to take you for another run real soon."

Killer barked, prancing around while Buddy, Butch, and Joey all flopped on the blanket Teilo had thoughtfully provided. "I didn't mean now," Raff said with a chuckle. "Go get some rest and we'll run later." Killer glared at him, making Raff laugh harder, but eventually he padded over to where Buddy and Butch were curled up together and plopped down on top of them.

"Have you seen Nereus?" Raff asked. He leaned his head on Teilo's thigh, looking over the choppy water.

"A few flashes of tail here and there," Teilo said. Raff felt a warm hand drop on his hair, stroking it. "It beats me why he doesn't feel the cold."

"He offered to teach me to swim this morning," Raff laughed. "I pointed out while we shifters run warmer than most, I'd still freeze in five minutes being in that water." He tugged his coat out from under Teilo's chair and put it on. A light breeze kept the sun from being truly warm.

"Are you okay? Are you happy here at Cloverleah?" Teilo sounded worried and Raff looked up at his warrior mate. It'd been almost a month since he'd found his home pack gone and Raff was ashamed to admit he'd gone to pieces for a while. But he smiled as wide as he could.

"I'm happy with you," he said softly. "I'm happy in our little house; I have loving mates, a caring pack and while I miss my home pack sometimes, I'm never going to be sorry that I'm still alive. If I hadn't left, I'd never have met you two and I'm thankful for that every day."

Teilo smiled. "I think about it sometimes, the events that brought you and Ner into my life. Who knew I'd have a serial killer to thank for meeting my mates? My dad told me over and over again as I was growing up that I'd never be worthy of anything, but meeting you have proven his words wrong. For the first time in a long time I have a home, my mates, brothers, and a pack. A wolf shifter doesn't ask for much else in his life."

"No, they don't, and I feel the same way," Raff looked back towards the water. "Nereus has been a long time. Oh wait, that must be him." He nodded to the bubbles forming about three feet from the edge of the pond.

"That's not him," Teilo sprang out of his chair. "That's... that's Lasse. Nereus's brother," he added as the tall blond stepped from the surf, the water streaming from his clothes and leaving him dry. "What's he got under his arm?"

Raff stood up too, his pups instantly on alert. Killer ran towards Lasse, barking, and growling, sniffing hard. Then he stopped, tilted his head and whined. Lasse laughed, a booming sound like waves crashing on the beach. "Hello, brothers-in-law. Greetings to you both, and your pack of course," he added as Kane and Shawn, Adair, Vassago and Marius all came hurrying over. "V man. Haven't seen you in an age. Ner tells me you're mated now. Who did you piss off?"

"I didn't piss anyone off, and it's King V to you now," Vassago said with a grin, giving Lasse a quick hug before he went back and wrapped his arm around Adair's waist. "This is my Consort Adair. You may see a family resemblance. Adair is Teilo's older brother."

Lasse inclined his head, his face still wearing a smirk. Then he turned to Kane and Shawn. "You must be the Alpha and Alpha Mate. Apologies for dropping in uninvited but my mating gift was upsetting Sei dreadfully." He held up a ginger bundle of fur which set Killer off barking again. "Meet Cutie Pie. Isn't he adorable?"

"Another dog? That's all we don't fucking need," Kane groaned while Shawn laughed. But Raff was enchanted.

"Can I?" He held out his hands but just then Nereus came storming out of the surf.

"What are you doing near my mates, Lasse?" Nereus roared. "You're in pack territory. You can't come wandering in here like you own the place."

"Brother," Lasse turned to greet Nereus and Raff's fingers itched. He wanted to examine the newest member of his puppy pack. Although Killer was acting weird; he'd have normally bitten Lasse by now, but he seemed more interested in getting to the little fluff ball. Buddy, Joey, and Butch all went back to their blanket, curling up with Ollie. But Killer seemed glued to Lasse's ankles.

"I brought you a mating gift," Lasse beamed, holding up Cutie Pie. "When I heard your little red wolf busy telling Sei about his mini dog pack, I just knew Cutie Pie would be perfect for you."

"This is a wolf pack! You can't just go bringing in new animals without checking with the alpha first." Nereus seemed to be having trouble with his temper. The waves on the pond got bigger.

"It's okay," Shawn said quickly, probably sensing a fight brewing. "Another wolf would need permission. I'm sure we'll all adapt to having one more pup around the house."

"Speak for yourself," Kane grumbled. "I'm going through a pair of boots a week. If I ever find out what Killer's doing with the left one; the left one mind, never the right, I'll... I'll...."

"You'll say thank you, Killer, for bringing the boots back," Shawn said, tugging Kane away. "Come on; let's get back to the BBQ. No one likes burned meat."

"Ah, love," Lasse said with a cheeky smile, but Raff noticed a hint of pain in his eyes as well. He hoped his brother-in-law would find a mate of his own one day.

"Come and put Cutie Pie down so he can mingle with the others; let them do the sniff and greet thing," he said, casting a warning look at Nereus. "We're having steaks, salads and I think salmon is on the menu, too. You're more than welcome to stay and eat with us."

"Why, thank you. I think I will." Lasse carefully put Cutie Pie on the ground and he and Killer eyed each other. Killer wasn't growling, which Raff thought was unusual. In fact, the poodle's whole body was shaking. Cutie Pie seemed equally affected and for a moment they were like two frozen statues.

"Er," Raff was just about to question the idea of keeping his lovely new pup when Cutie Pie growled and then barked. Killer barked back, his stance wide. Bark, growl. Bark, growl.

"Oh my goodness they are having a bark off.' Lasse slapped his thigh. "I bet they're mates. Oh, that's classic."

"Mates?" Raff knew Buddy and Butch were a couple. He'd rescued them together, and they were always side by side. Could Killer have finally found his match? It seemed so because suddenly Killer and Cutie Pie were rolling around together. The growls had stopped but there was some definite dominance play going on.

"Come on," Raff said, looping his arm around Nereus's waist and pulling them away from a situation which was moments away from doggie porn. "Let's go and get some food and leave these two to get acquainted."

/~/~/~/~/

Nereus stared out over the porch and sighed. The night sky was clear, the stars like diamonds piercing the darkness. The soft breeze was cool, carrying with it hints of pine, the earth and a trace of salt from his pool. He was quietly pleased Lasse had brought a gift to celebrate his mating. Perhaps, now he and Abraxas found their true mates, his twin might think of settling down. *A man needs a purpose.*

Memories washed gently through his mind. The armies he'd fought with, the ship's he'd captained. He and Sebastian spent a hundred lifetimes wandering the world, fighting for a just cause. *And now I have a real home.* He smiled as he listened to Teilo and Raff trying to herd the puppies into the spare room for the night. Raff was laughing; Teilo was grumbling good-naturedly which wasn't unusual where the puppies were concerned.

A loving home with mates of my own. Nereus mouthed a thank you at the night sky, before stepping back inside the house, closing the door firmly behind him.

"There you are," Raff smiled. "Everything okay?"

"If it's not, it will be in a minute," Teilo mock-growled as he swept

Raff off his feet. "Come on big guy, it's time for bed. Our little sweetness has been begging for a sound kissing."

I am a very lucky man, Nereus thought as he nudged his hardening cock and followed his mates into the bedroom.

Epilogue

The sound of vomiting filled the house. Seeing Raff turn green in sympathy, Dean yelled, "Close the damn door, Adair."

"I'm okay. I'm okay. It must mean it's 3 p.m. Teilo always barfs at 3 p.m. And 10 a.m. And 8 p.m. Like clockwork. How in the hell can you schedule something like that?" Raff's head hit the pillow again. Dean tucked extra pillows under his feet.

"There. That should help bring down the swelling."

"I don't care." Raff couldn't manage more than a whimper. "I can't get my shoes on. I can't get my pants on. I look like an overstuffed pregnant mongoose."

"No, you don't. I knew an overstuffed pregnant mongoose. You glow." Vassago plunked a tray down next to him.

Raff took a swing at Vassago and missed.

"So where is he?" Vassago plopped down beside Raff and Raff groaned. Every part of his unwieldy body ached.

"I don't know and I don't care. The bastard. That fucking bastard. He...."

Vassago stuffed a pickle-flavored ice cream in Raff's mouth. "Freshly made by the Fae. Isn't it good?"

Raff managed a nod although he could feel his eyes filling again. Vassago reached over to pat Raff's stomach and Raff didn't even try to hide his crying. "I can't do this. I can't. It... I... He needs to do this."

Dean pushed Vassago off the couch and muttered, "I told you to ignore the stomach. Any attention sets him off again. This started when Kane patted his stomach and said 'There there.' Shawn had to pry *him off Kane. Raff was screaming 'You bastards, you are all in this together. I know it.' Shawn got him calmed down and back here. I thought Raff was going to be our Alpha for a minute. Do NOT set him off."*

"Okay... ah... how about I feed the pups?" Vassago looked around while pointedly ignoring the lump... the Red Wolf on the sofa. "Where are they? With Luke?"

"No. They're sticking close, but they aren't stupid." Dean gestured to the other sofa. Five little heads appeared. Buddy brushed Butch and Butch bared his teeth and growled. Cutie Pie sent Killer a frosty glare. "And it appears the puppy couples think this is contagious."

"Contagious?" Vassago's voice was faint. "It might be contagious? It can't be contagious. It's a God thing. Nereus made that clear. It is a God thing. It has to be a God

thing. It can't be contagious. If it is... It isn't. It can't be. I...."

Vassago bolted out the front door.

Raff burst into tears. His life was over. Dean was awkwardly patting his arm, but it didn't help.

Adair dragged a half-dead Teilo toward the other sofa. "Where's my mate?"

"He ran away. He's worried this is contagious." Raff felt fresh tears run down his face. "Just like our mate. He ran away."

"Raff, you know Nereus went to Poseidon and Abraxas. He's trying to find ways of helping and to see if they know why this happened."

"I know how it happened," Teilo growled. "The bastard lied. He fucking lied to us."

Raff didn't know what to think. He loved both his mates equally but, he glanced down at his stomach which was impossible to ignore.

"He said we would be safe because we didn't carry a god-gene."

"HE LIED." Teilo roared his face red, his hair in disarray.

"Now, brother, I don't think he lied to you as such. I think he told you what he knew." Adair wasn't being very comforting. If Raff didn't feel like crying all the time he'd be pissed off too.

"And now that there is a question if this is contagious...," Dean said. Whoops. Adair went dead white. He didn't know. Although how he couldn't have thought the same thing... Raff giggled.

"Contagious? It can be contagious?" Adair sounded like every horror he'd ever thought of had come to life.

"Well, we're not sure," Dean said, trying to settle Teilo back on the pillows. "Um... Fafnir threw up this morning and Jax is worrying himself into an early grave."

"Oh, Gods." Adair covered his face with his hands.

"YES. THAT'S WHO'S FUCKING FAULT THIS IS. THOSE BASTARDS." Teilo's roar got louder.

Raff whimpered and tried to block his ears. He'd cuddle his mate, but the effort required to reach him was more than he could handle.

Teilo's yells ended in a dry retch. "Oh no, not again."

"It's okay." Adair patted his shoulder.

"Adair? Go into the kitchen and pour Teilo a big glass of Doctor Pepper and grab two plain donuts." Dean clearly knew what to do. "Do you want any, Raff?"

Raff shook his head. He couldn't bear the thought of eating. Although in another hour he'd be starving.

"Contagious. This could be contagious. I'm a dead man," Adair muttered the whole way out.

"Oh dear." Abraxas appeared in the middle of the room. "It wasn't this bad with Lasse or Nereus."

Raff glared at his father-in-law and Teilo growled.

Dean said, "It's only in the afternoon that..."

"Don't lie for us. We're..." Raff felt a sob rise in his throat and he lost it, crying so hard he couldn't talk.

"Yeah." Teilo whimpered and tears ran down the warrior's face. "We're elephants, crying, over-emotional elephants."

"You're not elephants," Abraxas said soothingly. "It's the hormones. It's perfectly natural; your bodies are going through a lot right now, trying to care for the pups. I went through the same thing when I was pregnant. And the fact you aren't

565

Mer or House of the Sun has probably made things a bit more difficult. Of course, one of the puppies you're carrying," Abraxas gestured to both of them, "might be your other mate's and not Nereus's. It's not unusual to have that happen when your genes are set up for carrying more than one pup... baby... at a time and you've had sexual relations with more than one person."

The room was deathly quiet. Even Dean didn't seem to have something soothing to say.

"More than one pup at a time?" Raff looked down at his stomach in shock.

"We could get pregnant from both our mates?" Teilo asked.

Raff stared at Teilo. Then he yelled, "You did this to me, you bastard."

"No, you did."

"This is Nereus's fault!" Teilo agreed with him on that.

"Just how many puppies are we carrying?" Teilo finally got his breath back to ask. "And how do you know?"

"Ah... Well...." Abraxas rubbed his hands together, a big smile on his handsome face. "This whole thing has caused a bit of excitement in certain circles and well... the guys upstairs are keeping a close watch on you. Zeus talked to the Fates and after a whole lot of flattery and bribery... I can tell you that Raff, my sweetness, is carrying five pups. And Teilo, you shocked absolutely everyone. It must be your wolf genetics but even then, there are very few female wolves that can do what you've done. You're carrying twelve of the little darlings."

A loud crash drew their attention to the door where Marius stood over the tray that had held dinner for them. "I don't want a mate. There's no way I'm having a mate. I don't want a mate. I don't...." He ran out the front door leaving Adair slumped in the kitchen doorway.

Raff's eyes got spots in front of them and he blacked out.

"Well, it's gotten quiet all of a sudden." Abraxas chuckled.

"Seventeen pups, there's going to be seventeen of them?" Dean shakily made his way to a spare chair and sat down with a thump.

"Well, they may not all be pups," Abraxas said, leaning over Raff and tapping his cheeks gently. "They could be Mers or Horses of the Sun. They'll be paranormal. Zeus checked and neither Raff nor Teilo have any humans in their family tree."

Raff came to and immediately searched for Teilo who was just waking up. "Seventeen pups between us, mate," he said, his throat raspy. "We're going to need a ton of diapers."

"You will be pleased to know all the babies will be born healthy and strong. You won't have any problems with delivery." Abraxas patted his knee but Raff still felt faint.

"That bastard is wearing a rubber from now on and so are you," Teilo said, accepting a glass of water from Dean gratefully.

"Hell, I'll glue the damn thing to my dick and yours." Raff was determined he wasn't going through this mess again.

Nereus appeared in the living room but before they could say anything, he ran for the bathroom. They could hear him throwing up. A box appeared in front of Abraxas who opened it and read the scroll inside. "Oh dear. It isn't seventeen pups. It's going to be twenty.

Nereus is pregnant with triplets. Poseidon is going to be thrilled."

"Nooooo!" Raff shot straight up, covered in cold sweat. Teilo had him in a death grip. Nereus pulled both of them against him. He felt his stomach. Flat. Muscular. No puppies. He panted. "Oh, thank the gods. I had the worst damn dream."

"I did too," Teilo said shakily, taking in deep breaths. "You were going to have five pups."

"You were going to have twelve!" Raff stared at him. "Please tell me this wasn't a premonition. We all had the same damn dream."

"I know; I'm still sweating over triplets." Nereus groaned. Then he raised his head. "Dad! Goddamn it, DAD. I don't care which DAD. One of you, I don't care which one, get your ass here."

"You can't get pregnant," Poseidon's voice sounded in the

room. "And no, I didn't send you a nightmare, although grandchildren would be nice... so long as they don't turn out like Baby."

Abraxas appeared. "It's okay. You aren't pregnant. You can't get pregnant. The Fates said no. Raff and Teilo aren't from a god line. Calm down and stop worrying. I'll make some hot chocolate. I guess Doctor Pepper and donuts are out of the question?" He disappeared in the direction of the kitchen.

Teilo looked at Nereus, "Your fathers have an evil sense of humor. Wait! How did they know about our dream?"

The three men looked at each other; the shock mirrored on their faces. "I think I need a hug," Raff said quietly. "But if either one of you think you're coming near me with a hard dick tonight, you'll be in for a hell of a shock."

"I doubt I could get it up," Nereus said and Teilo muttered in agreement. The three men lay huddled together under their blankets listening to Abraxas humming as he made hot chocolate in their kitchen.

"It wasn't a premonition, was it?" Teilo whispered.

"I'll find out first thing in the morning," Nereus said firmly.

Raff had a feeling it was going to be a long night.

The End

Oh, I did love these three men and I do hope you do too. This isn't the end, of course. Marius, although he didn't show up much in this story, will be the next man in Cloverleah to find his mate and we will learn more about Thomas, Ryan, and Wesley who've remained quite shadowy figures so far. There's still the talk, dark and dreary to find and he just might prove more dangerous than anyone in the pack can imagine. But you'll find out more in the next Cloverleah book.

Don't forget, the next book I will be releasing will be sweet Madison's story and his possible mating with Sebastian. This will be book one in the spin-off series, "The Gods Made Me Do It." You'll meet a lot of old friends in that series. Keep an eye on my blog and Facebook page for more updates.

Remember, if you felt kindly about this book, please leave me a review. Writing is my only source of income and every review helps with book rankings.

Hug the one you love

Lisa.

A Personal Note From Me ☺

Hi there, I hope you enjoyed my story. As with most fiction books, some of the themes in this book have relevance in real life. In this book, it's the scarcity and endangerment of Red Wolves. I personally have signed up with the Defenders of Wildlife and donate to them on a regular basis. I feel the animal extinctions in the last century are entirely human caused and should not be allowed to continue. I want my grandchildren to be able to have the chance of seeing one of these beautiful creatures in the flesh one day. If you want to help in any way at all, please check out the links below.

Defenders of Wildlife have facts sheets and information on what they are doing to help the Red Wolves and things you can do as well.

http://www.defenders.org/red-wolf/what-you-can-do

More information on what is being done for Red Wolves in the North Carolina area, which is where Raff was originally from.

https://www.nwf.org/News-and-Magazines/National-Wildlife/Animals/Archives/2014/Red-Wolves.aspx

This page has a lot of links about things that are being done well, and other things not so well. Honestly, if you want to help out then the Defenders of Wildlife link above should be your first call.

https://www.fws.gov/redwolf/evaluation.html

Other Books By Lisa Oliver

Cloverleah Pack

Book 1 – The Reluctant Wolf – Kane and Shawn

Book 2 – The Runaway Cat – Griff and Diablo

Book 3 – When No Doesn't Cut It – Damien and Scott

Book 3.5 – Never Go Back – Scott and Damien's Trip and a free story about Malacai and Elijah

Book 4 – Calming the Enforcer – Troy and Anton

Book 5 – Getting Close to the Omega – Dean and Matthew

Book 6 – Fae for All – Jax, Aelfric and Fafnir (M/M/M)

Book 7 – Watching Out for Fangs – Josh and Vadim

Book 8 – Tangling with Bears – Tobias, Luke and Kurt (M/M/M)

Book 9 – Angel in Black Leather – Adair and Vassago

Book 9.5 – Scenes from Cloverleah – four short stories featuring the men we've come to love

Book 10 – On The Brink – Teilo, Raff and Nereus (M/M/M) (you just read it)

Book 11 – (as yet untitled) – Marius and (shush, it's a secret) (Coming April 2017)

The God's Made Me Do It (Cloverleah spin off series)

Get Over It – Madison and Sebastian's story (Coming February 2017)

Bound and Bonded Series

Book One – Don't Touch – Levi and Steel

Book Two – Topping the Dom – Pearson and Dante

Book Three – Total Submission – Kyle and Teric

Book Four – Fighting Fangs – Ace and Devin

Book Five – No Mate of Mine – Roger and Cam

Book Six – Undesirable Mate – Phillip and Kellen

Stockton Wolves Series

Book One – Get off My Case – Shane and Dimitri

Book Two – Copping a Lot of Sin – Ben, Sin and Gabriel (M/M/M)

Book Three – Mace's Awakening – Mace and Roan

Book Four – Don't Bite – Trent and Alexi

Book Five – (as yet untitled) – Captain Reynolds and Nico (Coming March 2017)

Alpha and Omega Series

Book One – The Biker's Omega – Marly and Trent

Book Two – Dance Around the Cop – Zander and Terry

Book 2.5 – Change of Plans - Q and Sully – short story, (Coming soon)

Book Three – The Artist and His Alpha – Caden and Sean

Book Four – Harder in Heels – Ronan and Asaph

The Portrain Pack and Coven

The Power of the Bite – Dax and Zane

The Fangs Between Us – Broz and Van – a Portrain Coven and Pack Prequel (coming soon).

Balance – Angels and Demons

The Viper's Heart – Raziel and Botis

Passion Punched King – Anael and Zagan – coming March 2017

Shifter's Uprising Series – in conjunction with Thomas J. Oliver

Book One – Uncaged – Carlin and Lucas

Book Two – Fly Free (Coming soon)

About the Author

Lisa Oliver had been writing non-fiction books for years when visions of half dressed, buff men started invading her dreams. Unable to resist the lure of her stories, Lisa decided to switch to fiction books, and now stories about her men clamor to get out from under her fingertips.

When Lisa is not writing, she is usually reading with a cup of tea always at hand. Her grown children and grandchildren sometimes try and pry her away from the computer and have found that the best way to do it, is to promise her chocolate. Lisa will do anything for chocolate.

Lisa loves to hear from her readers and other writers. You can friend her on Facebook (http://www.facebook.com/lisaoliv erauthor), catch up on what's happening at her blog (http://www.supernaturalsmut.com) or email her directly at yoursintuitively@gmail.com.